Sparkledoll

Always Into Something

SPARKLEDOLL
ALWAYS INTO SOMETHING

▼

Dorrie Williams-Wheeler

Writers Club Press
San Jose New York Lincoln Shanghai

Sparkledoll
Always Into Something

Writers Club Press
an imprint of iUniverse, Inc.

For information address:
iUniverse, Inc.
5220 S. 16th St., Suite 200
Lincoln, NE 68512
www.iuniverse.com

Original cover design by Dorrie Williams-Wheeler
Author photo by Robert Williams

ISBN: 0-595-20805-3

Printed in the United States of America

This book is dedicated in loving memory of three beautiful young women.

Shanitha Thames-My dear friend, I wish I cherished you more when you were here.

Aaliyah Dana Haughton-You were so very beautiful and talented. I am sorry that you did not have the opportunity to see all of your dreams come true.

Cherica Addams-I wish that you could be here to enjoy raising your son.

CONTENTS

―――――――――▼―――――――――

Foreword

▼

Sparkledoll-Always Into Something is really good fiction kinda sorta based on a true story.

Sit back, and enjoy the ride.

You only live once, and I wanted to have fun-Sparkledoll

Acknowledgements

---▼---

I would also like to thank my parents and my family for always instilling in me that I achieve all of my dreams. I would also like to thank the following people-Mikal, Trina, El, Theresa, Carisa, Shekera, Sharon, and Donna for your constant support and belief in my talent.

IN THE BEGINNING

▼

I grew up in the Chicago suburbs in a small town named Park Forest South. I came from a successful middle class family. My father was a marketing executive and my mother worked in pharmaceutical sales. I had one brother. We lived in a modest 3-bedroom townhouse. I attended Monee Elementary School.

Monee Elementary School was a predominately white school in the middle of the cornfields of Monee, Illinois.

I was 5 years old when I started Kindergarten. I was so excited about the prospect of starting school. On the first day of school my mother dressed me in a pair of red corduroy pants and a fuzzy green shirt. The year was 1980.

The world was a much safer place in 1980 than it is now. I walked three blocks to the bus stop and waited in the September cold for the bus to come.

When the bus came, I walked onto the bus so proud. I carried my "Little House on the Prairie" lunch box with pride and sat down in the first empty seat that I found.

I looked out of the window as the bus pulled off. The bus made several more stops and the seats quickly filled up. We were one stop away from the school when we stopped at a farm.

I peered out the window and saw a little dark-haired White boy standing at the bus stop. He looked like he was about my age.

The boy boarded the bus and looked around for a seat. The only empty seat was the seat next to me.

"You can sit here," I said.

"My parents told me not to talk to or sit by any Niggers."

"Well, I didn't want you to sit by me anyway." I said. Screw this kid, I wasn't going to let him ruin my first day of school.

"Look, find somewhere to sit." The bus driver shouted. The little boy stuck his tongue out at me and sat down next to me.

Surprisingly, this wasn't my first experience with racism. I had to deal with racism in pre-school. I was the only Black girl in my pre-school. Most of the kids liked me and I made many friends, but there were always one or two kids that would want to cause a problem with me. Some parents took their kids out of the school when they found out there was a Black kid in the school with their kids. I never let racism bother me. Even at a young age, I looked at racism as a part of my life.

My life became twisted and distorted somewhere around 1984 when I was 8 years old. All of my thoughts started to become abstract and odd. I would lie in my bedroom all day long watching MTV and listening to my favorite cassette tapes. I was so captivated by MTV. I couldn't sleep at night because I didn't want to miss the videos. My favorite artists were Duran Duran, The Go Go's, and Culture Club. Let's just say I wasn't your average little black girl.

I would hide out in my room for hours styling my hair like a punk rocker or pretending that my Barbie dolls were having an exclusive rock concert.

When I wasn't playing with my Barbie dolls, I was writing in my journal. My favorite author was Stephen King. I wasn't your average 8-year-old. I always dreamed of being a famous writer. I was so passionate about my writing I would fill up whole notebooks in a day. When I wasn't writing I was creating artwork, painting on my easel.

I had three good friends. Two of them were Black, one of them was White. We didn't care about what color we were. We knew what we liked. We would hang out and watch videos and listen to Duran Duran's "Seven and the Ragged Tiger" album over and over, trying to make some kind of sense out of Simon Le Bon's lyrics.

School was a drag to me. I was highly intelligent, I had an IQ of 137, but school was not a challenge to me in the 3rd grade. They were teaching us how to spell words that I already knew how to spell.

I did like to write and in early October of 1983, my teacher Mrs. Carter announced that the school was holding a short story contest. The best short story would be re-printed in the school newspaper, and on top of that the story would be entered into a national short story contest.

I was determined to win the writing contest. I daydreamed about winning the contest. I could see myself reading my winning essay to the entire school in the auditorium.

The night before the entries were due, I still didn't have anything concrete on paper. I was suffering from severe writer's block. It was October, and Halloween specials were on television. I had an idea. I came up with a Halloween theme for my short story. I stayed up until 10:00 at night working on my story.

The next day, I was the first student to turn in their entry.

"Please read mine aloud Mrs. Carter, please!" I begged.

"Okay Lori, I will read your story aloud to the class."

All of the kids gathered in a circle on the floor and Mrs. Carter began to read.

> *Halloween time came to Monee School. All of the kids were very excited, until one by one children started to disappear. Where were all of the children? One curious student, Lisa, decided to get to the bottom of things. She walked down the dark hallway to look for her classmates who had all disappeared. She came across the janitor's closet. All of the missing children were tied up in the closet. Lisa rescued her classmates and headed back down the hall. "We have to find the teacher!" Lisa screamed.*

Mrs. Carter became more hesitant with her reading.

> *The children walked down the hall and into the dark principal's office. Much to their surprise, they found the teacher hanging from the ceiling.*

The class gasped in awe. Mrs. Carter stopped reading my story and put it on her desk.

"Lori, I want you to march straight down to the principal's office. This story is just awful."

"Mrs. Carter, you didn't even finish reading it. The teacher wasn't dead, it was just a prank to scare the children, please you have to believe me."

"Save it for the principal Lori Baldwin, leave right now. Don't even get your things, we will send them to the office later."

All of the kids started to laugh as I was sent to the office. As I was making the long walk to the principal's office I felt the tears welling up in my eyes. I couldn't understand why Mrs. Carter got so upset.

I walked in the principal's office and sat in the chair.

"Why are you here?" Asked the principal's secretary.

"Because my story was just awful." I said as the tears started to run down my cheek.

Mrs. Carter called my parents and I was told that I couldn't come to school until she had a conference with them. At the conference, Mrs. Carter showed my parents the story that I had written.

"Mrs. Carter, the teacher was alive in the end, it was only a prank." My mother tried to reason with Mrs. Carter. Mrs. Carter slammed her fist on the desk.

"What kind of eight year old child has a sick mind like this? What kind of parents are you? I am recommending that she start counseling immediately, and she must attend counseling before she returns to my class."

My parents argued with Mrs. Carter that I was only expressing my free speech. I was a straight "A" student. My parents and Mrs. Carter came to a resolution and was allowed to return to school. I also didn't have to attend counseling.

I couldn't understand why my story caused so many problems. Being that I was so young, I thought that the story was bad. I didn't really look at the fact that it was the subject matter that caused all of the problems.

After that incident I withdrew from my writing and delved further into the solitary insanity called my life.

In 1984, my family moved to Beverly Hills, California. My father landed a lucrative marketing position with a major television studios. Beverly Hills was a beautiful place. I attended Carthay Elementary School. I made many new friends.

Not everyone in Beverly Hills is a millionaire. We lived in a three-bedroom ranch style house. I fit in perfect in Beverly Hills. When I was a little girl my mother would take me shopping on Rodeo Drive. The shop owners would look at us crazy until my mother would pull out her Gold American Express Card.

In retrospect, I think about those early years, and my friends and I were so much more like little women that little girls. We would put on makeup and hang out at the mall. We would have our parents drop us off at Redondo Beach and we would play in the sun for hours. True, we were only 10 and 11 years old, but we were mature far beyond our age.

I guess life forced me to grow up. My father's job wasn't working out well. Life was not easy for a Black man working in Hollywood. To ease the pain, my father started drinking. My parents began to argue all of the time.

I had my own demons to deal with. I was extremely creative and intelligent and trapped in the monotony of the 4th grade.

My family and I spent 4 years in California. Those were the best and the worst years of my life. My parents were going through a divorce, which was more painful for them than for me. I wanted them to get a divorce. I was tired of all of the arguing. At home I was an introvert.

My friends were very important to me. I was so close to my friends, I felt like they were my family. I spent as much time at their houses as I could so I could escape the chaos of my home life. We would hang out and watch "Jem & The Holograms" and put on make-up. My friends were all White, but I fit in just perfect with them. I was totally content with my life. I loved my friends, and I loved California. I loved my life.

My parents divorce became final the summer after I finished the 7th grade.

My mother decided to move back to Illinois to be closer to her family. I was so distraught about having to leave my friends. I had made them my entire life. They were my support system.

Everything changed when we left California.

EARLY ANTICS

To understand the outcome you have to know a little bit about the beginning. My parents got a divorce when I was in the 7th grade. My mother, determined to make sure that we continued to have a nice life, moved us to the Chicago suburb of Schaumburg, Illinois. We moved to an upscale high rise apartment building. The building had a strict "no kids" policy. At the time, I was 13 ½ and my brother was 5. They decided to bend the rules because my mom had perfect credit and a really good job with Bausch and Lomb.

We moved to Schaumburg during the summer time and I was a bit depressed about moving away from California. I missed my friends and my dad. One day as I was sitting in the house playing Nintendo, a girl named Ivy knocked on my door. I knew who she was because she had introduced herself one day in the elevator. I opened the door and Ivy was standing there with a few Barbie dolls in her hands.

"Hi, remember me, do you want to play?" That was cool. I invited her in and Ivy and I hung out for the whole month of July. We went swimming and her seven-year-old little brother Jack hung out with my little brother Robert. Innocent children at play.

One day while we were outside we noticed a new Black family moving into the building. Prior to this time, my family was the only Black family in the building. I was excited at the prospect of having other Black friends, not that I didn't like my White friends.

The family moving in was the Greens. A single mother and her three children; a son Alexdon, a daughter Erica (who was the same age that I

-7-

was), and another son named Paul, who was around my brothers age. Ivy and I were sitting on the front lawn playing with our dolls when Erica Green walked over.

"Y'all live here?"

"Yeah, we live here. My name is Lori and this is my friend Ivy."

Erica waved at Ivy. Erica began sucking her thumb.

"Hey I'm 13 how old are y'all?" Erica had a thick Chicago accent. She seemed to be a tough kid.

"Well I'm 13 and Ivy is 12." Erica started to laugh.

"And you all are sitting her playing with Barbie dolls. I ain't played with no Barbie dolls since I was 7 years old. Do you all know how to jump rope?"

Erica continued to suck her thumb. Here she was making fun of me for being 13 years old and still playing with Barbie dolls and she was sucking her thumb. I didn't dare mention that because she seemed like the kind of girl that might beat me up. That day became the last day that I ever played with my Barbie dolls again.

The year was 1988 and rap and urban music was starting to cross over to the mainstream. Bobby Brown and New Edition were still doing their thing and rap artist such as Rob Base, Salt N Pepa and DJ Jazzy Jeff and the Fresh Prince were starting to influence young Black America. Me, I didn't know too much about rap or R&B music at that time. I was into Duran Duran, Madonna, and anything that came on MTV. When I started to hang around Erica, she introduced the Black culture to me. She was from an all Black neighborhood in Chicago and she was cool. She wore gold earrings and she had a huge collection of rap tapes.

Erica gave me a copy of an Eazy-E tape. I couldn't believe it. I had never heard music that had curse words. I wanted to be cool. I found myself starting to talk like Erica. I dressed like Erica. I am now embarrassed of the fact that I even got a Jheri Curl like Erica.

For a couple of weeks, Erica, Ivy and I tried to all hang out together. Ivy was a good girl and for the most part she had grown up in an all White world. She had only moved to Schaumburg a couple of months before me.

Previously, Ivy lived in a small town in Iowa. The family only moved to Schaumburg because her father, an architect, was working on a big contract. Ivy was nice and she was a good friend.

One day Ivy, Erica and I made the long walk to the mall. Normally, Ivy and I would have taken our bikes if we wanted to go to the mall, but Erica said riding bikes, "Wasn't cool". We walked in the scorching August heat to Woodfield Mall. I only had $2 on me. Everyday before she went to work my mom would give me $2 in case I wanted to go to 7-11 or if the ice cream truck came. Ivy didn't have any money. Her parents said that there was nothing that she needed money for. I guess they were right. They bought her clothes and they always had Popsicle's in their freezer. Erica didn't have a dime, which is why I didn't know why she wanted to go to the mall so badly.

We arrived at the mall and I was so glad to be in the air conditioning. Ivy wanted to go in the toy store and look at the toys. To be honest, I wanted to go in the toy store also, but I had to play it cool with Erica around.

"I need to get the new Slick Rick tape, let's go in the record store". Ivy and I followed Erica blindly. We didn't know what she was up to. We though that she had some money that we didn't know about.

Chi Town Records was a big record store. We walked in the store as a group, but we split up once we entered the store. Ivy went over to the magazines and started reading and article about The New Kids on The Block. Erica went straight for the rap tapes. The rap tapes were in the same aisle as the posters. I was browsing at the posters when Erica found the Slick Rick tape.

"Yeah this is what I been wanting a long time". She looked around the store. The clerk was helping another customer. Erica took the tape and put it in her purse. She looked around to make sure no one was looking. I couldn't believe she was stealing. Don't get me wrong, I didn't have these high morals that made me think stealing was bad, I just was afraid for us to get caught.

"Come on let's get out of here", Erica said in a low voice. I nervously followed behind Erica. Ivy saw us leaving and she put the magazine down and followed behind us.

I was scared shitless. I couldn't believe that she just put the tape in her purse.

"Hey Erica, I think we should get ready to go."

I didn't want to be in that mall one more minute.

We walked past a security guard and I was paranoid that he was on to us.

"Lori, we just got here what is the rush", Ivy said as she skipped through the mall.

"Yeah, just chill out, you're illin'", Erica patted me on the shoulder.

"Plus I need some new earrings."

I wasn't going in one more store with Erica that day. Erica walked into Gold & Diamond Emporium and Ivy followed behind here.

"Hey, I'm going to just sit here at wait for you all to come out." I sat down on the bench outside of the store. I saw Ivy in the corner looking at the necklaces. I should have warned Ivy that Erica was a thief, but Ivy would have freaked out. She probably would have even told the security guard.

Although I was outside on the bench, I could still see everything that was happening inside of the store.

Erica asked the clerk if she could look at a pair of earrings in the case. The woman behind the counter agreed to show her the earring but she had to go to the back of the store to get the key to the case. While the woman went to retrieve the key, Erica picked up a gold bracelet that was on display and put it in her pocket. The clerk retrieved the key and came back to the counter. She opened the case and put the earrings on the counter. The woman held the earrings up to the light.

"These are $89, they are 18 carat gold. They would look nice on you." Erica held the earrings in her hand. She carefully examined them as if she was checking to see how authentic they were.

Ivy was at the other end of the counter looking at birthstone rings. Ivy waved her hand to get the woman's attention.

"What is the birthstone for September, my moms birthday is in September."

The woman walked over towards Ivy, taking her eyes off of Erica and the $89 earrings.

"Well the birthstone for September is Sapphire, do you see something you would like to look at? We do have a layaway plan if you are interested." As the sales clerk was speaking to Ivy, Erica put the earrings in her pocket and walked out of the store. Ivy noticed Erica leaving. The clerk was a bit pre-occupied and she probably would not have noticed Erica walking away if Ivy would not have called Erica's name.

"Hey Erica, wait for me". The clerk still didn't notice that something wasn't right. She glanced at the counter and noticed that the earrings were gone. She started to yell.

"Hey come back here!" She yelled. Erica bolted out of the door. I jumped up off of the bench and bolted behind her.

"This has got to be a mistake, just wait a minute you guys" Ivy pleaded, but when the store clerk rang a security alarm, Ivy started running to.

The jewelry store was on the second floor of the mall. Woodfield Mall is a huge place. We ran down the escalator almost busting our asses. We ran through the lower level of the mall. Erica had a clear lead, I followed behind Erica, and Ivy and I were about neck and neck.

"Hey you kids, stop right now!" I looked back and now two mall security officers were chasing behind us. We ran faster and faster until we were outside of the mall.

We ran for awhile until we were about 500 feet from the mall. Erica slowed down to catch her breath and so did I. Ivy was crying and hysterical.

"What happened in there? Erica did you steal something. This is so terrible. I can't breathe, I think I am going to have an asthma attack."

Ivy sat down on the sidewalk. Erica had it all figured out. It was quite clear that she had stolen in the past.

"Look, once you are off of mall property they can't touch you, come on let's go. Ivy stop crying like a little baby."

We started walking again when we saw a police car pull around the corner. My first instinct was to run, but I was afraid that the police would shoot me if I ran.

"Freeze right there!" the officer screamed. He didn't point a gun at us, but I was scared. Ivy started to cry harder and Erica bolted. I've never seen anyone run as fast as I saw Erica run that day.

The police officer in the passenger's seat jumped out of the car and took off after Ivy. He was an older man in his fifties and he looked like he had been sitting behind a desk for a few years. He could not match the speed and quickness of a 13-year-old Black girl from the South Side of Chicago. Ivy and I sat on the curb and watched Erica out run the police officer until you couldn't even see her anymore.

The police officers took Ivy and I back into the mall. They took us to a security center in the basement of the mall. It was pretty high tech; they had cameras watching the people in the mall and surveillance tapes of the parking lot. We sat there for about an hour.

The police officer questioned Ivy and I separately. After about and hour and a half the jewelry store clerk came down and told her side of the story. Based on the clerk's statement and the surveillance video from the jewelry store, they determined that Ivy and I were innocent.

We would be free to go and the incident wouldn't go on our record under one condition. We had to give up Erica's name and address. The police weren't my friends and Erica was. I wasn't going to give her up. I told her that she was a girl from the neighborhood and I didn't know her name or where she lived.

"So you hang around with people whose name you don't know". He did have a point.

"You want to go to juvenile hall don't you." I hated to rat out Erica but I didn't have a choice. I sang like a canary and told the police officer Erica's name and address.

The police officer told us that we were banned from the mall for a whole year. The older police officer offered to give us a ride home. I didn't want my mom to find out what had happened.

As he was driving us home, Ivy and I sat in the back seat of the police car feeling real bad. We were good kids playing in the front yard with Barbie dolls just a month ago, and now here we were sitting in the back of a squad car like common criminals.

The car pulled up next the apartment complex and stopped. The officer came around the side and opened up the back door. The officer stuck his head into the back seat.

"Hey I have one question for you kids, if you hadn't done anything, and were innocent, why did you run from the security guard?"

As Ivy and I pondered the answer to the question the police officer said,

"The girl that you all were with is nothing but trouble. Based on the info you told us, we ran a background check. She has been arrested twice for shop lifting and she spent three months is the audi home." (The audi home is Chicago slang for juvenile detention).

"She's nothing but trouble and you girls shouldn't hang around her."

The officer stepped out of our way and Ivy and I walked into the building.

Ivy was pretty pissed off at me. She didn't speak to me the entire time we were at the police station. I had never seen Ivy so angry. She pressed the button for the elevator. The elevator opened up and we walked in.

"Lori you are so stupid. I know you knew Erica was a thief, but you wanted to be cool and hang out with her so bad you didn't even care. I don't want to be your friend as long as you hang our with Erica."

I had never seen Ivy like that, and her words cut like a knife.

"Look Ivy, I didn't know that Erica was a thief, I swear I didn't". The elevator opened up at the third floor.

"Whatever Lori, I just don't want to be your friend anymore." Ivy walked off the elevator. I couldn't let her have the last word. As the elevator was closing, I held it open with my hands and I yelled.

"I never liked you anyway Ivy, you need to grow up and stop acting like a baby". I knew that would hurt her feelings. I only wanted to hurt her because she had hurt me.

As I walked up to my apartment, I took my key out of my sock and opened the door. My mom was home. She was cooking dinner and she was in a really good mood because she had gotten a raise at work. She had even bought a cheesecake to celebrate. My little brother was sitting down on the floor playing Nintendo. What a day. My family was none the wiser. I lied to my mom and told her that we had been swimming all day long.

After dinner we were sitting down watching *Adventures in Babysitting* on video when there was a knock on the door. I immediately went into panic mode. Was it Ivy's mom? I knew Ivy was a wimp and that she had told her mom everything. Was it criminal Erica asking me to come and hang out? Who could it be? Surely it couldn't be the police. What would they want with me? I was innocent, remember.

"Who is it?" My mom peeked through the peephole.

"Good Evening Ms. Baldwin it's Officer Miller from the Schaumburg police department. Hot diggity, why were the police here? My mom was clueless about what had happened. She opened the door and invited the officer in. I tried to go hide in my room, but before I could get to the hallway, my mom motioned for me not to move.

"How can I help you Officer Miller?" I was in trouble. Damn. I could feel all of my phone privileges being taken away.

"It seems your daughter Lori and her friend Ivy have been hanging around with this young woman downstairs named Erica. Today, Erica was involved in several shop lifting incidents at Woodfield Mall, and your daughter and Ivy were with her. These two seem like good kids, so I wanted to stop by and talk to the parents about what happened. Now your daughter wasn't arrested, but she was banned from the mall for a whole year."

This was awful. The officer and my mom starting to converse and I just tuned their voices out. It was like I was in a tunnel.

My mom took away my telephone privileges for the rest of the summer. On top of that, I was grounded. I couldn't leave the house for the remainder of the summer. I spent the rest of the summer watching soap operas and videos on TV. Oh yeah, and I wasn't allowed to hang out with Erica anymore.

I was not excited about the upcoming school year. I didn't want to start a new school. I missed my old school and my friends. I was about to enter the 8th grade at a new school where I didn't have many friends. Ivy and Erica would be there, but I didn't really consider them friends.

When I walked into Jane Adams Junior High everything changed. The school was really nice. I remember being impressed that the hallways and classrooms were all fully carpeted. My first class of the day was English. I sat next to Jill Parker and Katie Powell.

Katie was something special. She had bleach blonde hair and she dressed in all black. She listed to The Cure and she was in love with Boy George.

Jill was just cool. She was a white girl that loved Black men and she had mega attitude. She lived with her mother who was a single mother.

The three of us met in class on the first day of school. After passing notes and talking for awhile we discovered that we all lived in the same neighborhood. I didn't know at the time, but those two became my best friends for the school year.

Jill was no virgin. I remember being so in awe of that. She had had sex with lots of guys. One day I spent the night over her house and she showed me her wrists.

"I tried to kill myself". I looked down at her arm. From the middle of her hand all the way down her arm was a zig-zagged scar. I stared down at her arm. She had to be lying.

"Get out of here, I don't believe you." Jill pulled her sleeve down.

"You know my mom caught me in the bed with a Black guy. She totally freaked out. She kept saying that she was going to send me back to the mental hospital." Back to the mental hospital? How come I always attracted people with so much drama in their life?

"Jill you never told me you had been in the mental hospital?" Jill put her hand in the air as if she was telling me to shut up.

"Let me finish, she kept telling me that she was going to send me back to the mental hospital, and I told her that I would fucking kill myself before I went back to that place. My mom went into the living room and picked up the phone. I used to carry a box cutter for protection. I took the box cutter out of my purse and slice-slice-slice." Jill motioned the way that she had used the box cutter to slice her wrist.

"My mom freaked, she called 911 and they didn't even take me to the regular hospital. They put a towel around my wrist and took me straight to the loony bin. I was there for 3 months, and that's how I spend my summer vacation."

I was mesmerized. That was a freaky story. Trying to kill oneself is definitely not a cool thing to do, but nonetheless, I was captivated by Jill and her story.

Jill and I became best friends. Katie hung out with us to sometimes. Katie was weird. She had an eating disorder. My mom used to hate for Katie to come over to our house because she would eat strange things. I will never forget. One day Katie went on an eating binge and she ate a whole box of garlic flavored croutons and then she went in the bathroom and threw up the whole box. My mom made a salad the next day and she couldn't find the croutons.

"Lori, where are my croutons, I just bought a whole box and I can't find them". I lied and said that I had "dropped them on the floor". My mom peeked in the garbage.

"I don't see them in the trash." I was found out.

"Look, Katie ate them, I didn't tell you at first because I was afraid that you would get mad." My mom stared at me in disbelief.

"You mean to tell me that girl ate my $3 box of croutons. She ate the whole box?"

After that incident my mom told me that Katie couldn't come over anymore. I didn't listen, I still brought Katie over when my mom was at work.

Jill was crazy cool and she was popular. She used to curse out teachers and get suspended. For some reason, I thought that was a cool thing to do. When I tried it I got suspended to, except I got an in-school suspension, which meant I had to spend the whole day in the office staring at the walls.

Jill introduced me to the world of boys. We would talk to guys on the phone all of the time. Jill always had a boyfriend. She still dated Black guys, but she kept it a secret from her mom. She would always tell her mom that she went out with me and my boyfriend.

We would always hang out with these two guys, Mike and Kyron. Kyron was Jill's boyfriend and Mike was his friend. I liked Mike, but Mike didn't like me. He said that he only dated White girls, which at the time I didn't understand. Here was another Black boy telling me that he didn't date Black girls.

Jill was getting me in trouble. I knew she was a bad influence but I just didn't care. I was having a blast and I loved hanging with her. When my report card came I had straight "C's". I had never done so poorly in school in my life. I still didn't care. To me, popularity was more important than grades. Jill was one of the most popular girls in school and I was her best friend. You couldn't pay for that kind of popularity. Jill cut class. That was cool with me. Jill cursed, that was cool with me. I didn't have sex though. Not because I was scared, but only because I was afraid I would get pregnant.

Believe it or not Erica was pregnant. As the fall came to a close I learned that Erica was 6 months pregnant. I couldn't believe it. She was in 8th grade and not only had she had sex, but also she was about to become a mother. There was a little more to the story. Her mother didn't know that she was pregnant.

My mom didn't allow me to hang out with Erica. I could have still been her friend if I wanted to, but hey, I had Jill, so why did I need Erica? Erica and I both were in the same science class. One day in class she leaned over to me and said, "Lori, you know I'm pregnant". She didn't look pregnant. The teacher was writing on the board. Erica lifted up her big sweatshirt and showed me her stomach. Her stomach was round and hard and she had stretch marks.

"Quit lying, you are just poking your stomach out like that." Her stomach did look different, but Erica lied so much I didn't know what to believe. She wrote me a note. The note said:

> *Lori-What's up. I'm still pissed off at you and Ivy telling the police my name and where I lived. You know I got arrested. But they never found the earrings or the bracelet.*

I stopped reading and looked up at her. She was wearing the earrings and the bracelet.

I continued to read.

> *My momma is so dumb. She can't even tell that I am pregnant. The father is this boy in Chicago that stays around my grandmother's house. His sister is 17 and she has a job. She says that she will take care of the baby. I see you hang out with that White girl Jill all the time now. You know there ain't but 6 other Black people in this school, you could still call me sometimes.*

> *Too Fresh For 88'*
> *Erica*

I never did call Erica.

Jill and I didn't really get in too much trouble. The month before graduation the weather started to get nice and we were looking forward to graduation. Most of the times we just hang out with Kyron and Mike. Jill's boyfriend Kyron had stolen a car. He stole the car in Chicago and brought it to Schaumburg.

How many people in 8th grade have a car? Jill and I hung out with Kyron and his friends for weeks in that car. We knew it was stolen, but we didn't care. We were kids having fun. Kyron would play NWA in the car. He would blast the song, "Fuck the Police" and we would all sing along.

One day after school Jill and I noticed that the Kyron's car was gone. Our first thought was that someone had stolen the stolen car. We then saw the police asking questions. Jill was worried sick about Kyron getting arrested. We walked around to the gym trying to find him to warn him, but he was gone already.

Jill and I went back to my place and ate nachos. We knew Kyron and Mike would call us. We had only been over at my house for about an hour when there was a knock at the door. It was Kyron and Mike. They came in and sat down on the couch. Kyron covered his face.

"The police got my car. I can't get arrested man, I am already on probation." "And I have a warrant", Mike said. I didn't want to see them get in trouble.

Kyron reached out for Jill's hand.

"Jill can we stay at your house for a few weeks and hide out?" Jill pulled her hand away.

"Get real, my mom would never go for that." The four of us sat there for an hour trying to decide where the boys would hide out. That is when Jill came up with the idea that led to my family getting evicted.

"Hey Lori, doesn't your mom have a storage unit?" Jill asked. The storage units were in the basement of the building. Each apartment was assigned a storage unit. The storage units were small, dark rooms. They were designed to store Christmas ornaments and boxes, not people.

"Yeah, we have a storage unit, I don't get it though it's dark and creepy down there." I didn't want to be a part of this.

"Yeah, that's sounds like a plan. We can hang out with our friends during the day and sleep in the storage unit at night. Let's go check it out!"

Mike exclaimed as jumped up off of the couch. The four of us took the elevator down to the basement. I used my key to open the room to the storage unit. Our storage unit was empty with the exception of one box. The unit was dusty, but the boys didn't seem to care.

That night Jill and I helped Kyron and Mike get settled into the storage unit. We gave them a flashlight and a battery operated radio. I packed Mike a little survival kit with food and water. Kyron gave Jill a great big hug and then he kissed her real tight. Mike gave me a pound and told me that "cool", and "Thanks for looking out".

The next day at school everyone was talking about Kyron and Mike. Word got around quick that the police were looking for them. The principal even made and announcement over the loud speaker.

"If anyone sees the young men in question, please tell the security guard or a teacher at once".

Jill and I didn't tell anyone that we were hiding Kyron and Mike in my building.

It was our little secret.

Three days passed and hiding Kyron and Mike became a part of Jill and my daily routine. We would leave school, go to Mc Donald's, buy food for the boys, and go hang out in the storage unit. We would act like silly kids. Mike liked to rap, so we would listen to the songs he made up. Kyron liked to dance, so he would impress Jill with his dance moves. We eventually turned the whole storage unit area into a little clubhouse. We would play Monopoly and listen to music all evening. I don't know how long we thought this could last.

One week after Kyron and Mike went into hiding they were profiled on the local news. The news listed them as "juvenile run-aways who were wanted for questioning."

Later that night as I was doing my homework my mom asked me about Kyron and Mike.

"Lori did you know those two boys that were on the news tonight? They went to your school." I didn't know if I should tell the truth or lie. It always seemed easier to lie.

"Yeah mom, I knew them, but not very well. They were in my gym class." I always felt bad about lying to my mom, but lying was always easier than telling the truth.

The day after the newscast I was sitting in Home Economics class when our school security guard Mr. Wilson came to my class and asked my teacher if I could be excused. What had I done now? I got up from my desk and walked toward the door. All of the kids in the class whispered, "Ooh you're in trouble".

I followed Mr. Wilson out of the classroom and down the hall.

"Am I in trouble?" I asked. He looked back at me.

"We'll talk in my office". When I got to his office my mom was in there. Shit. I was in trouble. Mr. Wilson took a sip of his cup of coffee and handed me Kyron and Mike's picture.

"Do you know these two kids?" My dad always told me that if you tell a lie you better believe it and stick with it until the end.

"Yeah, they go to school here. They are in my gym class and I saw them on the news." My mom started to cry. She always cried.

"Lori now is the time to tell the truth." I hated when people played games like with me. They obviously knew something, why were they harassing me?

"Look, whatever you know, you already know. What am I supposed to say?" I slouched down in the seat.

"Let me clear things up for you young lady. This morning these two boys were discovered hiding in your mothers storage unit. What we need to know is if they broke in or if they had assistance. They had a key and the storage unit had all of the amenities of home, except for a bathroom. They had a hot plate, blankets, radio; somebody was helping these two boys out. Was it you?"

Mr. Wilson stared me up and down. If I was going down, I wasn't going down alone, I had to take Jill down with me. I sang like a canary and told Mr. Wilson the truth.

The Schaumburg police considered charging Jill and I with aiding and embedding fugitives. Neither Jill nor I had a criminal record, so the police decided not to pursue the charge.

My mother was so disappointed in me. To make things worse, the next day the landlord served us with an eviction notice for breaking the terms of our lease agreement. If I knew that hiding Kyron and Mike would have caused so many problems I never would have agreed to it. My mom explained to the landlord that she didn't have the money to move into a new apartment. The landlord extended the eviction notice from 30 days to 90 days to give her enough time to save up a security deposit for a new apartment.

On May 18, 1989, Jill and I graduated from junior high school. I hated the fact that we would soon be separated. Jill's mom had just about all of Jill that she could take so she planned on sending Jill to Michigan to live with her father in August. My mom had to be out of our apartment by August 1st. Knowing that this would be our last summer together, Jill and I hung as much as we could. Kyron and Mike had been sent to juvenile hall so we didn't see them anymore. We spent most of the time sitting around the house ordering pay-per view movies and watching videos. We ordered *Bill and Ted's Excellent Adventure* three times in one day on one occasion. I had no concept of money in those days. Pay-per view movies were $4.99 a pop. We had a VCR, I could have recorded the movie the first time, but there was something so exciting about calling the cable company and ordering a movie.

We didn't have jobs or boyfriends and eventually watching TV got boring. We started hanging around Katie again for a minute, but we decided that she was getting to weird so we let her go. One day we saw an advertisement on television about a "Party Line". The television ad was colorful and included and teens dancing around on the screen.

Are you bored? Want to meet new friends? Call the party line! 1-900-555-2020. Only $1.95 a minute.

Jill and I decided to call. It was fun. We didn't even think about the fact that the calls were costing $1.95 a minute. We would lie on my bedroom floor laughing and giggling on the phone.

During one particular phone conversation we met these guys, Brad, Scott, and Rico. They were 18 and 19 years old. We were only 14, but we lied and told them that we were 16 and that we were sophomores in high school.

Jill and I were young girls playing on the phone. The boys asked us if we were virgins and we said "no". They asked us how we looked; I told the one guy Brad that I had "big breast" and a "big old booty". Jill told Scott that she was "A White girl that liked Black ding-a-ling". We would giggle after every word that we said. Scott had a deep voice and he said to Jill,

"Hey you all sound sexy and cute as hell. You all live 3 hours away, if we drive up there to see you all will you give us gas money to get home?"

We didn't think they were for real. It was all one big joke to us. Jill gave them my real phone number and address. I didn't know what she was thinking, why would she give these complete strangers my address.

"We're on our way." Brad said. We hung up the phone. I looked at the clock. It was 11:07 P.M. Surely, they weren't about to drive three hours to meet two girls that they had never seen before. Jill and I didn't think anything else about it. We went to bed.

At 3:39 my phone rang. I jumped to answer the telephone on the first ring so that my mom wouldn't wake up.

"Hello", I whispered into the phone.

"Yeah it's Scott, Brad and Rico. We are outside of your building come on down." I woke up Jill. I ran over to my window and peeked down. There was a teenage Black boy talking on the payphone. The boy saw me and waved. On the phone Scott said, "Yeah we're here, where's your girl at." I was so scared. I handed Jill the phone. "Hello. You guys want to come up here. Lori's mom is home and you can't come in." Jill paused. I heard Scott talking through the phone but I couldn't make what he was saying.

"Look don't get an attitude with me, we didn't make you all drive this far." Jill started to roll her eyes. Scott was screaming through the telephone.

"Man, fuck you." Jill hung up the phone.

"What happened", I asked. Jill got back in the bed. She pulled the covers over her and said,

"Lori, he was so arrogant. He said, "We drove all of this way you better let us come up at least give us our gas money."

The phone rang again. I picked it up and hung up right away. I knew they would call again so I unplugged the phone from the wall.

Jill had given them my address, but she didn't tell them the exact apartment number. I heard them in the hallway knock on several doors looking for the apartment that we were in, but they knocked on the wrong doors. My neighbors didn't answer their doors. Jill had no problems going back to sleep, but I was scared. What if they would have broke in and tried to rape us?

The next morning as my mom was getting ready for work she asked,

"Who called in the middle of the night?" I peeked from under the covers.

"I don't know". Another lie. I lied too much. The truth was just too much to fathom.

Jill and I didn't have school so we slept in late that day. At 10:00 AM there was a knock on the door. By then we had almost forgotten about the boys from the night before. Surely they had gone home. I didn't even ask who it was. I opened the door and there stood the three guys.

"Why did you all play us shady like that? That wasn't even cool. We drove all of this way to see you all. We had to sleep in a parking lot." The guy talking was

Brad. He was an attractive Black teenage boy, but he was too old for us. Jill was sitting on the couch eating a bowl of cereal.

"Hey come on in." Jill motioned for them to come in. I stood there as they walked past me into my living room.

Brad was about six feet tall and had a smooth caramel complexion. He was wearing a Chicago Bull's short set and black Air Jordan gym shoes. Scott wore glasses. He wasn't bad looking, but his glasses were so thick they took away from his face. Rico was short and bald headed. He was wearing a thick sweat suit and it was 90 degrees outside. Greg sat on the couch and put his arm around Jill. He started to kiss her on her neck and she smiled.

"Ooh baby don't stop." Jill cooed. Why was my friend so easy? Jill let Brad kiss her on her neck and he started to put hickeys on her neck. I was sitting on the floor next to the couch. Scott sat down next to me and tried to kiss me. He looked so gross. He opened his mouth real wide and all I saw was tongue and teeth coming at me. I turned my head and put my hand in his face. Rico witnessed this and started to laugh. Scott's feelings were hurt.

"Why are you tripping?" He tried to kiss me again and I got up and ran across the room.

Over on the couch Brad and Jill were getting kind of cozy. Brad whispered into Jill's ear,

"Come on in the bedroom with me, I want to make love to you." Jill stood up. "Whatever, I just met you and I am not having sex with you." Rico had been quiet up until this point until.

"You little bitches are tripping, we came all this way, you owe us, you owe all of us. You need to give up some sex." I was really nervous. There were three of them and two of us. They were men. They were stronger than we were. I was afraid they would try to hurt us.

"Look, you have to leave. My mom is on her way home".

"Sure we'll leave. Give us our gas money. We need $10 dollars to get back home", Scott held out his hand. I didn't have $10 and I knew that Jill was broke.

Scott was extremely persistent about us giving him $10 for gas money. I knew that my mom kept a little money under her mattress. I left Jill and the guys in the living room. I went into my mom's room and lifted up the mattress and took $10. I bolted back into the living room.

"Look here is your money, will you please leave now!" I slammed the $10 into Scott's hand. What happened next proves that Jill and I were definitely not as smart as we thought that we were.

Scott, Brad and Rico conversed among themselves. Brad then looked at us with his big brown eyes.

"Can you all come with us and show us the way to the highway?" I wasn't falling for this trick.

"You found your way here in the middle of the night, just retrace your steps." I put my hands on my hips and made a real tough girl face. Brad started to lay it on thick.

"We came all this way to see you beautiful ladies. We got lost. Show us the way to the highway, please. Once we see the highway, we will turn around and drop you back at home".

I had a bad feeling about the whole thing. Jill jumped up off the couch.

"It couldn't hurt, come on Lori." Jill put down her bowl of cereal. If Jill was down, I was down.

We walked out of the apartment building and we got in the car with the boys. Jill didn't have any shoes on.

"Jill, why don't you have any shoes on?" I asked.

"Lori we'll be right back." Jill opened up the car door and sat down. It was a beautiful Wednesday morning. The sun was shining and it was about 90 degrees outside. Rico was driving and Scott sat in the driver's seat. Brad was in the back seat with us. He was whispering in Jill's ear and sucking on her neck. She didn't seem to mind.

"If I give you my number will you call me?" Brad asked. I didn't hear Jill's reply because I was busy giving Rico directions to the highway. I wasn't even too sure how to get to the highway. I knew the highway was by the mall.

I led Rico to the 294 Exit and he kept driving.

"Hey you passed the highway!" I shouted as I pointed out of the window.

"Oh, I'm just going to drive down this way and turn around so that we can drop you all back at home" Rico said with a sly look on his face. Scott just sat in the passenger's seat smiling and looking out of the window. Brad was trying to stick his hands down Jill's shorts and she was starting to resist. I was starting to get a really bad feeling.

Rico kept driving for about 5 miles until we were in a forest preserve. He pulled over to the car and stopped.

"Why are we stopping?" I asked.

"Shut Up", Scott screamed as he stared straight ahead. With the car stopped Brad became more persistent with his sexual advances toward Jill. Rico turned off the ignition and turned around toward the back seat.

"Look we drove all this way. You little bitches are going to have to give us some sex. Head, pussy, something. No more games".

Scott started to laugh.

"Rico you are a fool." Rico leaned over the backseat and lunged toward me. Scared, I jumped out of the car and started to run. Rico opened his door and started to run after me.

What I did next puzzles me to this day. Perhaps I was acting out of fear. I ran towards the car and snatched the keys out of the ignition and started to run into the woods. Scott jumped out of the car and started to chase me. Rico opened the truck and pulled out an object. Meanwhile, Brad was trying to rape Jill in the back seat.

Scott caught me and pulled my arms behind my back. Rico had a crowbar in his hands.

"I'm tired of playing games with you little bitches, give me my god damn keys right now!" I threw his keys at him. He took the crowbar and swung it and hit me in my thigh. I fell to the ground as Scott dropped me. Jill was in the car kicking and screaming.

"Hey man, we're out of here," Scott said as got back in the car. Brad pushed Jill out of the car onto the ground. Rico slammed his door. He started the car and drove off. I was lying on the ground in pain. Jill stood up and dusted herself off. She extended a hand to me and helped me to get up.

Here we were in the middle of a forest preserve. It was 90 degrees outside and we had no water and no money. Jill didn't even have shoes on her feet. We didn't know what to do. We just started walking.

"Ouch, dammit!" Jill yelped as the sidewalk started to burn her feet. We walked for about an hour before we made it out of the forest preserve. When we emerged from the forest we found ourselves on a golf course. We walked along the golf course. We were trying to find our way home. We knew that we were still in Schaumburg and that eventually we would find a street or someone that we recognized. Jill was turning red from sunburn. Her neck was covered with hickeys that Brad had put on her. Her feet were burned and peeling from walking on the hot pavement. I also looked a mess. I was tired and exhausted.

The golf course that we were walking through was private property. We were running out of steam. I was going to collapse. We had walked at least five or six miles. A police car pulled up next to us we thought that we were rescued.

Officer friendly to the rescue. Not! The police officer on the passenger side rolled down his window.

"Hey what are you two girls doing out here? This is private property." I walked close to the police car and leaned over the edge of the window.

"We got lost, do you think you could give us a ride home?" The other police officer glanced over at Jill.

"What happened to your neck, and why don't you have any shoes on?" Jill rolled her eyes.

"I don't know where my shoes are, are you going to give us a ride home?"

We got in the police car, but the police didn't take us home. They took us straight to the Schaumburg Police station. They immediately separated us. They took Jill into one room and put me in another room. I remember the room I was in. I suppose it was an interrogation room. The room had a black window, which I later learned was one of those see through windows. I sat in the room by myself for about 45 minutes before the police officer came in to question me.

Why did I lie so much? Lying was my first instinct. I lied about my name. I lied about how we got out there. I told the police officer that my name was Lisa. I told him that "Me and my friend went on a bike ride and our bikes broke down and we decided to walk home". He didn't believe me, and in retrospect I can see why, that was a corny ass lie. After about 15 minutes of questioning the police officer invited a Black police officer to question me. The Black officer had more luck with me. He reminded me of a father type. He just broke it down.

"Look, I know you are lying. Your friend is in the other room lying to. Tell the truth. You are only hurting yourself".

I broke down like a baby. I told the police officer the entire story. I told him about the phone call, the $10, the crowbar, everything.

"What kind of car did these men drive?" the officer asked.

"I don't know, it was a big red car". The police officer made a few calls on the radio.

"So you don't know what car it was? What about your friend, was she raped?" I wonder what Jill had told the police. These police officers were good; they separated us before we could get our lie straight.

"No, she wasn't raped. She let the one guy put those hickeys on her neck".

To make a long story short, we spent about four hours in the police station. The police suspected us of being teenage prostitutes. That is what they told our parents. My mom was so disappointed me. I explained to her that it was all a big mistake when she came to pick me up but she didn't even want to hear what I was trying to say.

Jill's mom was furious. She had Jill's bags packed and in the car when she came to the police station to pick up Jill. The police released us to our parents. Jill's mom looked and me and then looked and Jill.

"Jill take a good look at your friend because this is the last time you will ever see her." Then my mom jumped in the conversation.

"Yeah, we had a long talk out here and we decided that it would be best to separate you two permanently

Our parents had talked like this before, but this time they were for real. Jill's mom drove Jill to Michigan that very evening. I spoke to Jill a couple of times by phone after she moved. Then our phone got disconnected. The phone bill came. The bill was $1627 dollars. I didn't realize that we had spent that much time on that 1-900 Party Line. Soon afterwards the cable bill came. It was $250 due to the fact that we ordered so many Pay-Per-View movies.

We soon moved to Chicago. My mother found us a new place to stay. We were moving to the south side of Chicago in a house 2 blocks away from my grandparent's home. I never spoke with Jill again. I heard from a friend of a friend that she is the single mother of two and that she is on welfare. I miss Jill. Sometimes I think about looking her up, but that was such a long time ago.

WILD CHILD

---▼---

The summer after I finished 8th grade we moved to the South Side of Chicago. I had spent my entire life living in predominantly white areas and suddenly I found myself thrust into an urban setting.

It took me a while to get used to the sounds of the city. The roar of the buses, the constant sound of motion would keep me up at night.

I was not at all happy about moving to the South Side. I felt like I was living in an area the was beneath the socio-economic level that I was accustomed to. Initially, I was very frightened of the city. I was scared of the people, I just knew I was a victim in waiting. I also couldn't get over seeing so many Black people. I had never been around so many other Black people in my life. I didn't know if I would be able to relate. I just didn't see how I would fit in.

We settled into our new home a week before I was scheduled to start my freshman year of high school. I didn't have any friends and I was depressed about leaving my old friends in Schaumburg.

My grandmother lived two blocks from my mother's new house on the south side.

I was in for the surprise of my life one afternoon when I went to visit my grandmother.

"Hey Grandma" I yelled as I walked in through the back door.

"Hey Lori, your cousin Ray-Ray is going to be living with me for a couple of months." My grandmother yelled back as she was in the front room watching "General Hospital".

Ray-Ray was my favorite female cousin. Ray-Ray was two years older than I was. Ray-Ray was from Atlanta. She was really ghetto, but she was cool people.

I hadn't seen Ray-Ray since I was twelve and she was fourteen. So you can imagine the shocked look on my face when I walked into the living room and saw the voluptuous grown woman Ray-Ray had become.

"What's up cuz" Ray-Ray gave me a hug. Ray-Ray was about five feet nine inches tall. Her bra size had to be at least a 42DD and the rest of her body was very shapely also. Ray-Ray was wearing a tight black Nike tee shirt and a pair of black Daisy Duke shorts.

I stood back and looked at Ray-Ray from a distance.

"You really have grown up." I said.

"No Lori, you have grown up. Look at you, we need to work on your hair and your clothes but you will be just fine."

"What's wrong with my clothes and hair?" I asked. I was wearing a pair of blue jogging pants and a white tee shirt. My hair was shoulder length and pulled back in a little tight ponytail.

"Well, you want to get a boyfriend don't you? You have to dress like a lady to get a man. Don't worry I'll help you out." Ray-Ray said.

I was 14 years old and I had never actually thought about having a real boyfriend. I had not yet started high school, and not many boys had ever tried to get with me.

All of that changed after a few days of hanging out with my cousin Ray-Ray.

The first thing Ray-Ray did was straighten my hair. With my hair straight I looked very nice with my shoulder length black hair sweeping off of my shoulders.

After we worked on my hair Ray-Ray and I went shopping. She bought me three short mini-skirts with matching tight shirts. She also bought me a pair of black biking shorts and a Nike tee shirt. Ray-Ray didn't have a job, but she always had money. I didn't ask where the money came from.

Ray-Ray was my favorite cousin and my best friend. Initially, I was hesitant about moving to Chicago, but with Ray-Ray by my side, I couldn't go wrong, at least I thought I couldn't.

Ray-Ray introduced me to a world that I had never been a part of. I had never had a boyfriend, wore make-up, or wore provocative clothes. When my cousin Ray-Ray and I would walk down the street all of the boys would take notice. I really enjoyed the attention from the opposite sex.

Ray-Ray was staying in Chicago with my grandmother because her mother was in jail in Atlanta for shoplifting. I was glad to have Ray-Ray around and I spent all of my free time with her.

School started the week after Ray-Ray and I started hanging out together. We both started school at Morgan Park High School on the first Monday after Labor Day in 1989. I was going to be a freshman and Ray-Ray was going to b entering the sophomore class.

I dressed like a hoochie in those days because Ray-Ray dressed like a hoochie and I thought it was cool. On the first day of school we wore the tightest black leather skirts we could find and tight red sweaters.

I had a big butt and a nice size chest, so of course all of the boys took notice to Ray-Ray and me as we entered the building. The women, they would just glare at us. Ray-Ray used to always tell me,

"Don't worry about bitches because you don't want them to like you. Do you see me hanging around any other females besides you? Hell no, because you can't trust them."

I was very nervous about starting school. I didn't see any White people. I had never been to a predominantly Black school before. I went to my first period class and sat at my desk. I felt completely lost and lonely. Ray-Ray wasn't in my class and it seemed as if everyone in the class knew each other from one place or another.

By the end of my first week of school, I hadn't made any new friends, but I did have three new phone numbers. I was a huge flirt with the opposite sex. Ray-Ray prepped me well for the dating game. She taught me how to walk sexy and how to pout my shiny red lips when I talk to boys.

Out of the three phone numbers I had, I only decided to call one of the boys. His name was Rick. Rick was a freshman and he lived in the Altgeld Gardens projects. He was a bad boy. He was in a gang, but I didn't care, he was attractive and I liked him.

Rick was about six feet tall and he had gorgeous brown eyes. His hair was long and he wore it in cornrows.

I didn't see it at the time, but Ray-Ray was a terrible influence on me. She was prepping me, a somewhat innocent 14 year old, to become a tramp.

The Saturday after the first week of school had finished, Ray-Ray and I planned a double date. We would be going to the movies with a guy that she met at school named Pookie and I would be going with Rick.

"Lori, if you hook up with this Rick boy you say that you like you have to have sex with him. If you don't you will lose him to another girl." Ray-Ray combed her hair as we got ready for our date. I looked down at my feet when Ray-Ray mentioned sex.

"Lori. Ohmigod, don't tell me you are still a virgin. Aren't you 15 years old?"

"I'm only 14, and of course I'm not a virgin, I've had sex plenty of times." I lied to Ray-Ray. For some reason, it just wasn't cool to be a virgin.

"That's good. I was about to say. You have to be ready to get it. Always use a condom though because you don't want to get pregnant by any of these bums out here." Ray-Ray always provided such wonderful advice.

The four of us took the bus to Evergreen Plaza movie theatre to watch a movie. I can't remember what we saw at the time. After the movie was over we all headed over to Pookie's house.

Pookie lived with his grandfather. His grandfather was deaf. So Pookie would always invite people over to his house to hang out in the basement and his grandfather would never be any wiser.

Pookie's basement was set-up like a low budget love shack. The basement was complete with two twin beds, a mini-fridge and a television set. Pookie also had a nice stereo system. Pookie dimmed the lights and turned on some slow music.

Rick and I were sitting together in the corner in a love seat. Pookie and Ray-Ray were laying on the bed kissing. Pookie was massaging Ray-Ray's breast as Ray-Ray stroked Pookie's back.

Rick stared at Pookie and Ray-Ray and leaned over and whispered in my ear.

"Are you scared to do what they are doing?"

"No, I'm not scared." I wasn't lying, I really wasn't scared.

Rick and I walked over to the other twin bed. Rick started to kiss me so hard. I remember just feeling his tongue deep down in my throat. I had never kissed a boy before, so I didn't know if I was doing it right. Rick wasn't complaining, so I guess I was doing okay. I tried to peek at Ray-Ray and Pookie. I couldn't tell if they were actually "doing-it" or not, but they were doing something. Ray-Ray's eyes were closed and she was moaning loudly.

As I was looking over at Ray-Ray and Pookie, Rick pulled my face close to his and started to kiss me harder. He lifted up my skirt and put his fingers inside of me.

"What are you doing?" I asked.

"Shhhh…just calm down," he whispered in my ear. What he was doing felt kind of good, so I didn't stop him.

Rick next pulled my skirt all of the way down and proceeded to pull his pants down. He opened up a little package, which I later found out was a condom package. Rick put the condom on.

I laid their thinking to myself. Is this really the way that I want to lose my virginity? Lying in some guy name Pookie's basement with my cousin Ray-Ray on the next bed getting poked herself? Then I thought to myself, "Hell, why not."

Rick pushed himself up inside of me and it felt really, really good. I had read all of these about girls losing their virginity and bleeding or being in a lot of pain, and my experience was just the opposite, I liked it.

The first time Rick and I had sex in Pookie's basement it lasted about 45 minutes. I remember that I was so paranoid about getting pregnant. I was so afraid.

After Rick and I were finished, Pookie and Ray-Ray finished. The two boys walked us back to my grandmother's house.

Ray-Ray and I stayed up all night talking.

"So do you like Rick?" Ray-Ray asked.

"Yeah, I like him. I did it with him didn't I?"

"Just because you did it with him doesn't mean you have to like him."

"Do you like Pookie?" I asked.

"He's alright. His thing is a little small, but he has a little money. I might mess round with him for awhile."

That night as I fell asleep, I dreamed sweet thoughts of Rick and I being together forever. I thought that since we had sex, that meant I was his girlfriend, and we would never break up. I was so naïve.

Monday I went back to school. I couldn't wait to see Rick. I went to my first two classes. At 9:40 as I was leaving my second class I saw Rick.

"Hey sexy." I looked up from my locker and there was Rick. Rick smiled and I looked up at him.

"Hi." I smiled so hard I thought my face would break.

"Let's get out of here." Rick said.

"What about class?" I asked.

"We'll be back before anyone misses us. What are your next three classes?" He asked.

"Gym, Art, and Biology." I said.

"Follow me." I grabbed my purse out of the locker and followed Rick out of the back door of the school. We ran straight to the bus stop.

"There is a bus at 9:45." Rick said as he grabbed my hand.

"Where are we going?" I asked.

"To my house." Rick said with a smile.

The bus came and we took the bus to Rick's house. Once we walked in the house he ripped off my clothes and we went at it. We had sex everywhere, in the bedroom, in the kitchen, in the living room. I really loved being with Rick. After we would make love, he would hold me tight and kiss me.

After our session ended, Rick and I would shower together and take the bus back to school. I would arrive at school just as Biology class ended. I didn't worry about the three classes that I would miss, but I was having so much fun with Rick, I didn't care.

Daily sex sessions with Rick continued for months. After awhile we got sloppy. Some days we wouldn't even go back to school after we had sex. Most days we didn't even use condoms. I was a smart girl, I knew I could get pregnant, but for some reason I thought it wouldn't happen to me. I was athletic, young and fit.

On New Years Eve of 1989, I was sick as hell. I thought I was dying. My mother had a party and had invited some of her co-workers. She was embarrassed because she thought that I had gotten into some of the alcohol. Ray-Ray held my hand as I threw up in the bathroom.

"When was your last period?" Ray-Ray asked.

"October." I cried.

"Damn, Lori! I think you are pregnant." Ray-Ray shouted.

"Shhh! My mom will here." I whispered.

"Fuck it, don't worry about it, we'll take care of things." Ray-Ray whispered.

I believed Ray-Ray, I thought she could fix anything. If I was pregnant, I didn't believe it. The sickness I was experiencing passed and I went back to my normal life.

"Did you tell Rick that you might be pregnant?" Ray-Ray asked me one day as we were walking in the park.

"No, I didn't tell him. I don't think I am pregnant." I said.

"Whatever, you period never came did it?" Ray-Ray asked.

"No, it didn't come back." I said as I looked at the pavement.

I was 14 years old. What was I going to do with a baby? I was really enjoying my life. I wanted to go to college or beauty school one day. Plus on top of that, my parents would kill me.

I went on with my life as usual. Ray-Ray would give me helpful hints on what to do if I was pregnant. She would say,

"Jump rope and drink lots of soda and that will make it go away if you are pregnant."

Ray-Ray's advice didn't work. By the time March rolled around, I was pretty confident that I was pregnant. Rick and I weren't doing well because I had decided that I like a boy around my neighborhood named Cliff. Cliff was cute and he was one of Pookie's friends. I broke up with Rick to go out with Cliff. Cliff and I lasted about three days because we argued about his dancing skills. He asked me if he was a better dancer than Mc Hammer and I told him that I thought Hammer was better. His feelings were hurt and we broke up.

When I broke up with Rick he told everyone that I was a whore and he spread rumors about all of the freaky things that I supposedly did to him. He even told people about how we used to sneak away from school to have sex.

My reputation was ruined and all of my so-called "sistas" at school talked about me like shit. Everyone was so judgmental. I didn't understand what the big deal was. I later came to the realization that the girls who weren't having sex, thought I was a threat to their relationships because I was.

I decided to get a job to pay for an abortion. I was only 14 when Ray-Ray and I went to the local wash named "Laundromat" looking for work. The man, who owned the Laundromat, Mr. Franklin hired both of us on the spot. My hours were Monday, Wednesday and Friday from 3:00-6:00 P.M.

My main responsibilities were simple. I would sweep the floors and give patrons change when they asked for it. I was concerned that I would be the only person in the store during my shift, but Ray-Ray promised that she would stay with me during my shift.

I called the abortion clinics around Chicago and they quoted me a price of $250. I only made $3 an hour at the Laundromat. I was so confused. I had really screwed up my life.

I didn't tell my parents about my condition and my mother couldn't even tell. My clothes still fit like normal and I felt great.

My second Wednesday working at the Laundromat was a nightmare. Around 4:00 P.M. we ran out of change. All of the customers were mad because they couldn't dry their clothes. All of the customers packed up their clothes and left to go to the Laundromat across the street. Ray-Ray had promised that she would hang out with me during my shift, but she spent all of her time over at Pookie's house. I decided to call her on the phone to tell her what happened.

I walked to the back of the Laundromat to use the telephone in the office. In retrospect, I probably should have locked the store, but I wasn't thinking.

I picked up the phone and started dialing Pookie's number.

"Hey, is Ray-Ray there?" I asked.

"Hold on." Pookie said on the other end.

"Yeah, what's up." Ray-Ray answered.

Before I got another word out I felt someone come up behind me. I dropped the phone and the person took the telephone cord and started to choke me with it. I put my fingers on the cords and pulled it to prevent it from completely cutting off my air supply. I turned around and kicked the person.

When I turned around I was face to face with a strung out woman. The woman's eyes were sunken in and her face skin was cracked. She was holding a black gun in her hands. I was hysterical.

"What do you want!" I cried.

"Open the motherfucking safe!" The woman screamed.

"I don't know the combination!" I cried as I faced the safe in the office. I could hear Ray-Ray screaming my name through the telephone.

"Well give me the money in the register!" The woman yelled. The woman walked me towards the front of the store. I opened up the register and gave the woman the $17 dollars in the register.

"Please don't kill me." I cried as I handed the woman the money.

"$17, that's all you have to give me." The woman grabbed my purse from under the counter. I don't know what I was thinking; I should have just been quiet and let the woman have the purse.

"Please don't steal my purse, I don't have any money. All that is in there is my school ID and my bus pass." I cried.

The woman opened up my purse and took out the bus pass. I stood there shaking and crying. I just knew I was dead.

The woman held the gun towards me. I continued to beg and plead for my life. The woman reached the gun high up in the air and struck me in the head with the gun.

She hit me so hard with the gun I thought I was dead. I just remember seeing black. I fell to the floor and that's all I remember.

I woke up, from what I can gather, about ten minutes later. I was laying on the floor of the Laundromat with Ray-Ray and Pookie standing over me. Ray-Ray had poured water on me in an attempt to wake me up.

By the time I regained consciousness, an ambulance had arrived. The ambulance took me to Roseland Hospital. My mother was waiting at the hospital when the ambulance arrived at the hospital.

I went through a series of tests at the hospital. I was in so much pain from the blow that I took to the head. The doctors performed a CAT scan. They determined that my skull had been fractured, but that it would fuse back together.

I remember sitting in the hospital room looking at the x-rays of my brain.

"You're a lucky girl." The doctor said.

"Yeah, I guess so." I said.

"Mom can I talk to you in the hallway?" The doctor asked.

What did he want to talk to my mom about? My head was spinning from pain. Then it dawned on me. They knew I was pregnant. Oh shit. What was I going to do? I thought about things. There was not much I could do. I just sat in the hospital room awaiting my mothers return.

As I suspected, the doctors told my mother that they suspected that I was pregnant and they asked for her consent to run a pregnancy test. My mother gave them the consent that they requested and not to my surprise the test came back positive.

My mother sat in my hospital room crying. She wasn't crying about my fractured skull. She was crying because her 14-year-old daughter was pregnant.

"You could have told me that you were having sex, I would have told you about how to protect yourself." My mother cried. I sat there in the hospital bed holding the covers close to my chin.

"I knew how to protect myself. I was just being stupid. I don't want to have it. I was trying to raise money to have an abortion." I whispered.

"Well that's good because you have no business having a baby and you can't even take care of yourself."

The following day I was released from the hospital my mother took me to a place I like to call "Sunny Brook Farm." When we left the hospital we got in the car and drove for what seemed like hours.

"Where are we going?" I asked.

"I'm taking you some place where they can get you out of trouble." My mother said as she drove.

About three hours later we arrived at "Sunny Brook Farm." The place was not really named "Sunny Brook Farm", but that was the first thing that came to my mind when we arrived.

We actually were at Sunnyvale Youth Counseling and Medical Center in Michigan. The place was bright and cheerful. As we walked through the sliding double doors the staff greeted us.

"Welcome to Sunnyvale." A blonde woman said with a smile on her face.

"Here is a clipboard for you mom and here is a clipboard for you." The woman handed my mother and I clipboards.

"Just have a seat and fill out the paperwork and someone will be right with you."

My mother and I took a seat at the first pair of empty seats that we found.

I looked down at my clipboard and started to read.

Welcome to Sunnyvale. You are here because you decided to take the first step in your recovery process. Please circle the reason that you are with us today.

Anorexia	**Bulimia**	**TeenPregnancy**
Alcoholism	**Drug Addition**	**Rebellious Behavior**

I circled teen pregnancy. My mother leaned over and circle rebellious behavior also. I felt like I was in the loony bin for sure. I continued to read.

By signing below you acknowledge that you are here on your own free will.

I looked over at my mom. Then I looked down at my stomach. I signed the form.

I was very frightened. Was I going to have to stay at this place forever?", What about school? What about Ray-Ray?

"Mom, am I going to be here forever? I asked my mother as she searched for her insurance card.

"No. Not forever." My mother said as she pulled her insurance card out of her wallet.

The blonde woman called are name and we went in a small room to talk to a counselor.

The counselor was a sort woman with curly brown hair. She seemed very friendly; but then again, everyone at Sunnyvale seemed friendly. I felt like I was in the fricken Twilight Zone.

The woman read over the documents that my mother and I had filled out.

"So Lori, you are pregnant. Would you like to have an abortion?"

"Yes, I would." I mumbled.

"And mom you wrote that Lori has been extremely rebellious since your divorce and that she has even been in some trouble with the police."

"Yes, that is true." My mother nodded her head.

"Well mom. We can help Lori. You understand that by signing the consent form you are allowing her to being under our constant care for medical attention and counseling. We normally determine the length of our patient's stay on the seriousness of the initial diagnosis and their progress during treatment. Just by taking an initial glance at Lori's paperwork I am recommending that she stay here at Sunnyvale for 45 days."

I leaned back in the chair and threw my arms in the air. I thought about saying something but I looked at my mother and just kept my mouth closed. I couldn't be quiet.

"What about school?" I said. The counselor opened a pamphlet.

"We at Sunnyvale coordinate your education with your school. You will meet with our tutors and your school will send us your lessons. You may actually find that your grades improve." The counselor explained.

We spent an hour talking with the counselor and then it was time for my mother to leave and head back to Chicago. I was very sad to see her go.

"I love you Lori. You'll be just fine. I will come to see you on visiting day." My mother kissed my forehead and walked away.

Immediately, after my mother left I was whisked away to my room. While at Sunnyvale I was going to be sharing a room with a 15-year-old girl named Carla who had an eating disorder. I changed into the standard Sunnyvale attire, which was an orange sweatshirt with matching orange sweat pants.

After I changed clothes, the counselor came to retrieve me to attend my first counseling session. I knew this place was going to suck. I didn't need any counseling I just needed an abortion. I didn't want to be there. I didn't want to hear what anyone wanted to say. I wanted to go home.

The counselor, who I later found out was named Ms. Dana, led me to a bright red room. The room was decorated with bright artwork. Beanbag furniture covered the floor. Eight other girls were sitting on the floor. The girls were all wearing the Sunnyvale outfits and they sat on the floor in a circle. I sat down.

Ms. Dana led the counseling session.

"Hello. This is all of you all's first day at Sunnyvale and I want you all to introduce yourself. You are all here because you are pregnant and have decided to terminate your pregnancy. We are going to help you through this difficult time, and through counseling and education you all can help each other."

I sat there silently as I listened to each girl tell their story. I wasn't the youngest girl there. Some girls were 12 and 13 years old. I remember feeling sad because the 12 year old had conflicting feelings about not having her baby. I didn't have any real emotions to share with the group. I was very nonchalant about the whole situation.

The entire group shared their story and it was my turn.

"Lori, are you read to share your story?" Ms. Dana asked.

I looked around the room. Faces of different races all in the same situation stared back at me. I didn't know what to say. I opened my mouth and the words just came out.

"Well at first I didn't think I was pregnant. Even when I had a pretty good idea that I was I pushed it to the back of my mind. I wasn't in love with my boyfriend. I liked having sex with him, but we broke up. I just no I don't want to have a baby. I still want to have fun." I looked down at the floor.

"Lori, thanks for sharing. I want to point out a few things about what you said. You ended your statement saying, "I still want to have fun" That is one of the subjects we are going to talk about while you are here at Sunnyvale. Selfishness. You all are going to learn how your actions impact yourself and the people around you."

I looked at the group. Then I looked at Ms. Dana. Yeah, this place was going to be the pits. I didn't even open my mind to what she was trying to tell me.

After three days of intense counseling the "abortion day" came along. At Sunnyvale they didn't call it an abortion, they called it, "the procedure." The day of the procedure the eight of us had an early morning counseling session with Ms. Dana.

"Now all of you be brave. We will meet back here at 4:00 P.M. By that time all of you will have had your procedure. We will discuss your thoughts and feelings about the procedure."

Ms. Dana walked all of to the medical corridor. Some of the girls were crying.

"I don't want to kill my baby!" A 13-year-old girl named Farrah shouted in the corridor.

"Stop acting like a baby. Be a woman. You don't have to do this if you don't want to." A girl named Ursula shouted.

"Yeah, you are making me nervous." The 12-year-old said.

We arrived at the medical facility and we all sat down. One by one they called us back to the operating room.

The nurse called my name and I walked into the room. I climbed up on the table and put my feet in the stirrups.

I looked up at the bright light on the ceiling. The doctor walked over to me and shook my hand. He was a tall White man with a silver beard.

"Hi, Lori. We are going to put you to sleep and you won't feel anything." The anesthesiologist put an IV in my arm.

"How old are you Lori?" The doctor asked.

"I'll be 15 next week." I said.

"Do you have a dad?" The doctor asked.

"Don't be stupid, yeah I have a dad. He is a.."

I fell asleep. I was out cold.

When I woke up I was in the recovery room. The "procedure" was over. All of my newfound Sunnyvale friends were in the recovery room with me. The 12-year-old was crying hysterically. Me, I was chilling. I felt like a weight had been lifted off of me. I was ready to hit the streets and hang out with Ray-Ray again.

The next month at Sunnyvale was the pits. I spent my days attending counseling sessions and working with a tutor on my schoolwork. My roommate was a nutcase. She would steal food from the cafeteria and stare at it.

"Why does food cause me to have the problems I do?" She would say to herself, as she would stare at a Twinkie.

"I don't know. You are stronger than the food." I would say as I read a magazine.

I did form strong relationships with some of the girls I met in Sunnyvale. Sunnyvale had strict rules. We were not allowed to exchange phone numbers or addresses. We could not make any attempts to contact each other upon our completion of the program. I guess they figured that if we all hooked up we would get in trouble again.

While I was there I made a pact with myself that I would try my best to not disappoint my parents in life. I felt as thought I had been given a second chance and that it was up to me to make a difference with my life.

The counselors at Sunnyvale really felt like they had made some progress with me. Ms. Dana and her cohorts felt like they had cured me of my rebellious behavior. In all actuality, the peace and serenity of Sunnyvale only made me long for my old life. I couldn't wait to get back to Chicago. I missed Ray-Ray and I even wanted to have sex again. This time I would be protected. I didn't want to go through all of the drama of getting pregnant again.

Forty-five days after I entered Sunnyvale I left a free woman. My mother and my brother picked me up. We stopped at Wendy's and I ordered a Single with Cheese Combo. That was the best Wendy's meal I had ever had. Sunnyvale didn't have the best food in the world.

Sunnyvale didn't cure me, or at least I didn't think that it. It didn't take me long to get back to my old self.

My mother didn't want me hanging around Ray-Ray so for two months I played it cool. I would only talk to Ray-Ray on the phone. I would go to school everyday and come straight home. At the end of the school year I brought home a report card with good grades.

Summertime came and my mom got a new job. Her new job required her to travel a lot. This meant that I had more freedom. It didn't take long before I was up to my old tricks with my cousin Ray-Ray.

During the summer of 1990, I was 15 years old. Ray-Ray was 16 going on 17 and we felt like the world was ours. Ray-Ray was still dating Pookie and I was single and ready to take the world by storm.

I would put on my tight skirts and short shirts that would show off my belly button. I would walk up and down the street like a young girl in heat. Ray-Ray and I spent the whole summer outside it seemed.

Our summer was relatively "trouble-free" until the 4th of July weekend. Pookie borrowed a car from a drug dealer named Silkie. Silkie was fine and he always had nice cars. He would drive up and down the street and blast Ice Cube from his speakers. Pookie borrowed a 1990 Chevy Blazer from Silkie. The Blazer was souped up with rims and a hot ass sound system.

"Let me drive." Ray-Ray asked Pookie as we stood outside of his house.

"Hell no, you can't drive." Pookie said.

"We are only going to go around the corner." Ray-Ray pleaded.

"I'm not letting you drive Ray-Ray, you can forget about it."

Pookie jumped in the truck.

"I'm going to the liquor store. I'll be right back."

Pookie and his friend Trey drove off.

Ray-Ray and I sat on Pookie's back porch with his sister Ricca.

Ricca was a fast little girl. She was 13 years old and she drank and smoked weed. She also had a 17-year-old boyfriend who sold drugs on the block. Ray-Ray and Ricca didn't get along very well, but they tolerated each other.

Ray-Ray and I sat on Pookie's front porch and waited for him and Trey to return from the store.

Almost an hour later, the two still hadn't returned.

"Lori, this is some bullshit. Let's go to the park. I'm not going to sit around here and wait on Pookie all day."

Ray-Ray got up and I followed her.

The walk to the park was a short one. The park was two blocks from Pookie's house.

It was the 4th of July and the park was filled with picnic tables and families barbecuing. The basketball court was packed with fine men playing basketball.

"Ray-Ray, let's go over to the basketball court." I said.

"Yeah, let's go over there."

Ray-Ray and I walked over to the basket ball court and sat on the benches and watched the boys play basketball. We had only been their fifteen minutes when we looked across the park and saw Pookie's truck pull up. As we looked closer, we realized that Pookie was not in the truck with Trey. He was in the truck with another girl.

As soon as Ray-Ray realized what she was seeing she jumped up and ran across the park. I ran behind her as fast as I could. Pookie saw us coming and he drove off.

"Damn him, come on Lori, come with me to grandma's house." Ray-Ray said in an out of breath voice.

"Why are we going there?" I asked.

"Because I know who that girl is and we have to take care of her."

We went back to my grandmother's house and went to the basement. In the basement we put on our "fighting clothes." We put Vaseline on our face and took off our jewlery. Ray-Ray grabbed a steal baseball bat and handed me a tie iron.

"What are we going to do with this?" I asked.

"We are about to get our scrap on." Ray-Ray bolted out the basement door and I followed behind her.

Our destination was Church Street. 1414 Church Street. We were headed to Shawna Taylor's house.

"How do you know that was Shawna in the truck Ray-Ray?" I asked. I was nervous. I had never had a fight before, let alone a fight with weapons.

"I know that was her." Ray-Ray shouted. I felt the steam coming from her.

Shawna's house was enclosed with a metal gate. We opened the gate and walked up the steps. Ray-Ray rang the doorbell. No one answered. I swung the bat aimlessly in the air.

"No one is here. Come on let's go." I said as I retreated down the steps.

As we were walking out of the gate the door opened.

"Ray-Ray why did you come over to my house you fat bitch." We looked up and there was Shawna Taylor. Shawna was a thin light-skinned chick with long Black hair. She used to always tell people that she was mixed with Indian, that is why her hair was so straight.

"I want to know what you were doing with Pookie. That is my man." Ray-Ray screamed.

"Why yawl got bats? Yawl came to fight? So I rode in the car with Pookie, big deal. He asked me to. You better go home before you all get beat down."

We looked up and three of Shawna's friends came out of the house.

"Bitch, we ain't scared!" Ray-Ray screamed as she waved the bats. I was scared.

Shawna and her friends ran out of the gate, sans weapons and attempted to beat us down. I swung my bat and hit a few people until someone took the bat from me. Ray-Ray was going crazy with her bat; she was swinging it like crazy. She almost hit me.

The fight lasted about fifteen minutes. After the fight was over, Ray-Ray and I ran back to our grandmother's house to recuperate.

When we looked at each other after the fight we couldn't do anything but laugh. Ray-Ray's hair was a mess and my clothes were torn. We were young and fighting did not seem like a bad thing. We ended up fighting those girls every time that we would see them for the remainder of the summer.

After the fight, we changed clothes and I put on one of my cute outfits. While I was changing clothes I thought about Sunnyvale. I had only been out of there a couple of months and I was already up to no good.

Later that evening, Ray-Ray and I went over to Pookie's house. She confronted him about having Shawna in the truck with him and he claimed that Shawna was "just a friend." Ray-Ray and Pookie made up. She never stayed made at him for long.

It was the 4th of July and the sun had set. The sky was lit with fireworks. Ray-Ray, Ricca and I sat on Pookie's front porch. Pookie was washing the truck that he had borrowed from Silkie.

"Let me drive the truck." Ray-Ray asked.

"Hell no. You can't drive." Pookie playfully sprayed the water hose in our direction.

"I can drive. My uncle taught me to drive. Come on Pookie, we'll bring it right back. We'll only go around the block." Ray-Ray pleaded.

Pookie had just gotten out of the doghouse for riding around with Shawna earlier in the day. He wanted to get 100% back in Ray-Ray's good graces.

"Okay. You can drive the truck. But you have to promise to bring it right back. Take Ricca. If you bring Ricca I know you will be right back."

Ray-Ray, Ricca, and I ran towards the truck. Ray-Ray sat in the passenger's seat and Pookie handed her the keys through the window.

"Be careful and don't get into any trouble." Pookie kissed Ray-Ray on the cheek.

Ray-Ray turned up the radio and sped down the block. We drove all around Chicago. We had no destination in mind. We were young, it was the 4th of July and we had wheels.

Ray-Ray drove onto the Dan Ryan Expressway and headed towards downtown Chicago. I remember she was going 90 miles per hour down the highway, pumping Digital Underground in the stereo.

I was having the time of my life. At the same time I was worried that we would get pulled over. I knew Ray-Ray didn't have a license and I feared that the truck was probably hot. The truck belonged to Silkie, and chances are he had stolen it.

We drove around for two hours. When the truck was almost out of gas, we decided to take it back to Pookie.

"Hey drop me off at home." I said.

Ray-Ray drove down my block and I said my "good-byes" and walked into the house. My mother was fast asleep on the couch.

I went into my bedroom to take off my make-up when I saw a light flickering from the window. I walked over to my window and I peered out.

Outside a police was had pulled over Ray-Ray in the truck. I wasn't scared for Ray-Ray and Ricca; I was scared for myself. I turned off all of the lights in the house and I got in the bed.

Fifteen minutes later, there was a knock at the door. It was Ricca and a tall, handsome Black police officer.

"Lori, tell them that you were in the truck with us?" Ricca said. I looked at Ricca, then I looked at the police officer. Then I thought about my mom on the couch sleep.

"No officer, they came by to visit me, but I told them that it was too late for me to come outside." I lied. I sold out my cousin and Ricca.

"Goodnight." The officer led Ricca by the hand and walked her to the squad car.

I peered out of my window through my mini-blinds. Outside I saw that the police had Ricca and Ray-Ray up against the squad car. Both of them were handcuffed. I watched outside for as long as I could. The police eventually placed both of the girls in the squad car and drove off.

I had to do something. I snuck out of my window and ran to Pookie's house. It was 1:30 in the morning, and here I was running three blocks through the mean streets of Chicago, by myself. I was only 15 years old and I feared that I would get raped or abducted on my way to Pookie's house.

I made my way to Pookie's house. I knocked on the basement window.

"Pookie, it's me." Pookie came to the window.

"Hey, Ricca and Ray-Ray were arrested in front of my house. I don't know why. Let's go to the police station and find out what happened."

Pookie called his friend Trey. Trey came over in his father's car and the three of us went to the police station. We walked into the police station and we immediately saw Ray-Ray and Ricca handcuffed to chairs.

"Awe, bitch, I know you didn't come up here." Ray-Ray screamed at me. Why was Ray-Ray mad at me?

"What did I do?" I said as I pointed to myself.

"Ricca told me how you lied and said that you weren't in the truck."

"What was I supposed to say." I whispered.

"Oh shut up you sold us out." Ricca scowled at me.

"Oh officer, she was with us, come handcuff her." Ray-Ray shouted to an officer.

"I told you. I didn't see her in the car. I can't touch her. I saw you driving and the other young lady in the passenger seat." The officer said as he filled out paperwork.

I was really shocked that Ray-Ray and Ricca were so mad at me. I felt that if the situation had reversed they would have done the same thing.

Turns out that the truck we had been riding around it had been stolen. A pregnant woman was car-jacked at the 7-11 on 127th and Western Avenue. Two men pulled up next to the woman and pulled her out of the car. The woman went into premature labor. Her and the baby survived the ordeal.

The police knew that Ray-Ray and Ricca had not stolen the car. However, the way that the facts unfolded proved that they were in a stolen vehicle. They were locked up until their trial dates. They were charged with a number of offenses, including joyriding and possession of a stolen vehicle.

Ricca was only 13. She was sentenced to 90 days in juvenile hall. Ray-Ray was 16. She was charged as an adult and she spent 9 months in a woman's correctional facility in Moline, Illinois.

I wrote Ray-Ray while she was locked up. She never wrote me back. Ray-Ray was angry with me for a very long time. Ricca never spoke to me again. Pookie hated me because he felt that I "sold-out" his little sister. I couldn't understand why it was so important to them to see me go down with them.

When Ray-Ray was released from jail, we saw each other from time to time. After all, she was still my cousin. Things were never the same. We didn't hang out anymore.

I don't regret lying to save my ass. I only regret that so many people were hurt in the process.

Young Thug

---◆---

Trouble used to always come my way. I used to think that world had it in for me, but now that I reflect on things I realize that I brought a lot of trouble on myself.

I sit here writing with a clean criminal record. How that is, is a miracle to me considering all of my run-ins with the law. The first time that I saw the inside of a squad card was during the summer before 8th grade. My friend and I were picked up for suspicion of shoplifting. Then I was suspected of being a teen prostitute. (See Earlier Chapters for the full scoop on those incidents.)

I next found myself in trouble in high school. I attended high school on the south side of Chicago. My high school had your mix of students. You had your athletes, your smart kids, the popular kids; it was your average American high school demographically.

I don't think that I fit into any one category. I wasn't necessarily a smart kid, but I wasn't stupid either. My favorite class during my junior year was Physics. My physics teacher Mrs. Tallman had faith in me. She felt that I was very smart, but that I didn't apply myself in school because I was too preoccupied with boys. I would ace every physics test with a 100%.

Mrs. Tallman felt I had enormous potential so she signed me up for a college prep physics course at the University of Chicago. I was very honored to be chosen to participate in this program. Along with myself, Mrs. Tallman also enrolled 4 other of my classmates in the program. The college prep course would meet every other Saturday for 4 hours. The other students selected included a boy who was nicknamed Yoda, another boy name Leon, who was very smart, another girl named Shantrice who was very quiet, and a girl named Contessa. Contessa was someone that I didn't know very well. She wasn't in my physics class. I was in Mrs. Tallman's morning class and Contessa was a student from her afternoon class.

I was anxious for the class to start. Our first meeting was on the first Saturday in November. The class took place on a big college campus in an auditorium. The course was all lecture, but it was very interesting to me. It got me thinking about my future. I knew that I wanted to attend college one day, but I had no idea what I wanted my course of study to be.

Students from other high schools in the city of Chicago attended the college prep course. The grand total of class attendees was an even 100. Five students from 20 Chicago Public Schools. All of the students from my school sat together, except Contessa and Shantrice, who sat in the front row. The first class lasted about 3 ½ hours. After the class, my classmates and I decided to stop at the pizza parlor on campus and share a pizza. We talked about class and we talked about school. They were a pretty cool bunch and I enjoyed their company.

The second meeting of the college prep course took place in late October. This particular class I found very boring. I decided to go and hang out in the bathroom. I messed around with my hair and made some adjustments to my make-up. The bathroom had a small couch in it. I sat down on the couch and realized that I was sitting on something.

I reached underneath my behind and discovered that I had been sitting on a wallet. The wallet was black and it was made of real leather. It was a woman's Coach wallet. I looked around and even looked under the stalls to make sure that no one else was in the bathroom. I didn't see anyone so I opened up the wallet. Inside of the wallet was a crisp $20 bill. There also was a brand new 40-ride bus pass, several receipts and pieces of paper in the wallet—along with a few loose coins. The wallet did not contain any identification, so I decided to keep it.

The honest thing to do would have been to go back into the auditorium where the class was being held and to ask if "anyone had lost a wallet." I didn't do that, though. I liked the wallet and I needed the $20. I didn't have any money for our after-class trip to the pizza parlor.

I took the $20 out of the wallet and put it in my pocket, then I hid the wallet in my bookbag.

After class, my classmates and I met for our bi-weekly gathering at the pizza parlor. We ordered our food, ate, drank, and had a good time. When the bill came, I took out my $20 bill, and the rest of the group took out their money.

Contessa patted the left pocket of her jacket.

Then she stood up and felt her pants and the right pocket of her jacket.

"My wallet is gone, I can't find it. My money was in there and so was my new bus pass."

It didn't take long for me to put 2 and 2 together and figure out that the wallet that I had found was Contessa's. I didn't want to speak up. How would that look? "Oh yeah, I found this wallet today, but instead of asking anyone if they lost a wallet I decided to keep it and spend the money." That would never work. I took the phony route,

"Contessa, don't worry, I'll pay for your portion of the bill."

"Oh thank you Lori," she said.

"Do you all mind if we go back to the college and look for my wallet?" Great. All I needed was to search a 300-seat auditorium for a wallet that I knew was in my bookbag.

I played along with the game. The others and myself went back to the college and looked for Contessa's wallet. We looked in the bathrooms and under every seat. Contessa was so distraught. To me, it was just a wallet, a bus pass, and $20, but to Contessa it seemed like it was very important.

"I had all of my lunch money in there for the next two weeks and my new bus pass." Contessa cried.

"How much money did you have in there?" Yoda asked.

"I had at least $35 dollars in there." Contessa said.

She was lying. I knew there was only $20 in the wallet but I didn't say anything. Contessa called her mother from a pay phone and asked her to pick her up at the college. We all waited with Contessa until her mother arrived very upset.

"Contessa, how could you be so foolish?" she shrieked at her daughter.

"I don't have the money to just buy you another bus pass. How did you lose your wallet?" Contessa was crying as she got into her mother's car.

"Someone stole it mama—I just know it," she said.

"They must have reached into my pocket and pulled it out. I always would let the Coach tag hang out over the side of my pocket."

I watched the car pull away. Yoda, Shantrice, Leon and I waited at the bus stop.

In the days that followed I felt bad about having "acquired" Contessa's wallet. One evening when I was at home, I took a real good look at the wallet. I noticed the initials "CDK" engraved onto the wallet. Contessa Denise Kilgore.

Hey, I wasn't going to give the wallet back. Contessa's mother was a teacher and her father was a garbage man. They could afford to buy Contessa a new wallet. I decided that I liked the wallet so much that I was going to buy a purse to match it. I took a box cutter and tried to neatly scrape away Contessa's initials.

I rarely showed the wallet in public. Most school days it was neatly tucked away in my purse. Contessa talked about the wallet constantly. Sometimes we would eat lunch together and she would say,

"Ooh, I can't wait until we go to the college prep class because I am going to find out who stole my wallet, just watch." She wasn't going to let this wallet thing go. Her parents had bought her a new Coach wallet and a purse to match. I didn't understand why she was so concerned about the wallet that she had lost.

"Contessa, did you ever stop to think that maybe you lost the wallet?" I asked.

"Even if I lost it, no one made any attempt to return it,' she answered. "So it was stolen."

"You didn't have any ID in the wallet so how was someone supposed to return it?" I asked.

Contessa paused.

"How did you know I didn't have ID in the wallet?"

Uh-oh.

"I remember you saying that." I said, barely missing a beat.

"No," Contessa countered. "I never said that"

"Yes, you did, at the pizza parlor!"

"Okay," she said. "Maybe I did".

I had slipped up. I couldn't let that happen again.

The day of the class Contessa scanned the audience for potential wallet thieves. She even asked the instructor to make an announcement.

"If anyone had any information leading to the return of a black Coach wallet with the initials CDK, please let me know," the instructor said. "The owner of the wallet is offering a $50 reward."

A $50 reward!

How could I return the wallet and collect the reward money without being discovered as the person who took the wallet in the first place? I couldn't.

I decided that the risk was too great. But I hated to see that reward money go to waste.

As usual, the five of us went to get pizza after class. We were all having a really good time. We ordered the pizza and then we took turns playing the pinball machine in the parlor.

When we were finished eating the waitress brought the check over. The bill was $20.01, so that meant we each owed $5 towards the bill. Contessa got out her new wallet, and the boys took their money out. Shantrice hadn't come to class this particular day.

Then I made the most foolish slip up in history. I took the wallet out of my purse to get my money.

I was having such a good time I didn't even realize the mistake that I made. I had opened the wallet to take out a $5 dollar bill when Contessa said, "That's my wallet."

"Oh shit," I thought to myself.

"No Lori, that is my wallet," she said when I made no apparent attempt to give it to her.

"Let me see it."

Contessa held her out her hand. I began to lie my ass off.

"Contessa, do you know how many black Coach wallets there are in the world?" I asked.

"This is not your wallet."

"No, Lori," Contessa fired back.

"I know that is my wallet because I saw where my initials had been scratched out."

Damn, she had good eyes. I had only taken the wallet out for a split second and she noticed that!

"Look, Lori," Yoda said.

"If you let Contessa see the wallet once and for all, she will see that it is not her wallet and that will be the end of things."

I tried to talk my way out of the situation.

"Contessa if you were my friend you would just trust in the fact that I didn't steal your wallet," I shouted. Contessa looked as if she getting very angry.

"Show her the wallet" Leon said.

"Screw all of you," I said.

"I'm not showing anybody anything." I slammed my $5 dollar bill on the table and left the restaurant.

The following Monday in school, Contessa told everyone that I was the one who had stolen her wallet.

I stuck with my original lie. It was my wallet. My father always told me, "If you tell a lie, then you better stick with it and believe it as if it is true."

I told my side of the story to a group off my peers during gym class.

"It's my wallet," I said.

"Contessa just freaked out because she thought it was her wallet. Do you know how many black Coach wallets there at in the world?"

I continued campaigning to my peers in Algebra class.

I attempted to win Shantrice over by writing her a note in class.

> *Shantrice-*
>
> *Too bad you missed class on Saturday. I DID NOT STEAL Contessa's wallet. She just freaked out because she thought that I had her wallet. My wallet looks like hers— that's all. Do you know how many black Coach wallets there are in the world?*
>
> *You should have been at the restaurant. They were attacking me—"Show me the wallet, show me the wallet."*
>
> *You believe me, don't you?*
> *Lori*

I took a few notes in class and waited for Shantrice to write me back. Surely Shantrice would believe me.

Shantrice took a long time to write me back. She was writing one long note.

Finally she passed it to me.

> *Lori,*
>
> *I do believe that you stole Contessa's wallet. She told me that a couple of weeks ago you told her that the wallet didn't have any ID in it. How would you know something like that?*
>
> *Also, if you didn't steal the wallet, why wouldn't you show Yoda, Leon, and Contessa your wallet at the restaurant? Plus, I heard that the initials on the wallet were scratched out in the exact same place where Contessa's initials should have been.*

Lori, just confess and give Contessa her wallet back before everyone turns against you. It's never too late to tell the truth.

Shantrice

I thought about what Shantrice had said. Could I tell the truth? I had told my lie to so many people, even if I would have told the truth no one would have believed me. On top of that, the truth was even worse. Sure, I had found the wallet. But when I discovered that the wallet was Contessa's I didn't even tell her. I even put up a guise and helped her look for the wallet.

I couldn't tell the truth. I was sticking with my story.

After algebra class I went to my locker to retrieve my history book. I opened my locker and someone came up behind me and slammed it shut. I looked up and I saw a big light-skinned chick. Who was this and why was she slamming my locker shut

"Excuse me, who are you and why did you just slam my locker shut?" I asked. The girl leaned up against the locker and said,

"My name is Casey Kilgore and you stole my little sister's wallet," she said.

Oh, so this was Contessa's big sister. I knew that Contessa had a brother and a sister that went to school our school, but I didn't know who they were.

"Look, I didn't steal your sister's wallet, it's all been one big misunder-standing," I said.

"If you didn't steal it, then let me see the wallet in question?" Casey held out her hand.

"Look, I didn't even bring it to school today" I was getting nervous but I didn't let Casey see it.

"How about this. Today is Wednesday. You have until 3:30 on Friday to come up with my sister's wallet, the $20 that was in the wallet and a 40-ride bus pass."

"If you don't me, my brother and my sister and going to stomp your ass." Casey pushed me on the shoulder as she walked away.

The news of the Kilgore family preparing to stomp my ass spread around school like wildfire. I pretended that I wasn't afraid, but deep down I had my concerns. I couldn't believe that all of this drama had started about a little wallet.

The girls in gym classed asked me as they looked for an expression of fear on my face.

"No, I am not scared. What do I have to be afraid of?"

I played it cool like I didn't have a care in the world but I was quite afraid.

After gym class I went to see my guidance counselor Mrs. Samson. Mrs. Samson was a heavyset Black woman. She had short hair and she always had good snacks at her desk. Mrs. Samson was looking down at a legal pad writing when I walked into her office.

"Can I come in?" I asked.

"Sure Lori, have a seat. What's going on?"

"Contessa Kilgore thinks I stole her wallet. My wallet only looks like her wallet. Now she has gotten her family involved. Her sister said that if I don't come up with the wallet, the money that was in the wallet, and a bus pass by 3:30 on Friday that they are going to beat me up."

Mrs. Samson thought long and hard about what I had told her.

"Lori, I know the Kilgore family. The mother and father go to my church. I just couldn't imagine Contessa, Vincent, and Casey starting a fight with anyone, especially over something petty like a wallet. If Casey said something to that effect to you, surely she was just teasing."

Just teasing? It was clear that talking to Mrs. Samson was not the answer. I needed another plan of action.

Friday finally arrived. I wore a black denim skirt and my favorite red sweater. The whole sophomore class was ready to see the Kilgore family pulverize my ass. Would I stand there and fight like a woman? Would I run? Would I get my ass kicked and call it a day? I had no intentions of giving up the wallet or any money.

My last class of the day on Friday was English. The class met from 2:40-3:30. All eyes were on me as I sat in class. People looked at my face to see if they could sense any fear. I sat next to a boy named Eddie Lewis.

Eddie was mad cute and I had been digging him the whole school year. He was a big flirt and he always dressed nice. Eddie was about 6 feet tall and he had a smooth caramel complexion. Eddie was tall and lanky but he was very attractive. He had short curly black hair and he wore a six point star earring in his right ear.

He was only 16, but he had a nice brand new Grand AM. His mother and father had been killed during a robbery at a restaurant that they owned. Eddie and his siblings inherited a large inheritance. They also profited from the sale of their parent's restaurant Eddie always had the fly-est clothes and nice jewelry. He usually left school early and cut English class. On this particular day he was in class.

"Hey Lori, are you ready for the fight? I heard Contessa and her people are going to dig up in your ass." Eddie whispered to me as he leaned over towards me.

"Thanks for the confidence Eddie. I am not scared." I said.

"I have all of the confidence in the world in you baby girl. But you are no match for three people. That's why I brought a little sumthin-sumthin for you."

Eddie reached in his pocket and pulled out a large red pocketknife. Eddie handed me the knife. I didn't want my English teacher to see what was going on so I hid the knife under my English book.

"What am I supposed to do with this Eddie?" I whispered.

"You're a smart girl Lori. If things get out of hand use it. I mean don't pull it out right away, but if you get in over your head, pull it out. And if you pull it out, you better use it. Don't kill anybody just hurt them".

I took the knife and put it in my pocket. I prayed that I wouldn't have to use it, but Eddie had a point.

"Thanks, Eddie"

"No problem, baby girl"

3:30 came and the bell rang. My heart was beating so fast. In the back of my mind I was hoping that I could just sneak out of class and just go straight to the bus stop unnoticed.

No such luck. As soon as I walked out of English class Contessa and her family were outside waiting for me. On top of that, a large crowd was outside waiting to watch the big fight.

"Do you have my wallet and my money?" Contessa asked.

"No, I told you I didn't steal your wallet, bitch" I said.

With those words Contessa swung and punched me hard in the face. Her sister Casey grabbed me. Contessa swung to take another punch at me but she missed. The crowd was cheering Contessa on. I broke free from Casey and reached in my pocket. I pulled out the knife and opened it up.

The crowd was silent as I stood there with the knife pointed at Contessa.

"What are you going to do with that, you are going to cut me or something?" Contessa asked. With those words I lunged at Contessa with the knife. Slice! I cut the right side of Contessa's face with a long deep swipe of the knife. Contessa felt the blood trickling from her face. She lunged towards me and holding the knife firmly in her hand I cut deep into the left side of her face. I could feel that my skirt and had raised up and my panties were showing, but I didn't care. Blood was pouring from both sides of Contessa's face.

Before I knew what was had happened her brother Vincent ran up behind me and knocked the knife out of my hand. He picked me up and started to shake me. Casey ran over to Contessa and attempted to stop the bleeding.

As Vincent swung me around in the air like a paper doll I peeped Eddie pick the knife up off of the ground. The crowd was so large and the scene was so congested no one knew what was going on. Eddie kicked Vincent in the back of his knees and he fell to the ground.

I broke free and started to run. Some other kids chased after me, but Eddie grabbed my hand and we took off.

We ran to the other side of the building. We went into the boys locker-room. The locker room was empty. Eddie turned the lights off and locked the door. Once we got into the locker room Eddie grabbed me and kissed me real hard. The kiss was so exciting will all of the adrenaline running though our bodies.

"Baby girl, I can't believe you used the knife, you made me proud. I was afraid that you would be scared." Eddie held me close to him.

"Why did you help me?" I asked.

"Because I like you"

"Since when do you like me? You never told me you liked me," I said.

"I've liked you since I met you. You always dress real cute and you're smart. You always had a boyfriend, and now you don't so maybe you can give me a chance."

Eddie pulled me close to him.

"I'm in a whole lot of trouble now. What's going to happen to me?"

"Don't worry, everything is going to be okay" Eddie kissed me again.

Eddie and I hid out in the locker room for about an hour. Judging by the sounds outside the police had arrived. Eddie held me tight. I was really scared. I imagined that I would go to jail. I didn't want to go to jail. I was so stupid to pull that knife out on Contessa. Now I was in deep trouble.

We heard voices in the hallway.

"Yeah, she probably managed to get on the bus and go home amidst all of the confusion after the fight. We'll send a squad car to her house," a voice said from the hallway. We heard footsteps walk past the door and the voices stopped.

"Eddie what am I going to do? They aren't going to just stop looking for me. They are even sending the police to my house!" I was a nervous wreck.

"You can stay with me."

"Stay with you?" I asked.

"Yes, stay with me."

"What about your parents?"

"Well, it's just me and my brother. My mother and father are dead."

I knew his parents were dead, but when he said it out loud it made me feel sorry for him. I wondered what it was like to be a teenager and not have parents.

We waited inside of the locker room until 4:45. By that time the only person left in the building was the school janitor. We didn't want to take a chance and go into the hallway. We climbed through the locker room window and ran to Eddie's car and got in. His car was really nice. He had a CD player, which was a big deal to me considering the year was 1991, and most people still had cassette players in their cars. He popped in a DJ Quik CD and we sped away.

I was so afraid; I didn't know what to do. My mom was away on business for the weekend and my brother was staying with my grandparents. My mom was always away. This particular week she was in Atlanta at a conference. She didn't too much worry about me because she knew that I was a responsible young adult. I could have stayed in my house and hid under the bed for the weekend. I was afraid to go home so I took Eddie up on his offer.

Eddie lived in a modest three-bedroom home on the south side of Chicago. The house was like a boy's fantasy home. There was a black light in every room. The living room table was covered with video games and 40-oz beer bottles. Two men were sitting on the living room couch.

"Hey, Lori, this is my brother Nate, and his friend DeMarco. Lori is going to be staying with us a few days." I waved at the men. Melvin was young. He was maybe a year older than Eddie, that would make him 17. I couldn't imagine the freedom that they had. They didn't have anyone to tell them what to do, they could eat what ever they wanted to, and stay out as late as they wanted.

Our first night together was a blast. The four of us played spades and listened to the radio until 11:00. After we had had enough of that we jumped in Eddie's car and rode down to the lakefront. I really liked Eddie. I had been in serious relationships before but they never lasted more than 3 months. I really wanted to be with Eddie.

Many of the girls at school said that Eddie was a player and that he was good, but I saw something special in Eddie. People at school spread a lot of rumors about him the way that they spread rumors about me. Everyone at school used to say that I was a ho because of the way I dressed. In all actuality, I had only had sex with one boy at school. That hardly made me a ho.

I think they were jealous of people like Eddie and I because we lived our lives the way that we wanted to and didn't worry about what other people said. Sure we were in high school. But this was the 90s. A good 75% of the student body was sexually active. I can't judge my feelings at that time. I was only 16 years old; I didn't know trouble when I saw it. I probably should have listened to the rumors about Eddie and not gotten serious with him.

When we got back from the lake front I was exhausted. Eddie had a gorgeous bedroom. He had a king sized bed with a satin comforter. I wanted to have sex with Eddie, but I couldn't give into him on the first date, I didn't want him to think I was easy. Eddie took a shower before he got into the bed.

"Hey, you're all fresh and clean what am I going to sleep in?" I asked.

"You don't have to sleep in anything." He said.

"Eddie, I really like you and everything, but I can't have sex with you on our first date."

"Who said anything about sex? I could just hold you."

"You're sweet," I said.

"Thanks. There is an extra towel in the bathroom. If it makes you feel comfortable, you can wear one of my T-shirts and a pair of my shorts to sleep in." Eddie tossed the clothes at me.

I had never been in such a nice house that was under the complete control of teenagers. Eddie had his own private bathroom. Most high school boys aren't the neatest people in the world, but Eddie was different. His bathroom was immaculate, and it was even decorated. The bathroom had a plush blue carpet with a matching shower curtain.

When I came out of the bathroom Eddie had completely transformed the room. He was burning incense and the room was dimly lit with candles. He was lying in the bed wearing only a pair of boxer shorts. I got in the bed with him. He held me real tight and kissed me for what seemed like hours. We didn't have sex. Eddie held me tight all night. I felt so warm under the covers with him. I almost completely forgot about the trouble that I was in.

The next day I woke up and Eddie wasn't in the bed with me. The aroma of bacon and eggs filled the room. I assumed that Eddie was in the other room cooking. I took the opportunity to call my mom in Atlanta.

"Hey, Mom, how are you doing?"

"I'm fine, Lori, but I talked to your grandmother. You are in serious trouble, young lady. I heard that you were in a fight at school."

She knew.

"Look mom, I just wanted to call you and tell you that I was staying with my friend, Megan. I can't talk on Megan's phone long distance so I will see you on Monday." I quickly hung up.

Eddie came into the room. He was carrying a food tray. He was so damn sexy. I just wanted to stay at his house forever.

"You cooked breakfast." I said.

"Yeah, I thought I would fix us something to eat." Eddie sat the food tray on the dresser and hopped into bed with me.

"Did you call your mom?" He asked.

"Yeah, I don't know how I'm going to get out of this mess"

Eddie had scrambled some eggs. He put a few pieces of egg on a fork and fed the eggs to me.

"Lori, let's worry about your problems on Monday."

I learned a lot about Eddie that weekend. His brother Melvin was a high school drop out. Melvin was also dyslexic and collected disability checks for some slight mental problems. His sister, Tanisha lived in Ft. Campbell, Kentucky with her husband.

Eddie and each of his siblings had collected about $50,000 each from their parent's life insurance policy. At the age of 16, $50,000 sounded like a huge amount of money. I imagined that I could have lived off of that much money for the rest of my life.

Our weekend was carefree and fun. On Saturday, we met up with some of Eddie's friends and went roller-skating. After we left the skating rink we went to the mall and Eddie bought me several outfits and a gold Mickey Mouse ring. Sunday, we slept in the bed until noon. At 12:00 we walked to the liquor store and Eddie bought a 40-oz.

Eddie drank beer all the time. Sometimes he drank hard liquor like Vodka. It bothered me at times because my father had been an alcoholic. Eddie didn't change when he drank though, so I didn't bother him about his drinking. As we walked back from the liquor store we talked about our lives and future together.

"Eddie what's going to happen to us?" I asked.

"What do you mean baby girl?"

"I mean am I your girlfriend now?"

Eddie stopped walking. He looked angry. As a matter of fact he looked really pissed off.

"Lori, do you think this is a game? Do you think I would just do all this shit for you if I didn't want to be with you?"

I gave Eddie a hug.

"I just don't know, I've been hurt so many times, I just want to make sure that me and you are going to be for real. Plus, I'm in all this shit at school, I might go to jail." My tears started to fall.

"Lori, look. Trust me. I'm not going to let anything bad happen to you. I will take care of things."

I had only been close with Eddie for a few days but for some reason I really trusted him.

That Sunday afternoon Eddie and I made love for the first time. Many times when people here about young people having sex they imagine that they are young and inexperienced and that it doesn't last very long. Eddie and

I were nothing like that. We both knew what we were doing and we had sex for hours locked away in his bedroom listening to a Jodeci CD on repeat.

Sunday night came and we decided to go to the Red Lobster at Ford City Mall to eat dinner. I wore one of the new dresses that Eddie had bought me.

"So what should I do tomorrow. Should I go to school, or should I hide out a little bit longer?" I asked. Eddie was eating his shrimp and he didn't seemed as concerned about my problems as I was.

"I have a couple of friends that work at the police station around the school. One of my guys, Chico, is a cop. I called him this afternoon. This is how it is going to go down tomorrow. You are going to get on the bus and go to school. When you get off the bus at 7:15 A.M. there will be a police car will be waiting in front of the school. When you walk off of the bus, Chico is going to grab you by the arm."

"Don't worry, he won't hurt you, I told him you were my little baby girl. He is going to take you into the school office and ask if you are the student they were looking for on Friday. Of course, they will say yes. Chico will then place the hand-cuffs on your hands and take you to your house."

I thought about Eddie's plan.

"So he won't arrest me, he will only make it look like I was arrested."

"Yeah."

"What about the school won't they want to follow up?"

"Chico or someone else will call the school, tell them that they had no weapon, and no eyewitnesses, and since it was your first offense, you were released into your parents care."

"Eddie, I sliced up Contessa's face with a knife. You think they will just let that shit slide?"

Eddie got angry. He slammed his fork on the table. He had a terrible temper. Here we were at Red Lobster, on a Sunday, during dinner and he was causing a commotion.

"Lori, damn, can you just give it a try?" Do you have a better idea?" He did have a point. I didn't have a plan of action.

The next morning, I prepared to go to school. Eddie drove and he dropped me off at the bus stop. He didn't think that it would look good if we arrived at school together. I got on the bus and I was nervous the whole ride.

At 7:15 the bus pulled up outside of the school. I peered out of the window. A police car was outside exactly as Eddie said. I was the last person to get off of the bus. I looked at the office inside of the squad car. The officer was a Puerto-Rican man. He looked like he may have been all of 23 years old. Was this Chico? What if our plan backfired? What if this was a real police officer coming to drag my ass to jail?

The door to the police squad car opened and the tall, handsome, man opened the door. He nodded his head as if he was giving me a signal that it was he was Chico. Chico played the role very well. As I was walking into the building he grabbed my arm.

"Excuse me, is your name Lori?" he asked.

"Yes," I said.

"You are wanted for questioning regarding an altercation that took place on Friday. Come with me." He gently pulled me by the arm into the school office.

"Thank God you all have found her. Mr. Sullivan. They have Lori!" The school secretary shouted. They acted like I was a career criminal.

Mr. Sullivan, the school principal came walked up to the counter where Chico and I were standing.

"Where did you find her?" He asked.

"I found her on her way into the school. I'm going to arrest her based on the witness statements. Did you all ever retrieve the weapon or view the surveillance video?"

"Well, we never found the weapon in question," Mr. Sullivan said.

"Some of the students said it was a red knife. The surveillance video is no good. It didn't pick up that corner of the courtyard. Do you have enough to arrest her?"

"Yes sir, we'll take her in."

Mr. Sullivan pointed his finger at me.

"Lori, you are such a bright girl." Mr. Sullivan gave me a scornful look. "I am so disappointed in you."

"Mr. Sullivan, I told my guidance counselor that they were going to beat me up and she told me that the Kilgore kids went to her church and they would never do anything like that. I am disappointed in this school for failing me. I asked for help and no one helped me." I felt tears welling up in my eyes.

"Lori, I am sorry, but you are expelled."

"Whatever," I said.

Chico placed the handcuffs around my wrists and escorted me out of the building. He opened the door to the squad car and helped me into the car.

"So how did you end up hooking up with little thug-ass Eddie?" Chico asked with a laugh.

"Eddie is cool. I like him. He goes to school with me. He really looks out for me. How did you end up being friends with Eddie?" I asked Chico.

"Oh, Eddie is cool. He does some work for me. I won't get into details. If he thinks that you are worthy enough, he will let you in on all his little secrets."

What kind of business could Eddie possibly have with a police officer?

"Look at you girl, you are so curious. I had you going, you thought I was Mr. Crooked Ass Cop. Eddie's sister and I went to high school together. Eddie and I hang out and play basketball sometimes. That's all. I did this thing for you and his as a favor, so don't go running your mouth, cool?"

"Yeah, cool"

By this time we were at my house. My mom's car was in the driveway. She wasn't due to get back until Monday night. I guess she decided to come back early. I went in the house and told my mom the whole story. I didn't exactly tell her the whole story, I told her what I wanted her to know. I didn't tell her that Eddie gave me the knife and I didn't tell her that I had spent the whole weekend with Eddie.

I did tell her that I was expelled. My mom wasn't mad at me, she was furious with the school for not doing anything about Contessa and her siblings when I first mentioned it to them.

The next day my mother, her lawyer and our family minister went up to the school to have a conference with the Kilgore's and the school administration. Not much was resolved. My mother threatened to sue the school for not doing more to protect me. The Kilgore's threatened to sue us for the amount of money spent on Contessa's medical bills and future medical expenses.

Contessa. I felt so bad about what I had done to her. She had to get 26 stitches on the left side of her face and 33 stitches on the right side of her face. Her parents said that unless she had plastic surgery she would be scarred for life.

I didn't want to scar anyone for life. I started to feel bad. Then I thought about the fact that she and her siblings had tried to jump on me. After I thought about that I didn't feel bad anymore.

Due to my mothers increasing legal pressure, Mr. Sullivan revoked my expulsion and changed my punishment to a two-week suspension. He also kicked Contessa and I out of the college prep course.

Those two weeks away from school were horrible. I was so bored during the day. I would just watch soap operas like "All My Children" and "One Life To Live" every day. I would live for 3:45 to come around. When 3:45 arrived Eddie would come and pick me up and take me to his house. Sometimes we would stop at McDonalds to grab a bite to eat. Other times we would go to Evergreen Plaza and go shopping.

At the time I didn't have a job of my own. Eddie would buy me anything that I wanted.

It didn't take long for me to figure out that Eddie was in a gang and that he earned money from various sources. In Chicago, the "Folks' or Gangster Disciples wore blue and black and turned their hats to the right. (At least they did in 1991) Being Folks and putting in work was a favorite conversation around Eddie's house. Eddie and his brother Melvin also sold weed and crack cocaine. People would knock on the kitchen window all day. Melvin, DeMarco, or Eddie would walk to the window, reach out and grab money in exchange for drugs. Eddie also had a gun, a 38-caliber revolver.

One night in bed I asked Eddie a few questions about his lifestyle. That was one of the few times that I asked questions. I was personally against gangs and selling drugs. But I liked Eddie and I liked spending his money. He always had a gift for me.

"Eddie, why do you sell drugs and why are you in a gang?" Eddie rolled his eyes when I asked him about his lifestyle. He started to shake his head.

"I thought you were down, I guess you aren't, do you want me to take you home."

I grabbed on to his arm as he started to get out of the bed.

"Eddie, I am down. I just wondered. I mean you got all of that money when your parents died. Why do you have to sell drugs?" Eddie leaned back in the bed and lit a cigarette.

"I didn't get as much money as you think. $50,000 after taxes is about $43,000. I bought my car, brand new off the lot. That was about $17,000. I bought the rims and the sound system. That was another couple of thousand dollars. We had to pay off some of my parents' debt. That was almost another $10,000. With the rest of my money I made an investment. Since I made that investment, I have seen my money triple."

"You invested in drugs?"

"You are so naive acting. Aren't you from the south side? Don't you know how things work? Some of my Folks, Esco or Chico, you met Chico, they get me the work, I sell it, we split the profits. It's just like a big circle."

Chico was the police officer. I could believe that he was involved in selling drugs, something about him looked crooked.

"Well why are you in a gang?"

"Lori, my whole block is Folks. How would I look not being down with them? Them Niggas would kick my ass. It's not what you might think being in a gang is like. We don't go around looking for trouble all of the time. Being Folks is just a way of life for me."

Eddie put the cigarette out and laid down in the bed. He leaned over and kissed me and started to massage my breast.

"Lori, you aren't scared of me are you? I don't want you to have to worry about anything, as long as you are with me, things are going to be just fine." Eddie leaned over and kissed me.

I didn't worry when I was with Eddie, I felt safer with him than I had ever felt with anyone in my entire life.

When I returned to school after my 2-week suspension things were very different. I was two weeks behind in all of my classes. I was afraid that I wouldn't make it through my junior year. I wasn't that popular with people before the fight. Now I was truly alienated. My teachers looked at me with disdain. My favorite teacher at the time was my gym teacher Mrs. Hill. One day after class she asked me if she could talk to me. Of course, I agreed.

"You want to talk to me Mrs. Hill, is it about the make-up assignment that you assigned me? I should have it done by tomorrow."

"No, this is not about the make-up assignment, it is about your behavior. I am so disappointed and ashamed of you. You know you could have killed Contessa. Then you would be in jail right now. And I heard that you are dating Eddie Lewis. Is that true?"

"Yes, but what has Eddie got to do with anything?"

"It's only been a year since his parents were killed. That boy has done nothing but go downhill since then. I heard he is in a gang"

"Mrs. Hill, I don't want to be rude, but this is really none of your business."

"Lori, your attitude has changed. You are going to let that boy bring you down. Rumor has it he gave you the knife that you used during the fight with Contessa. Don't let a man drag you down, because if you let him he will drag you all the way down into the gutter"

"Mrs. Hill. I have to get to my next class." As I was walking away Mrs. Hill grabbed me gently on the arm.

"Lori, it may seem like we are all picking on you, but we are concerned. You are a bright young girl with your whole future ahead of you. We just don't want to see you go down a bad path." Mrs. Hill let go of my arm and I walked away.

As I was walking down the hallway I saw Contessa and a few of her friends. The scars on each side of Contessa's face were long and deep. As I walked past her she didn't speak, she just gave me a really dirty look. I felt bad every time I looked at Contessa.

What would I have done if Eddie hadn't given me the knife? Had I made a mistake? I didn't know what to think about what I had done. I was so confused about my actions that I just didn't think about them. It was easier to block out the pain if I just didn't face any of my problems head on.

Every one of my teachers that first day back lectured me on my bad behavior. It got to be so annoying I didn't know if I would even be able to continue to attend that school. Everyday I thought about transferring. But then I thought about Eddie. If I transferred I wouldn't be with Eddie.

Eddie was popular. He wasn't an athlete, and he wasn't the smartest kid in school. Eddie was popular for a lot of the superficial reasons. He had the best clothes. Whatever fashion trend was popular Eddie had it. He had money and nice jewelry. He was the only student in the sophomore class with a new car. Before Eddie and I hooked up he, was a big flirt. He had never dated anyone at school before. A lot of girls would try to get with Eddie, but he never took things past the flirting level.

When Eddie would walk down the hallway with me on his arms all of the students would stare in awe. Some were jealous. Most wondered why he was with me of all people. After the fight many people looked at me as a deranged person. I had used a knife to bring bodily harm to another one of my classmates. Looking back, maybe that was a big deal. But to me, it was just something that happened I got over it, so I felt that everyone else should have gotten over it.

I spent all of my time after school with Eddie and his friends. Eddie had two close friends. Fred was his best friend. They had a lot in common. Fred was also Folks, and Fred had recently lost his mother to complications to diabetes. Eddie's other close friend was Anthony. Anthony was the total opposite of Eddie. Anthony didn't drink, he wasn't in a gang, and he didn't sell drugs. Anthony was just a cool guy. He and Eddie met freshman year and they just hit it off.

By December, about a month after Eddie and I had hooked up, I moved into his house. I was 16 years old, and I moved out of my mother's house. To a degree my mother had pretty much given up on me. She knew that if she didn't let me go willingly, that I probably would have ran away. She only made three request of me.

1.) Don't get pregnant
2.) Stay in school
3.) Come home & check in at least once a week

I could live with those terms. Prior to me moving in with Eddie, I had spent almost every night over at his house. In the morning, he would drive me to my house so that I could get ready for school, and then we would go to school together. It was just a big inconvenience.

We spent the holidays together. I cooked a big meal for Eddie, his brother, and some of the other guys on the block for Christmas. For Christmas Eddie bought me a 14K gold necklace. The necklace had a charm with his initials on it. What did I buy Eddie? I bought him just what he wanted, a pair of brass knuckles. It wasn't easy for me to get my hands on a pair of brass knuckles, but Fred told me where I could buy them.

After the holidays our relationship started to go downhill a bit. His brother Melvin did not like the fact that Eddie had welcomed me into their inner-circle. Eddie still sold drugs and it had gotten to the point where I would help in the operations. I would chip away the rocks from the large chunk of crack-cocaine. I would bag up the weed. I would count the money. Sometimes I would even go to the window and sell the drugs. Eddie would give me a cut of his cut of the money.

Eddie's best friend Fred resented the fact that I was always around. He always complained to Eddie about me. Fred felt that I was turning Eddie "soft" Of course, Fred didn't have a girlfriend of his own.

Eddie and I started to argue frequently. He felt like I was always underneath him. We started to have less fun and I felt that we were headed down a bad path. There were also many things sexually that I wasn't ready or willing to do that Eddie was interested in. He was obsessed with having a "threesome."

He wanted to have sex with another woman and me while he videotaped the whole thing. Whenever I would tell him about a friend of mine or someone in class he would always say, "Do you think she would be down for a threesome?" The whole threesome things started to consume our sex life. Every time that we had sex he would always whisper in my ear, "So are you going to find another girl or do I have to?" I would always say, "Eddie, I don't feel comfortable doing that." He would either get mad and stop making love to me, or he would try to do it to me real hard like was trying to break my insides in half.

Eddie had lots of friends, but I was pretty much a loner outside of my cousin Ray-Ray. Ray-Ray and Eddie didn't get along, so I didn't dare bring her around Eddie. In February of 1992, I befriended a girl named Tabitha. Tabitha was a black girl that lived around my grandmother's house. We met one day when I was visiting my brother over at my grandmother's house. Tabitha was 15 years old and she was a nice looking girl.

Often I brought Tabitha over to Eddie and I shared. It was nice to not be the only girl around. Eddie's best friend Fred liked Tabitha. The two of them instantly hit it off. This was good for me, because Fred stopped complaining about me being around him and Eddie. Many times Eddie and I would go on double dates with Fred and Tabitha. Tabitha was a bit "out-there" sexually. I remember one day Eddie and I were in the living room watching "House Party" on video. Tabitha and Fred were on the other couch kissing. She took her shirt off and Fred started to suck on her breast. Tabitha then took her skirt off. She wasn't wearing any panties. Eddie was just staring at Tabitha's ass while Fred was grabbing her ass. I am a very jealous person.

"Tabitha, why don't you and Fred go in the room?" I said in a pissed off voice.

Tabitha giggled and her and Fred went into the empty third bedroom and started to have sex. Tabitha was moaning and the love making sounds only got louder and louder. Eddie wasn't even paying attention to the movie, he was to busy listening to Tabitha and Fred. I was pissed off.

"Lori, you are to jealous, why are you so jealous? You know you are the only girl for me." Eddie kissed me on the cheek.

I never forgot the way that Eddie looked at Tabitha that day. I limited my interaction with her after that incident. Soon after her and Fred broke up. Fred said that Tabitha was "too much" for him. I was back to being friendless. I was 16 years old and believe it or not, I really did want to have a future. I decided to get a job.

I wanted a good paying job. I didn't want to be a waitress or work at a fast food restaurant. I looked in the classified section of the Chicago Tribune every Sunday. One Sunday I saw an ad that the telephone-company was hiring. They were looking for new "dial 0" operators. The ad said that there would be on-the spot interviews on Tuesday.

Tuesday arrived. I went to the phone company and filled out and application. I lied on the application. I said that I was 17 years old and that I had graduated from high school. I got the job. My hours were 4:30-8:30 PM Monday-Thursday.

Eddie was highly pissed off about me getting a job. He felt that he provided for me, I didn't need money of my own. He didn't look at the big picture like I did. I couldn't imagine spending the rest of my life selling drugs out of a window. I had big dreams; I wanted to go to beauty school. I even wanted to own my own beauty shop one day.

I started training the very next day. The job was a challenge, but it was interesting. That job gave me discipline. We had to plug into our workstations at the exact time that we were given. If we were late, chances are we may get fired.

Eddie would pick me up from work everyday. We would then go to the McDonalds drive through to pick up dinner. We would then go back to the house and talk about our day. We were only 16 years old, but we felt like an old married couple.

Training lasted two weeks. On the last day of training we had a "graduation party". The office provided us with certificates of completion and cake and ice cream. They even let us off early.

It was 6:30 when I got off of work. I called Eddie at the house but there was no answer. I assumed he was out with his friends. The telephone-company was on the same bus route of our house, so I decided to take the bus home.

I arrived at the house at about 7:00. Eddie's car was in the driveway. I opened up the door and the living room was dark. Melvin wasn't home. I heard music coming from our bedroom. I opened the door and I was completely flabbergasted.

There on the bed was Eddie butt ass naked pumping Tabitha doggystyle. Tabitha was moaning the same way that she was in the room with Fred that day. I couldn't believe my eyes. I didn't know what to say. I stood there in shock.

"You fucking asshole," I screamed at Eddie. Eddie pushed Tabitha off of him. Tabitha ran for her clothes. I was just in shock. I couldn't even move. I couldn't even breathe. I loved Eddie, how could he do this to me?

"How could you do this to me?" I cried.

"Lori, I am so sorry." Tabitha cried. She was more hysterical than that I was.

"You were supposed to be my friend, and Eddie you used to be my boyfriend." I picked up a lamp off of the dresser and threw the lamp at Eddie. The lamp hit a wall and it shattered.

"Bitch, that was my mothers lamp, now look what you've done!" Eddie screamed.

Tabitha grabbed her clothes and ran into the living room. I ran towards Eddie and just started pounding on him with all of my might. He tried to restrain me, but I was so angry. I was crying, I was a wreck.

"Lori, I am so sorry, just let me explain." Eddie cried as he tried to restrain me.

"I don't care what you have to say, I'm moving out and going home."

"Lori, baby no, don't leave, just let me take her home and I will explain everything." I lied on the bed and just cried and cried.

Eddie left to take Tabitha home. I was so shocked. I couldn't believe that Eddie had cheated on me.

I should have left Eddie. I had seen him cheating on me with my own eyes. He came back and explained that he only had been with Tabitha because he was "lonely because I worked too much". I wanted to leave him so badly. He wasn't good for me, but I just couldn't leave. He promised me that he would "never do it again" and I believed him. I loved him so much.

I kept my job. However, I was consumed with the thought of Eddie cheating on me. I would call home every hour to check on him. Needless to say, I cut Tabitha out of my life.

While I was working at the telephone-company, Eddie was coming up with ways to make more money. His drug operation wasn't going well. Chico had been busted and was in jail. His other connection Esco was also in jail. He still had a weed connect, but selling weed is only lucrative if you are moving weight, and Eddie was strictly small time. His brother Melvin's best friend DeMarco had started a legit job as a manager at McDonalds. One evening after Eddie and Melvin picked me up from work they stopped to pick up DeMarco from McDonalds.

We pulled up alongside the Mc Donald's on 87th and State Street and Eddie blew the horn. DeMarco had taken off his uniform and he opened up the back door and got in the car.

"How was work Mr. McDonalds?" Eddie said.

"Man, that job is shitty. I come out of there smelling like a big ass french fry every night. They make bank though. Tonight I counted $5000 and put it in the safe, and that was just the money from my shift".

"McDonald's makes money like that?" Melvin said in disbelief.

"Hell yeah!" DeMarco said.

"We need to hit them up" Eddie said as he stopped at a red light.

"We could do that shit to. You'll come up to the spot, walk up in like,

"Freeze, open the mother-fucking safe. I'll act all scared and everything, open up the safe."

"And we'll split the money 3 ways" Melvin said.

"3 ways, what are you going to do Melvin? You are too scary. You can stay outside in the car. 40% for DeMarco, 40% for me and 20% for you."

"Fuck that Eddie, I get 40% too man." We all started to laugh.

"Melvin, 40% times 3 is 120%. Nigga you shouldn't have dropped out of school."

Eddie said as he laughed.

"I know that if I don't get my cut, all of you'll gonna be in jail cause I am going to trick. Excuse me officer, I know two black males who robbed McDonalds."

"Quit playing Melvin, you'll get your cut Nigga, we was just playing with you."

Eddie pulled into the driveway.

I didn't know if Eddie, Melvin and DeMarco were serious about the McDonalds robbery. Honestly, I didn't want to know. When we got in the house, I took a shower and went straight to bed. Eddie, Melvin and DeMarco talked about their plans for hours.

Eddie was crooked like that. He always talked about what he was going to do. He would always talk about the "perfect robbery." He would dream of stealing new cars off of car lots.

Three weeks later, I left my job at 8:30 and Eddie was no where around. I called the house and there was no answer. A co-worker gave me a ride home. I turned the key to open the door and the door flew open. It was Eddie.

"Hurry up and get inside."

He pulled me in and shut the door. Money was everywhere. Eddie, Melvin, and DeMarco were sitting on the floor counting a huge pile of money. They counted the money for what seemed like hours. It was exactly $7,523 dollars. They had robbed the McDonalds. Things went exactly the way they had planned.

"Did you here me say that shit? I said, "Nigga freeze, open up the motherfucking safe right now!" Eddie shouted, pretending to hold a gun.

"You looked a little too serious, I was starting to get scared" DeMarco said with a laugh.

I had been with Eddie long enough to know not to ask any questions. I just watched them count the money. DeMarco kept the biggest cut, $3300 dollars and Eddie kept $3,000 and Melvin had the smallest cut of the money. Melvin was really pissed off about the money.

DeMarco was so stupid. The next day he didn't show up for work and that cast suspension on him. The police went to his house to question him about the robbery and he was gone. DeMarco had taken his cut of the money and caught a Greyhound bus to Tallahassee, Florida to be with his babies mother. The police questioned Eddie and Melvin, not as suspects, but as DeMarco's friends. They were almost certain that DeMarco had an accomplice, but they had no evidence.

Money had been tight for awhile. Our bills were high and I only was making $7 an hour and the phone-company. We had a good time with the robbery money. We went out to eat and we bought new outfits. Word on the street was that the police had located DeMarco in Florida. Eddie was scared that DeMarco would tell the police on him.

I knew that being with Eddie was bad. Not only was he in a gang, he sold drugs, he was a thief, and he had cheated on me. But I was blind to all of this and I stayed with him.

When senior year came around Eddie and I were still and item, but the spark was gone. I started to look at other men, and we argued more than we made love. I also started spending more time at home with my mother and my brother.

During the second week of school Eddie was expelled. He was caught selling weed to an under-cover police officer on campus. I thought that under-cover police officers only existed in TV shows such as 21-Jump Street. Eddie was arrested, but he quickly posted bond.

Everything fell apart at that point. Social Services got involved and placed Eddie in a foster home. Melvin and Eddie ended up losing their parent's home. They were behind in the mortgage and the mortgage company took the house from them. The police seized Eddie's car because he was in the car when he sold the drugs to the undercover officer.

With Eddie in a foster home, I moved back home with my mother. I was happy to be home. I had to think about myself for once. I wanted to have a future. I was a senior in high school and I was even thinking about going to college. I felt that college would give me the opportunity to get away from Eddie and all of the bullshit in Chicago.

Eddie spent his days studying for his GED and awaiting his trial date for the drug case. His foster mother was cool, she would let me come and visit him. One day as I was visiting Eddie I decided to share my future plans with him.

"Eddie, I'm thinking about going to college." I whispered.

"College huh. Where are you going to go, Chicago State?" Eddie smirked.

"Well, I'm thinking about Southern Illinois University. It is far away from here and it is cheaper that the University of Illinois. Plus I don't think my grades are good enough for me to get into U of I." I was excited about my plan.

"I thought you were going to stay here and go to beauty school?" Eddie asked.

"I just want to get away"

"What about us, you are just going to throw our relationship away?" Eddie and I had talked about our futures before. It was always a sensitive subject because we both wanted different things in life.

"You can come and visit me anytime" I said.

We argued for the rest of the afternoon. We broke up that day. Eddie felt that if I was going to eventually leave, we might as well break up now. He was so dramatic. I didn't care. I wasn't going to throw my future away simply to appease him.

Two weeks later Eddie was sentenced to spend 6 months at a halfway house for boys. The halfway house was in Bloomington, Indiana. Eddie would spend his days going to re-hab for his drinking and studying for his GED.

I went on about my life. Things were going good for me. I had saved enough money from my telephone company job to buy myself a car. I was a teenager again. I realized that I had given up so much of my youth to Eddie and all of his drama. I started dating again, and I was truly happy and looking forward to the future.

In December of 1992, Eddie's friend Anthony asked me on a date. Anthony was cool. Sure he was Eddie's friend, but by this time Eddie had already been gone away for almost 3 months. Anthony and I went on a date to see the movie "The Bodyguard". It was an icy and cold evening. I remember Anthony letting me hold on to him tight so that I wouldn't slip on the ice.

Anthony and I started to see each other. We did "wholesome" teenage things. We did the things that Eddie and I used to do. We went roller-skating and we would go play miniature golf.

It didn't take long for word to get to Indiana to Eddie that Anthony and I were dating. Eddie had called me collect from the halfway house several times. One day he called and he had a major attitude.

"Hey what's up?"

"How are things going in Indiana?"

"Cool. Are you still going to send me that new Dr. Dre tape?"

"Yeah, I'll send it when I have a chance."

"I heard that you are fucking my boy Anthony." Eddie said in a pissed off tone of voice.

"Eddie, you and I broke up."

"But still Anthony is my boy, how could you do that."

'Easy, the same way you fucked Tabitha. Look I have to go."

I hung up the phone and I didn't expect to ever talk to Eddie again.

Three months later Eddie was at my doorstep. He had completed his program and he wanted to get back together with me. I just didn't see any future in our relationship. He didn't have the same dreams and goals as me. I wanted a successful career, Eddie wanted a lot of money and he didn't care what he had to do to get it. I still loved Eddie. I just didn't want to go down that path again.

I went on to graduate from high school and Eddie got a job as a taxicab driver. I went on to college and I left Eddie and his memories behind me. Eddie was a bad boy. Perhaps that is why I was so drawn to him. Whatever, it was that attracted me to him I was definitely past that stage.

Anthony and I didn't last long either. We broke up after high school. He wanted me to stay in Chicago and marry him. I wasn't interested in being married at such a young age, I already felt like I had been married and divorced to Eddie.

I don't have any hard feelings towards Eddie. I look back on the times and think about how I could have been killed or in jail due to being with Eddie. I thank God that the outcome was brighter. Three years after I had seen Eddie last, he was almost killed in a robbery when someone tried to rob him as he was driving his taxi. Eddie was shot three times.

His injuries forced him to quit being a cab driver. His leg was injured so he collected disability. Eddie enrolled at a junior college and tried to make a future for himself. He got a young woman pregnant and went back to selling drugs to try to provide for his family. Unfortunately, he was arrested. When he got out of jail he had a hard time finding a job, and he ended up hooked on the same drugs he used to sell.

I saw Fred one day at a party at my college. Fred had joined a fraternity and some of his frat brothers had a party at SIU. Fred told me that Eddie was strung out on heroin and that he had stopped by his house once asking to borrow some money.

I felt bad about how things turned out for Eddie. But I was glad that I eventually took Mrs. Hill' advice.

COLLEGE BOUND

▼

I decided to attend Southern Illinois University for several reasons. SIU was inexpensive. My grades weren't good enough to get into the University of Illinois, my parent's alma mater, so SIU became a natural decision for me.

I planned to major in film production. Growing up in Southern California, and having a father who worked in the entertainment industry exposed me to the industry. I wanted to become a famous Black female director.

Carbondale, Illinois is a small town in Southern Illinois. Outside of the university, Carbondale doesn't have much to offer. Carbondale is a beautiful town. Carbondale has four seasons and it is a peaceful and quiet place, most of the time.

I arrived in Carbondale, Illinois on August 17, 1993. It was my first time away from home and I was so happy to be on my own. This was going to be a chance for me to start over and to leave all of the drama of high school behind me once and for all. My first car was a 1992 Toyota Paseo, but you couldn't tell me it was a Ford Mustang.

I pulled up to the dormitory at about 10 o'clock A.M. I realized that the building I was in was four floors and that it did not have an elevator. The temperature outside was 90 degrees.

As always, I counted on my good looks and sexuality to get me out of this situation. I looked up to the sky at the sun and then looked around for the tallest, strongest man my eyes could see. There was Vic. I had met him during new student orientation and he was helping new students move into the dorm. Should I ask him to help me? Should I just hope that he would see me struggling trying to carry the mini-fridge that weighted almost as much as I did?

I attempted to pick up the mini-fridge and I dropped it on the sidewalk. Vic came running over.

"Hey, do you need some help," he asked. I was so grateful.

"Yes, I do."

That morning Vic helped me move all of my belongings into my new dorm room. I was very grateful and offered to cook him and his roommate dinner sometimes. Why I was offering to cook and I didn't have a stove I don't know, but it sounded like a nice gesture.

Roommates. Unless you come from a wealthy family or just have it all figured out, chances are most people have had roommates at one point in their life or another. I initially looked forward to the idea of the college roommate. I envisioned this roommate as someone that would be a good friend and that we would grow to be best friends and continue the journey of life together.

What a sweet vision of a roommate. It didn't take me long to realize that the college roommate and the word "hell" might as well be one in the same. I had so many roommates while in my late teens and twenties. I always went into the situation with an open mind, but eventually I realized that the roommate thing definitely was not for me. I've never had a "good" roommate experience.

I knew that I had a roommate. Over the summer they send out these little post cards that have your roommates name, age, and general information, such as course of study. I received my post card in July. My roommates name was going to be Shanika Buckley, she was 19 (a year older than I was), and she was from East St.Louis, Illinois.

Being the frantic, excited, future college freshman that I was, I called my roommate a full six weeks before classes began. I dialed the number carefully; the phone rang about 5 times before a woman picked up.

"What's up?" It sounded like a young girl on the other end, maybe this was the roommate.

"Hi, this is Lori, is Shanika home?" The phone was silent, for a few seconds. "This is Shanika, who the fuck is this?" Okay, this was different.

"Oh well I am going to be attending SIU this fall and I am going to be your roommate." The girl on the other end started laughing.

"Oh, my bad, oooh I am so sorry, I thought you were this girl that thought I was messing around with her boyfriend calling my house playing on the phone".

Now that we had gotten all of that out the way, I figured we would talk about roommate stuff. I didn't know how to break the ice after such a shocking introduction.

"Are you a freshman?" I asked.

"Oh no, don't tell me that stuck me with a freshman, no I am a sophomore". This conversation wasn't going to well.

"Well, I am bringing a mini-fridge and I have a television set, do you think you can bring a microwave?" I was afraid to ask this girl anything; I didn't know what to expect.

"Look, bring whatever you want, and I have my own mini-fridge. I like to have all of my own stuff. Plus I don't plan on keeping a roommate long. Once consolidations start I'm getting a single room."

She was a very special person. I was ready to end this conversation.

"Well I guess I will see you when school starts".

Six weeks later, I sat in the dorm room unpacking my belongings. I put a few posters on the wall and set up my mini-fridge. I went to Wal-Mart to buy a microwave because I had no idea what to expect from my new roommate.

After, I returned from Wal-Mart, I decided to take a nap. I was so pleased with my accomplishments for the day. I had moved in the dorm room and I was all settled in.

Then the door opened. In came my new roommate Shanika and her friends. She was a very petite Black girl. She couldn't have weighed more that 95 pounds. Shanika didn't have to say a word for me to see that she was all attitude. She looked around the room in disgust.

"You just made yourself at home, you didn't even wait to see how I wanted to set things up". Well she did have a point, but I got their first.

"Well we can always change things around if you don't like the way things are set up", I said in a confident voice even though I was a bit nervous.

Shanika's friends seemed as unpleasant as she was. One was tall, light-skinned and looked like a model. The other one was a short dark-skinned girl. They didn't speak to me; they just looked at me as if they were checking me out. I could tell this was going to be quite an experience.

Shanika unpacked her belongings and her and two friends caught up on each other's summer vacations. I sat on the bed, attempting to include myself in their conversation, but every time I said something they would pause, and then resume talking as if they didn't care what I said in the first place.

"I need to go to Wal-Mart. I don't have any soap, or deodorant, Kelly can you run me to the store real quick?" Shanika asked the tall girl who looked like a model.

"Girl, I have practice, I'm sorry, can I take you tomorrow?" Shanika looked a little pissed off.

"Damn Kelly it won't take but twenty minutes, what am I supposed to do with no soap or deodorant, I can't be walking around all funky and shit".

"I can take you to the store", I said meekly.

The whole paradigm of the conversation shifted. Shanika smiled and her friends just kind of looked at me.

"You have a car?" Shanika asked. Her other friend, not the model chick but the short girl said,

"I thought freshman couldn't have cars?" These people were being nice to me for the first time all day, at least so I though. Back then I was to naïve to see that they were only plotting on how they were going to use me.

"Yes, I have a car".

"How did you manage to pull that one off?" Shanika asked.

"Well you see, I told them that I didn't have anyone to bring me to school because my mom had to work so that I would have to drive myself down here. They gave me a green parking sticker, so I can't park in the lot behind the building, but I can park behind the cafeteria."

Shanika was smiling.

"Roommate has a car, we are going to get along just fine", she said as she put her arm around my shoulders.

I took Shanika and her short friend, who I later learned was named Tasha to Wal-Mart. Shanika and I picked out groceries for our little mini-fridge's. I started to think that she was really cool. I felt that these were going to be my new friends.

While we were at Wal-Mart I saw Sheree. Sheree was a girl that I met when I worked at the telephone company in Chicago. We weren't very close in Chicago. We knew that we both would be attending SIU in the fall.

Sheree only worked with me a few weeks because she got fired for making to many outgoing calls. (I mean think about it, a telephone operator is supposed to receive calls).

"Hey girl!"

Sheree gave me a big hug. We conversed about our first day away from home and she introduced me to her friends April and Michelle. Shanika said "Hello", but her whole aura was this "I'm so tough" attitude. Sheree and I exchanged numbers. Shanika, her friend, and I continued to shop.

"I don't hang out with to many girls, women are nothing but trouble. Women will try to play you, steel you man, talk about you behind you back, you'll see," Shanika said as she tossed a box of Tide into her shopping cart. I found a statement like this strange coming from another woman. I didn't say anything, what was I supposed to say about a statement like that. It was my first day of college and I was not trying to analyze my roommates psyche'.

We left Wal-Mart and soon arrived back at the dorms. We unpacked the groceries and talked about trivial things like music and celebrity gossip. Shanika was a little rough around the edges, but I thought we could be friends.

"Hey do you want to go to Beach Bumz?" Shanika asked me as she was hanging up a LL Cool J poster she bought. Beach Bumz? What was this girl talking about?

"What's Beach Bumz?" I asked.

"It's a club on the strip," Shanika said as she straightened the poster she had just hung up. Wow, I was going to be hanging out with my new roommate, things were looking good.

"Yeah that's cool."

"Oh yeah, you're driving". Well I kind of assumed I was driving since I was the one with the car. Shanika picked up her cordless phone and started dialing.

"Tasha, call Kelly at work. We're going to Beach Bumz, roommate is driving and we are going to get drunk tonight".

Okay, did I offer to drive her and her friends? And what's all this about getting drunk? I just went with the flow, I was happy to have been invited.

We stepped in the club. All eyes were on Shanika, Kelly, Tasha and me. For some strange reason that night I had on a pair of neon yellow denim shorts and a black body suit. Hey, it was 1993, but that is still no excuse for such poor fashion taste. My roommate was really popular, every time I turned around someone was like, "What's Up Shanika, how was your summer". Shanika was cool. She introduced me to everyone that crossed her path.

"Hey, this is my roommate, she's a freshman. She's from Chicago." She never said my name, which I thought was odd. She was putting away Long Island Ice all night.

Someone came up behind me and put their hands over my eyes. I turned around and it was Sheree and her friends whom I had seen earlier at Wal-Mart. They weren't drinking, we were only 18, but if we wanted to, we could have. Sheree and I weren't that cool in Chicago, but now that we were in a different environment things were different. Plus, I liked her friends. April was about 5' 6. She was light skinned and a very pretty girl. She had a huge scar going across her chest and she also had a long scar that ran all the way down her arm. You couldn't look at her and not notice the scars. She was a very nice girl, and beautiful despite her scars.

Michelle was a year younger than us I found out, but she was funny and definitely the life of the party. I liked hanging out with them. We danced and met guys and had a great time. We had a really nice time dancing and meeting people. I was glad that I had made so many new friends on my first day in town.

As the party was dying down, my drunken roommate came over. I was standing with my new friends near the exit. Her eyes were glazed over and she was sweating profusely from dancing.

"Hey, Lori, are you coming back to the room tonight?". Am I coming back to the room tonight? I live there; I had classes the next day, why would I not be coming back to the room.

"Yeah, I have class at 8' o clock."

"Can't you stay with one of your friends?" My newfound group of friends shared a look on their face like; no she can't spend the night in our rooms.

"Why don't you want me to come back to the room?" I asked, once again too naïve to see what was going on. Shanika starting smiling.

"See there is this guy I like on the football team named Jimmy and I invited him back to the room". Okay, it was already close to 2AM and she invited this Jimmy guy back to our room. Shanika put me in a real uncomfortable position. On the one hand I wanted to stay friends with my new roommate and then again, I needed to go back to my room.

"Shanika, I need to get ready for tomorrow".

"Fine whatever." She walked away. She was backed to being the queen of the attitude again. I followed behind her.

"Hey do you and your friends still need a ride home?"

"Forget it roommate, we'll find a ride". She was walking too fast for me to keep up with her. Whatever. I gave my new friends that had walked a ride home.

I beat Shanika back to the room and took over my clothes and got in the bed. I was exhausted. I couldn't imagine how I would make it to class the next day.

About twenty minutes later Shanika came in the room. She had a man with her, I can only assume that this was Jimmy. Shanika was giggling,

"Shhh be quiet, my roommate is trying to sleep". I pretended to be asleep but I was wide-awake. Shanika walked over to her bed and turned on the television set.

"Do you want something to drink?" she asked Jimmy.

"No baby, I'm straight, so what's up with you".

The two began chit chatting, which was really interrupting my sleep. The next thing I heard was kissing sounds. I opened my eyes and peeked out. Shanika was sitting on his lap with her legs straddled around him kissing him. Jimmy picked up the remote control and flicked off the television. The next thing I heard was Shanika asking Jimmy, "Do you have a condom?"

Get out of here! I know she was not going to have sex with him with me in the room. I was in shock. They had sex with me in the room and they weren't quiet about it or anything. I lay there listening and I thought to myself, "Welcome to college kid".

Shanika and I only remained roommates for about two weeks. We got into an argument because she found out that I had sat on her bed while she was at class. Her words were, "I don't want your fat ass sitting on my bed, I don't know where your fat ass has been". So soon after that I moved into a single room across the hall from Sheree and her friends in the other building.

When I moved to the other building life became one big party. Sheree, April, Michelle and I would hang out all hours of the night. We would have slumber parties and take turns doing each other's hair.

I experienced the most fun in my entire life during the first semester of my freshman year. For the first time in my life, I had a close circle of female friends. We were a team, and we were inseparable. My friend provided me with a support system that I had not experienced since I lived in California.

We had a little too much fun perhaps. At the end of the semester grades were released, I failed all of my classes with the exception of theatre.

CHERRY BERRI

For some reason I always found friends that had a whole lot of drama and shit going on in their lives. Perhaps it was because my life was always so crazy I was drawn to people who weren't playing with a full deck.

I met Cherry Berri in the spring of 1994. Cherri Berri was about four foot eleven. Cherry was very cherubic looking. Her real name was Hannan Sharaa. Hannan acquired the nickname "Cherry Berri" in grammar school. People used to tell her she looked like a Strawberry Shortcake figurine.

For months I thought that she was Hispanic, but I eventually learned that she was from Kuwait. She was from a very affluent family who had sheltered her for her entire life. Her parents were very strict. When Cherry went away to college, she got "buck wild" and was completely out of control.

Actually, I cannot remember exactly how we met. I think we had a friend in common. It just seemed like all of a sudden we were friends. When I met her she was so in love with this guy named Quentin.

"Lori, ohmigod, you have to meet Quentin, he is so god damn sexy. He is gorgeous".

She drank a lot and smoked weed, but more than anything she was just a blast to hang out with. She was so much fun. She lived in the dorms across the street from my building. For the first few weeks that we were friends we were inseparable. I was relieved to finally have a friend that I didn't feel inferior to. For once, I felt like I had the upper hand in the friendship. Cherry looked to me for guidance, advice and support.

We had a little restaurant in the basement of the cafeteria named the Snack Bar. One evening after I left the Snack Bar after grabbing a sandwich, I went back to my empty single room to crash. This was a night that I was not going to think about any of the misfit men in my life or the classes that I probably was going to fail. No sooner than I hit the room, the phone rang. I answered the phone and on the other end was Cherry Berri screaming.

"Ohmigod Lori you won't believe it." I threw my bookbag onto the floor and listened intensely.

"What is it Cherry?" Cherry was sobbing and hysterical on the other end.

"I got arrested my parents are going to kill me!"

"Wait hold on, calm down, what did you get arrested for?" Cherry was a mess but I wanted to try to make some kind of sense about what was going on.

"It's Quentin, he's only 14!" I couldn't believe it.

This guy that she had went on and on about for weeks was only 14. I had never met him, but I never would have imagined that he was only 14.

"Hey Cherry, he's 14, wait a minute, finish telling me why you got arrested."

"Lori why don't you come over, please I can't be by myself like this."

Cherry was so very dramatic. I couldn't believe all the drama that she was having. So much for my peaceful night. I grabbed my bookbag (which I always carried, like I was really going to study) and headed over to Cherry's room.

When I arrived to the room, Cherry's face was all red like she had been crying. Her roommate Beth was sitting on the bed consoling Cherry. Cherry looked a mess and she was smoking a cigarette.

"Man Cherry, tell me everything that happened?" I sat down on the bed and Cherry began to tell me her wild and crazy story.

"Well you know how much I liked Quentin and how he is so fine and everything. Well I had been calling his house and a lot of times his mom would answer the phone and she would always say, "He's not here". So when I would talk to him, I'd ask him, why is your mom always trippin like that? And he said his mom didn't like him dating girls that weren't

Black. So I thought that is why the mom wouldn't always have an attitude with me on the phone. So tonight I was over at his house, and we were kissing and stuff, and he asked if he could kiss me on my breast, and I was like, "hell yeah do that shit". So he was kissing me on my breast and I let him put his fingers in my panties and his mom walked in".

Cherry was talking about a mile a minute, she was so frantic, but this story sounded like it was getting good.

"Lori, Let me tell you, his mom was like, "Bitch, get away from my son, you are 19 years old and he is only 14, you bitch, don't move."

"The next thing I know his mom picks up the phone and dials the police and they arrest me for Reckless Endangerment of a Minor, and for committing a lewd act with a minor".

Reckless Endangerment of a Minor. I couldn't believe it.

"Reckless Endangerment of a Minor, man Cheri, did you know he was 14?"

Cherry wiped the tears on her face with her shirt.

"No Lori, I didn't know he was 14, he told me he went to Township, but I didn't know that that was a high school, and to make things worse, I had weed on me when I was arrested, I know my parents are going to find out. I should just kill myself know." Cherry was crazy.

"Girl don't talk like that, things will be fine," I said in an attempt to console Cherry.

Cherry's roommate got a phone call and left in the middle of the night to go spend the night over at a guy's room. Cherry and I stayed up talking the rest of the night. She went on and on about how fine Quentin was and how she can't believe that a fine ass Nigga like that was only 14. She always referred to Black men as Niggas, yet she wasn't Black. She only dated Black men, and sometimes it offended me when she used the "N" word, but I never complained.

Cherry did make the cover of the school paper for her antics with Quentin. She really didn't care, as long as her parents didn't find out and till this day I don't think that they found out.

As April turned to May, Cherry and I became very close friends. She was the only person I had every met that was more naïve about things than I was. This made her vulnerable and weak and she was often preyed on upon people with strong personalities.

I was never into drugs. Being the child of an alcoholic, I saw how alcohol destroyed my father for about ten years, so I never really felt the need to alter my mind with drugs.

Cherry was different though. She would try anything. She was free with her sexuality, mind and spirit. Perhaps there was a part of me that envied Cherry's free spirit. Maybe that's why we were friends, because when I was with her, I could live a little on the wild side.

One day I was coming back from a pizza parlor with Sheree, and some my other friends. As we walked around the corner, we saw a girl lying on the sidewalk. We walked faster to see if we could offer her any help and much to our surprise it was Cherry Berri laying on the sidewalk outside of Neely Hall.

Sheree's friend April walked up to Cherry and tried to lift her up, I ran over and helped and we pulled Cherry to the side. She was conscious, but just barely.

"Cherry what's wrong?" April asked.

"It's that Nigga Ty, he got me all fucked up." Cherry was barely audible and she was tearing up a little.

"Cherry, what happened?" I asked.

"Well I was in my room and Ty called on the phone and he asked me what I was doing, and I said nothing. He asked me if I wanted to smoke some weed and I said hell yeah. Well he came and picked me up and he took me to a hotel room. Man, we got there; he had me drinking, smoking weed and smoking crack. He got me all fucked up, had sex with me and he dropped me off at the corner, he wouldn't even take me back to my room. I tried to make it but I fell asleep on the sidewalk."

I was so embarrassed. Here I was with Sheree and my new friends, who I wanted to think highly of me, because I really liked them, and here was Cherry, drunk, high, and incoherent in front of my building.

"It will be okay Cherry, come on up to my room". I pulled Cherry up and walked her to the door of Neely Hall. Sheree and her friends stayed outside talking. I just knew they were talking about me.

The next day at lunch Sheree and her friends told me that if I wanted to stay friends with them that I would have to stop hanging out with Cherry Berri because she had such a bad reputation. I wanted to be friends with them, but I couldn't let Cherry go like that. Cherry was my friend, I liked hanging out with her, and plus I felt like she needed me.

After that experience with Quentin, and the experience with Ty, I should have known that Cherry was nothing but trouble. Added drama to my already complicated life. But I just couldn't let her go. Hey after all, we were all young; perhaps she was just going through a phase. Anyway, who was I to judge Cherry? I had my own drama.

May rolled around and the school year was about to end. Cherry had planned to attend summer school, but when she found out that she had failed all of classes, so she had to make other plans. Cherry was going to attend a junior college over the summer so that she could bring up her grades and come back to SIUC in the fall.

Cherry hated being at home with her parents. Her parents were very strict Muslims. They moved to the U.S. from Kuwait shortly before the Gulf War started. Cherry's father was an executive for an international bank and her mother was a doctor. They only wanted what was best for Cherry, but she saw things different.

"Lori, if I have to spend the whole summer at home with my parents I will probably kill myself," Cherry said as she packed her bags for the summer.

"Cherry I am sure that you will not kill yourself, that would be so stupid. It couldn't be that bad."

"Lori you don't know. They put my brother in the mental institution because he smoked cigarettes and started hanging around with a bunch of skate borders. I hate them". Cherry sat down on her suitcase in order to close it all the way.

"Look before you know it, it will be time to come back to school. Just chill, everything will work out. Trust me."

Would Cherry make it a whole summer with her parents? It couldn't be that bad. Cherry only dated Black men and she said that her parents were not to keen on Black people. I was going to miss Cherry. I had other friends, but Cherry was my road dog. She was always down for whatever. We heard a horn blow and we knew it was Cherry's parents ready to pick her up and take her home.

It was a beautiful day outside. It was one of those days were it wasn't too hot. I was nervous about meeting Cherry's parents. She had participated in a lot of wild antics this past semester and I didn't want them to think I was a bad influence.

Cherry's parents were in there forties and although they had only been in the U.S. for five years, they were very Americanized. Cherry's father had on a pair of Nikes and a jogging suit. Her mother was wearing a simple black dress.

"Hi, I'm Lori, and I am very pleased to meet you." I reached out to shake her mother's hand and her mother apprehensively shook my hand, her father on the other hand seemed eager to shake my hand.

"Lori, Cherry has told us so many good things about you. You have been such a good influence on Cherry"; Cherry's mother shocked me by making a statement like that. I was afraid that they would accuse me of totally corrupting their daughter.

"Mom, Lori is my best friend in the world." Cherry gave me a big hug. I'm not one to cry in public, but I felt myself tearing up. Life was going to be different without Cherry around.

"Cherry, put your bags in the car we must go. I want to be home before it gets dark", Cherry's dad said in an authoritative tone. Cherry packed her bags into the trunk and slammed the truck shut.

"Well, Lori, it's been real. See you in the fall." Cherry waved and got into the car. Cherry's parents got in the car and they were about to drive off when Cherry's mother rolled down the window.

"It was very nice meeting you Lori. We don't normally like Cherry to hang around Black people, but you seem very nice."

"Oh thanks". I didn't know how to take that compliment.

Cherry shrugged her shoulders as if she were to say, "See what I mean". The car pulled off and I watched it until it was out of view. It finally felt real to me that the summer was coming.

I went about life as normal. Without Cherry and a few of my other friends I made new friends. I didn't here from Cherry again until late July. I had moved into a little apartment on East College Street. The place was so small. All I had was a bed, a TV, a stereo, a table, a stove and a refrigerator. I didn't even have a desk, so you know I didn't do any real schoolwork that summer. I was laying up with this guy named Issac when the phone rang. This was before the days of Caller ID, so I picked up the phone.

"Hello".

"Hey Lori, it's me Cherry, what's going on?'

"Hey girl what's up." I hadn't heard from Cherry for a minute.

"Lori, I can't take it anymore, if I have to stay here one more minute, I am going to kill myself." Cherry was on the other end of the phone hysterical.

I was about to get my groove on with Issac before the phone rang, but I was always there for my friends.

"What is wrong now?"

"I can't believe, it happened again. I was with this guy and his mom called the police on me. We was just friends, chilling smoking weed and his mom came home and called the police."

I tell you with that Cherry Berri there was a never a dull moment.

"How old was this guy Cherry?"

I waved at Issac signaling that I would only be on the phone for one minute.

"See Lori, he was 16, but his mom called the police and said I brought the weed over there. It's just a big mess. My parents told me I have to go. Lori, I don't have any money or anywhere to go can I come down there and stay with you, please. I'll get a job and help out."

I looked around my one room place. I didn't have room for Cherry, and I was really enjoying my summer fling with Issac. Cherry would definitely put a damper on love life. I thought about it though. Cherry was so nice. If the situation had reversed, se wouldn't have hesitated in letting me stay with her. I was so easy.

"Okay Cherry you can come down here," I said letting out a big sigh.

"Thank you so much, I am going to pack my stuff and I am going to have my friend take me to the bus station. I'll see you tomorrow."

Why did I agree to something like that? What had I gotten myself into?

Cherry Berri arrived the next day on the bus. I was happy to see her and we once again became the best of friends as if no time had passed. The remainder of the summer was peaceful. Cherry didn't have any drama and we took turns sleeping on the floor of my one bedroom apartment.

As fall approached I prepared to return to the dorms. I had only signed the apartment lease for the summer. I was eager to return to the dorms. Dorm life was easy. I didn't have to worry about bills or where I was going to get my next meal.

Cherry never did enroll in the classes at the junior college. Her G.P.A. was a 1.2, which meant that she couldn't return to SIU. Cherry needed a job and a roommate. For awhile, she had talked about living in my dorm room with me the whole semester. I pretended that that could be an option, but deep down, I knew I couldn't succeed in college and live with Cherry Berri. She was a good time girl. Everyday had to be a party.

I feel guilty for introducing Cherry to her future roommate.

The Saturday before the start of the new school year, Cherry and I went to a keg party. I introduced Cherry to Wanda Simpson. Wanda was a 23 year old Black female. She had dropped out of SIU two years earlier and was living in Carbondale. To earn money Wanda took in college students as roommates and worked as an unlicensed hairdresser on the East Side of Carbondale. I knew Wanda because she had styled my hair on several occasions. I explained to Wanda that Cherry was looking for a roommate and that she didn't have much money. Wanda seemed eager to help. She told Cherry that she could move in with her ASAP. Wanda didn't even care that Cherry didn't have any money. Cherry had good credit and Wanda asked her to get the telephone and the cable cut on in her name since Wanda had long since ruined her reputation with those two utility companies.

I felt like I had really done a good thing. I didn't just leave Cherry out there. I helped her find a roommate and she was going to be okay. Now I could go on with my sophomore year of college without having to do the roommate thing.

When school started I started to realize that I didn't hear from Cherry as much. Whenever I called Wanda's house, Wanda would say, "Cherry's busy" or "She's not here". I started to feel a little jealous. Cherry was my friend first. She was my number one road dog, and now she was with Wanda all the time. I even felt like Wanda purposely tried to alienate me from Cherry.

I started to hear rumors about Cherry around campus. People would walk up to me and say, "Lori, your girl is out there", "Lori your friend Cherry is a dike", "Lori your friend Cherry is a crack-head", "Lori your friend Cherry gives good head", "Lori your friend Cherry is a prostitute".

Normally, I just let things roll off my shoulders. Could these rumors be true? Well I did know that Cherry was promiscuous and that she did do drugs, but people were basically telling me that she was totally out of control.

It was now fall, and in Carbondale it gets cold in the evenings. I didn't have any gas in my car, or any money for gas, so I decided to take the long walk from the dorms to Cherry and Wanda's house.

I arrived at the shabby two-bedroom house. The screen door had a big tear in it and you could smell the weed for miles. I knocked on the door, but the music was too loud and no one heard me knocking. I finally decided to take my chances and to just open the door.

"Hello," I said as I peeked my head through the door.

Cherry was lying on the couch, obviously high. She had on a tank top and a pair of shorts. Wanda was sitting on the couch with Cherry playing in Cherry's hair. Two guys were sitting on the other couch. They also seemed high out of their minds. No one even noticed that I had come in the room.

"Hey what's going on?" I said in a louder voice.

The place was a mess. Dirty dishes and old pizza boxes on the floor, panties and bras on the couch. Wanda looked up,

"Hey Lori, what's up, you don't never come see nobody", Wanda mumbled.

"Yeah, I was never invited, I never hear from Cherry, so I thought I would come and check her out."

Cherry didn't even seem like she was aware of her surroundings. These people were definitely on more than just weed.

"Hey, Lori, didn't Wanda tell you on the phone that I was fine. I'm fine. You were supposed to be my girl and you are never there for me. You aren't never down for me. Wanda is my girl. She gave me a place to stay, she takes care of me," Cherry said in an angry tone.

Cherry was not making sense. I hadn't done anything wrong to her in order to be angry with me.

"Shorty you want to sit down," the big fat guy on the couch asked me.

"No, I'm fine." I was scared that if I would have sat down a roach would have crawled in my clothes.

The whole aura of the room was weird. I didn't feel like I was supposed to be there. I was worried about Cherry. Maybe I should have just let her go. Being the person that I am, I wanted to save Cherry from herself.

"Hey Cherry, why don't you come outside and talk to me for a minute?"

I didn't know if she would take me up on my offer but it was worth a try. Cherry sat up and lit a cigarette.

"Anything that you can say to me, you can say in front of Wanda," Cherry said as she puffed on the cigarette.

"It's not that I don't want to say anything that I can't say in front of Wanda, it's just far to smoky in here for me, my contacts are drying up."

I didn't even wear contact lenses at that time. It's true I didn't trust Wanda, and I didn't want to talk to Cherry with her around.

Cherry and I went outside and sat on the porch. I didn't waste anytime, I wanted answers.

"Cherry, what's all this stuff about you being a lesbian and a crack head whore?" Cherry got heated.

"Now, Lori. You know them Niggas be lying' on me, I just be chilling, hanging out."

Cherry didn't have a job and she wasn't in school. Who was I to pass judgement on her? I was just trying to be a friend.

"Well Cherry are you doing okay, you don't look good." I hoped that wasn't a bad thing for me to say, but I was being honest. Cherry had cut her hair real short. She had a large bruise on her left and the clothes that she had on looked like she had been wearing them for weeks. Cherry looked down and started to cry.

"Fuck you Lori, I don't have parents that send me money. I can't afford nice clothes." Cherry started to cry.

"Cherry, I didn't mean to hurt your feelings. It's just, look at you, and look at this place. Where do you sleep, and who were those two guys sitting on the couch?"

The temperature started to drop. I folded my arms around myself and rub my hands together,

"Those guys are our roommates. They sleep on the couch I sleep in the bed with Wanda." Cherry looked ashamed.

"Do you like sleeping in the bed with Wanda, don't you want your own place to sleep?"

"Look Lori, you want to know the truth? You want to know the truth?" Cherry shouted at me.

"Wanda takes good care of me, she gives me drugs, food and money and a place to stay. I just have to go down on her before we go to bed at night, I don't like it but I do it because she is good to me."

I couldn't fucking believe what Cherry had just told me. This was so crazy. "Cherry if you don't like it, don't do it. You don't have to live like this. This is crazy. You would be better off at home with your parents. You aren't doing anything good down here. That girl is using you. Just because she helps you out doesn't mean that you should have to do something that, the next time she asks you to do that, just don't do it anymore, tell her no."

Cherry and I sat outside talking for hours. I missed my friend. Wanda had completely brain washed Cherry against me. After our long talk, Cherry assured me that she was going to get a job, and get her own place. I wasn't expecting a miracle. If she would have cleaned herself up that would be good, but I wasn't going to hold my breath.

The night after our long talk it was raining cats and dogs. I was laid up with a guy (as usual), when the phone rang. It was Cherry.

"Lori, that god damn bitch put me out." Cherry was on the phone screaming.

"Calm down, what happened?"

"Lori that Wanda is a slick one. She called my parents and told them I was a crack head, and that I had sex with Niggas all the time and that I stole from her so she was putting me out. She only really put me out because I stood up to her like you said. I told her I wasn't doing that shit anymore."

Now Cherry was homeless, the whole conversation I was hoping that she wasn't going to ask if she could come and stay with me. I played it cool.

"Cherry are you okay?" I asked.

"Yeah, I'm cool, I'm staying in Mae Smith with my friend Missy. We're in room 103. Are you coming over tomorrow?" Cherry asked.

"Sure thing, I'll stop by after class." I went back tending to my company and didn't think anything else about Cherry for the rest of the night.

After my 3:00 class I decided that I would go check out Cherry at her friend Missy's dorm room.

When I arrived the girls were sitting on the bed watching a talk show. Cherry seemed happier than I had seen her in awhile. She was still under the influence, but she was cool. She had on decent clothes and had even put on some make-up.

Missy was a white girl who was pretty cool. She only dated Black men and she acted like a Black girl. She styled her hair like a Black woman and all of her friends, with the exception of Cherry were Black. We were just sitting around watching television. No one was tense, and nothing could prepare us for what was about to happen.

There was a loud knock on the door. Cherry got frightened, as if she knew that the person behind the door was looking for her. She ran and hid under the bed. Missy walked to the door.

"Who is it?" Missy asked in a pretend half-sleepy voice.

"It's the R.A. and campus security Melissa open the door," roared the voice from behind the door.

"I'm sleep right now, do you think you can come back later?" Missy pointed at me to go and hide in the closet. Why was I hiding? I hadn't done anything wrong.

Before I had a chance to get to the closet the door opened. Get out off here! I couldn't believe it. It was the resident assistant, campus security and Cherry's parents.

The security went straight for the closet and Cherry's father went straight for the bed. He saw Cherry's leg sticking out and he physically pulled her from under the bed by her leg.

"You little whore, you shamed me, you shamed your mother, you are a disgrace to your entire family," he shouted at Cherry as he slapped her across the face.

I thought her mother was coming to her rescue, but her mom joined in with the father. They took turns slapping, kicking and pulling on Cherry. The RA and the campus security officer stood by idle.

"You can't fucking do this to me, I'm 19 years old, you can't make me go, you can't make me go, somebody stop them," Cherry screamed.

Cherry's father picked her up and threw her over his shoulders like she was a little girl and walked out of the room. Cherry's mom walked over to me and said,

"Lori we thought you were a good girl, you are trash, just like Cherry." What had I done to deserve that? I wasn't the one responsible for Cherry's behavior. Then again, I did introduce her to Wanda.

The entire floor came out of their room and watched Cherry being carried away by her father as if she had been naughty.

Cherry's parents took her back home, and I didn't hear from Cherry for about 8 or 9 months. I was at my mothers house in Chicago for Labor Day and Cherry called. I was so excited to hear from her. She told me that she had been "working at Burger King" and that she was "doing well". Cherry had also enrolled at a local community college and she was in the process of raising her grade point average so that she could come back to SIU in the spring. We caught up old times and it was really good talking to her.

That was the first phone call. About three hours later Cherry called me for a second again. She asked me if I wanted to go to a party with her on the North Side of Chicago. I passed because I kicked it too much at school. I was at home with my family in relax mode.

In the wee hours of the next morning I got a third phone call from Cherry. She called me at 3:00 AM. I answered the phone on the first ring because I knew my mom would trip about the phone ringing so late at night.

"Hello," I whispered into the phone.

"Lori, it's me Cherry. I came home and my dad was just snapping on me. He told me I had been out to late and he just slapped me in the face for no reason. I can't take it anymore, I met these guys at the club, they are cool and they rap and shit. I'm going to move in with them. They are on their way to come and get me," Cherry said as she cried into the phone.

Cherry had lost her mind. I tried to talk some sense into her.

"Cherry, you can't move in with some guys you met a couple of hours ago at a club".

"Look Lori, page me tomorrow, if I don't call you back, that means something ain't right, but things will be cool, I'll talk to you tomorrow. Look my dad is coming I gotta go".

Cherry hung up the telephone and that was the last time that I ever talked to her in my life. I did page Cherry the next day and the day after. She never called back. I didn't know what to do. I called her parents. They told me that they hadn't heard from Cherry and they didn't care if they ever heard from her again. Weeks turned to months and no one heard from Cherry. I called her mother and would beg for information and she would always say, "Lori, don't call here anymore". Then she would hang up.

Where was Cherry? I used to imagine that she was just high somewhere or that she just wasn't around a phone. Till this day, no one is 100% sure what happened to Cherry. She had been missing for about six months when the Chicago Police found her purse and a bloodied sweatshirt of hers in a dumpster.

That was in 1996. No one had ever heard from Cherry again. She is "presumed dead" by the Chicago Police Department.

Sometimes I wonder who really cared about Cherry besides me. Her parents were very cruel to her. They only cared about her if she behaved the way that they wanted her to. The men in her life only used her and the women to if you think about the Wanda situation.

I remember when I finally found out that Cherry was missing; I called everyone in my phone book. Most people didn't remember Cherry. Some didn't even care. Bad things had happened to me plenty in my life, but losing Cherry hit me hard. She was so pretty and just clueless about the world. She was my greatest project. I just really wanted to turn things around for her. Most of all I remember all of the fun that we had together.

CRIMINAL BEHAVIOR

▼

I opened up my first checking account when I was a freshman in college. I opened up the account with a $250 refund check that was issued to me from the financial aid office.

I planned on using the checking account to pay my bills. I was going to be a responsible citizen. I would write out a check every month to my creditors and pay all of my credit card bills on time.

I wrote my first bad check when I was 18 years old. I was broke. I knew that I didn't have any money in the bank and I wanted to go to a party with my friends. It was homecoming weekend and I was broke. My mother and father refused to send me money because they felt that I should have been working.

I didn't know that I could get into legal trouble for writing bad checks. I thought I would just get bad credit. My credit was already bad.

I walked to the Student Center and wrote out a check to myself for $50. My hand was shaking as I signed the check. The clerk typed into the computer. Was she on to me? I thought with fear. No. She handed me the money and I quickly walked away.

The check bounced and the bank sent a notice to my dormitory. I tore up the notice. Writing bad checks became a habit for me. Every time I needed money, I would take out the checkbook and write a check.

It didn't take long for my check writing habit to get out of hand. I would go to the mall and go on shopping sprees. I would buy clothes, shoes, make-up, you name it. If the stores sold it, I would write a bad check for it. My most expensive purchase was a $350 television set.

Carbondale is small town. They circulate a list called "The Bad Check List." The list is distributed among all of the local stores. The cashiers hang the list next to their registers. It didn't take long for my name to show up on the list. With my name on "The Bad Check List" I couldn't write anymore checks.

I put my bad check writing days behind me and decided to get a legitimate job. My first legitimate job while in college was typing papers. I would type term papers for $1 dollar per page. I suppose I should have charged more money.

Typing papers did not make me rich. I only made enough money to hang out with my friends or to get my hair done. I still had my car and I was two months behind on my car insurance. I needed a way to make money. I had to bring home at least $400 dollars a months to pay all of my bills.

My next big idea was "Lori's St. Louis Taxi Service." I would drive SIU students to St. Louis for the day. The cost was $20 per person. Every Saturday, I would pack up my car with three other students and drive to St. Louis. I would drop them off wherever they desired. By, 4:00 P.M., I would pick everyone up and we would head back to Carbondale.

The rides to St. Louis became stressful. I was putting too many miles on my car and by the time the weekend was over I was exhausted.

During my sophomore year I had a math class named Introduction to Contemporary Math. I sat next to the finest boy. I looked forward to going to class just so that I could see him. I didn't know his name. He was about five foot nine and he had the most gorgeous brown eyes that I had ever seen.

The class met Tuesdays and Thursday's from 11:00-12:15 P.M. One Tuesday, I made up my mind. I was going to get his name and number before the class let out.

This particular Tuesday, I wore a red tennis dress and a pair of white tennis shoes. I put my hair up in a large pony-tail and dabbed on my sweetest smelling perfume.

It was a beautiful sunny fall day. I was casually late for class and smiled at the young man as I sat down. He smiled back. My heart almost jumped out of my chest.

After class he grabbed his books and headed to the door. I ran behind him. I knew he could tell that I was following him.

"Wait!" I screamed. I felt so foolish. Why did I say that? What was I going to say now that I had gotten his attention?

He stopped and looked at me. He was so handsome. I melted.

"Are you talking to me?" He asked.

"Yeah, I was wondering if you wanted to study sometimes."

I was such a nerd. How could I let something so lame come out of my mouth? He smiled.

"I don't know about studying. This class is so easy. We can hang out though. Do you want to go to the movies sometimes?"

Was he asking me out?

"That would be great. I don't know your name though, or your phone number," I said.

"You don't waste a minute do you little mamma. Walk with me to my car."

He grabbed my hand and we walked to the parking lot. I was so nervous. He held my hand tight. He stopped in front of a black Dodge Viper. The car was hot.

"Nice car!"

"Thanks." He opened the door on the driver's side and took out a piece of paper. The paper already had his name and phone number written on it.

"Call me sweetie." He smiled and drove off. I looked down at the piece of paper. His name was Tavares.

I didn't want to seem to anxious, but at the same time I wanted to call him. I called Tavares four hours after he gave me his phone number.

"Hello." He answered the phone in a deep sexy voice.

"This is Lori, from your math class."

"I knew it was you," He said.

"How did you know it was me?" I asked.

"Because, I don't give many people my private phone number. What made you talk to me today after class?"

"I had been wanting to talk to you for awhile but I was scared. I'm a little shy at times," I giggled. I always giggled when I was nervous.

"You are not shy. Let's go to the movies. I want to see *Above the Rim*"

"When do you want to go?" I asked.

"Right now."

"I live in the dorms are you going to pick me up?"

"Yeah, meet me down in the parking lot in about 30 minutes." I hung up the phone.

I only had 30 minutes to shower and get dressed. I was so broke I hadn't washed clothes. I pulled a dressed that looked clean out of the hamper and ironed the wrinkles out of it.

I took a quick shower and pulled my hair up in a pony-tail. I grabbed my purse and my keys and went downstairs to meet Tavares.

As soon as I reached the parking lot Tavares pulled up. I hopped in the car and he drove off.

"You look nice." He said.

"Thanks." I smiled. Tavares massaged my leg as he drove. He was so sexy.

We watched the movie. I remember the whole time I was watching the movie I was desperately hoping that he would lean over and kiss me.

Tavares didn't kiss me in the movie theatre. He squeezed my leg a couple of times. He was a perfect gentleman.

After the movie was over he dropped me back at the dorms. This was the first time in a long time that a guy didn't try to take me back to his house after a date.

The next afternoon around 4:00 P.M. Tavares called and invited me over to his house. I accepted and I drove my car to his house.

Tavares lived in a gorgeous three-bedroom townhouse outside of Carbondale. There were two cars and a truck in the driveway. I parked my car on the street and rang the doorbell.

Tavares answered the doorbell.

"This place is phat. Your parents must be rich," I said as I stared at the white carpet and the glass furniture.

"Just the opposite. My parents are not even together. I bought all of this stuff on my own." Here I was with a man that had money and I was broke as a joke.

I sat down on the white couch in the living room. Tavares sat down next to me and put his arm around my shoulder. He picked up the remote control and turned on the television set.

"I don't want to sound nosy, but how can you afford to live like this. You don't sell drugs do you?" I asked with a smile.

"If I did sell drugs you wouldn't want to hang out with me anymore?" He asked.

I sure knew how to pick them. There was a drug dealer or a gang banger in every town and I always knew how to find them.

"I knew you sold drugs," I laughed.

"Hey, don't go telling everybody. I have a new plan. I'm a senior. I'm about to graduate. I need to make a quick $10,000 dollars before I leave town."

Tavares was talking about big money and I was interested.

"Tell me your plan." I asked.

"Why are you going to help me?" He said with a smile.

"That all depends. Will I get in trouble?" I giggled.

"Baby girl you won't get in trouble." Tavares held my hand.

"Tell me all about it." I asked.

"I have a plan. You can get a job working in the financial aid office. You will have access to everyone's social security number. If you can get me about 50 names, birth dates and social security numbers of white male students, I will give you $2,500."

That sounded like a stupid plan. I had no idea what he was up to.

"Tell me more." I asked.

"No, I don't want you to know too much." He grabbed my hand.

"So are you going to get the job?"

"I'll look into it next week." I was hesitant. I didn't need any trouble in my life.

We spent the rest of the evening watching movies and talking. He didn't try to put the moves on me, which I thought was odd. I had done my best flirting with Tavares and he wasn't responding.

The next day, which was a Saturday, Tavares and I went to a SIU baseball game. I found baseball absolutely boring, but it was a sport Tavares enjoyed.

"Why haven't you tried to kiss me?" I asked Tavares as the sun beat down on us in the stands. Tavares took a sip of his soda and pulled his baseball cap down.

"Lori, I have a girlfriend," Tavares whispered. I couldn't believe this. I had been having a blast hanging out with him for three days only to find out that he had a girlfriend. I couldn't hide my disappointment.

"I'm glad you told me," I mumbled.

"It's not like you think. I'm from Atlanta. That's where my girlfriend is. She's not here in Carbondale. I love hanging out with you. I really enjoy your company." Tavares put his arm around my shoulder. It was cool. I liked hanging out with him.

"I'm glad that you told me. You didn't have to tell me."

"I'm an honest kinda guy," Tavares said as he held my hand.

Later on that evening, Tavares and I went out to dinner. I wore a new dress that he bought me earlier that day when we stopped at the mall. I was wearing my hair down and I felt really beautiful. Too bad he had a girlfriend.

Just when I thought that Tavares had forgot about his plan, he mentioned it.

"Are you still going to get that job at the financial aid office?" He asked as we waited for our dinner.

"First thing Monday morning." I was very uncomfortable. Stealing social security numbers sounded serious. I knew that the financial aid office had cameras. I was scared. I could have just told him no, but I was weak.

Monday morning I went to the financial aid office and applied for a job. I was interviewed on the spot by an older White woman named Mrs. Gordon.

"Why do you want to work here Ms. Baldwin?"

"Because I need a job." I said with a giggle. I was young. I didn't know that giggling and stupid answers aren't standard protocol for interviews.

"We have two positions. Both positions require you to work with student records. You will have to pass a background check before we could hire you." No problem

I thought to myself. I had never been arrested.

I filled out the consent form and handed it to the interviewer. I went in the lobby and started to read a magazine. I waited in the financial aid office for what seemed like an eternity awaiting the results of my background check.

Finally, Mrs. Gordon came out of her office.

"Ms. Baldwin. I regretfully have to decline your application. It seems that you have several warrants for your arrest. You are also on "The Bad Check List." I could call the campus police and you would be arrested. You seem like a very nice girl. I think you should try to work out your problems as soon as possible."

I felt like a heel. I was a college criminal. What did I have a warrant for? Could it be for the bad checks?

"Did they say what the warrants were for?" I asked.

"They were for writing bad checks to Wal-Mart and to Target," Mrs. Gordon said as she looked down at the paper.

I left the office and tears ran down my face. I was so embarrassed. I had warrants for my arrest. I feared that the police would come and bust down my dorm room door and haul me away to jail.

Later that night I called and broke the news to Tavares.

"I can't get a job at the financial aid office because I have a warrant for my arrest. I wrote some bad checks and they caught up with me."

"That's cool. Don't worry. I'll get the information I need somehow."

"Do you think I will go to jail?" I asked.

"Just pay off all of the bad checks." He made things sound so simple.

"I would if I had the money. I never would have wrote the checks if I had money in the first place."

I started to cry. I was in college because I wanted to get an education but I was so tired of being broke. College sucks when you don't have money to survive.

"I'll help you out if I can," Tavares promised.

The next few weeks I didn't see Tavares as much as I would have liked to. A part of me had lost interest in him because he had a girlfriend. He promised to help me out and I hadn't seen a dime.

I pushed the fact that I had warrants for my arrest to the back of my mind. The school year was coming to a close and I didn't want to fail all of my classes. I studied when I could in hopes of passing at least 4 out 5 of my classes.

Tavares stopped calling. He didn't come by. He even missed class.

Two weeks after I hadn't seen nor talked to Tavares he stopped by my dorm room.

"Long time no talk to," I said sarcastically as I welcomed him into my room.

"Lori, are you mad at me? I hope you took good notes for me." Tavares gave me a big hug.

"Where were you?"

"Well I spent a week in Atlanta. I have a new job. I've been working as a janitor in the Admissions & Records building."

"You have money. Why are you working as a janitor?"

"Shhh. You talk to loud." Tavares was paranoid.

"I've been working there so that I can get on the computers at night time to get the information I need. I have everything I need now. I'm going to quit in a few days."

"What are you up to? Why won't you tell me?" I begged.

"Lori, the less you know the better."

"Give me some money." I stuck my hand out playfully.

"How much money do you want?"

"$20 dollars!" I smiled.

"You have to earn it." Tavares said slyly.

"How?" I smiled.

"Introduce me to some of your friends." What was he thinking about?

"Are you trying to be freaky?" I asked.

"No. I know you have some friends that smoke weed. Introduce me to some of your friends."

I called my friends Sheree, April, and Michelle. I invited them over to my room.

We all lived on the same floor, so it didn't take them long to arrive.

"Hey, this is Tavares. He thinks we should all hang out." I was terrible at making introductions.

"He's cute, is this your boyfriend?" April asked.

"No, Lori is just my friend," Tavares said as he came up behind me and gave me a big hug. He kept saying that I was just a friend but I definitely felt sexual energy between the two of us.

My friends didn't get high until Tavares smooth talked them into buying weed from him. I was down to. I had never smoked weed until that day. I liked being high. I was already silly and being high made me act even sillier.

My sophomore year was almost as my freshman year. I did worry about my grades, but I still had fun. I just had fun and lived my life one day at a time.

After my friends left Tavares gave me the $20 dollars I asked him for.

"Tavares, they only spent $15, and you are giving me $20 anyway?" I was puzzled.

"They may have spent $15 today, but they will be back for more. You just got me some new clients."

Everything made sense. Over the next few weeks, I introduced Tavares to every one I knew. He already had a nice clientele, but now he was supplying most of the sophomore class.

May rolled around and Tavares prepared for graduation. After graduation he planned to move back to Atlanta. Tavares was a computer science major and he had a job lined up at IBM. The day before his graduation, Tavares let me in on his plan.

Tavares called me on the phone and invited me over to his house. I drove to his house on a Friday afternoon after my last class.

The glass furniture was all packed up and most of the house was empty. The couch was gone and the art work had been removed from the walls.

"I'm going to miss you," I said as I gave Tavares a big hug.

"I'm going to miss you too." Tavares reached into his pocket and pulled out a large wad of money. He put the money in my purse.

"What is this for?" I asked.

"It's for being such a good friend." I didn't count the money because I didn't want to seem frantic.

"Is this money from the secret operation?"

"Lori, you just have to know. I'm going to tell you, but you have to promise me on everything that you love that you will never tell anyone."

"You didn't tell anyone about my warrants. I promise I won't tell anyone."

Tavares and I sat down on his living room floor.

"Remember I told you that I was working at Admissions & Records?" I nodded.

"Well, I broke into the computer system. I found names that I thought were Caucasian, because most of the time, White males have good credit. I applied for about 60 credit cards in these other peoples names. My partner Fred works in the mailroom. When the credit cards would come, he would hold them to the side for me. Once I received the card, I would go to the ATM and withdraw the maximum cash advance amount on the card." I stared in awe.

"You have far too much time on your hands to think up a plan like that. Do you know if you get caught that you will be in big trouble?"

"I'm not going to get caught. Tomorrow is my graduation and I am leaving Carbondale and I am never coming back here again."

"Tavares, I'm curious. How much money did you get?"

"Each card had a maximum cash withdrawal of $1000. So I got about $50,000. I gave Fred $3000, and there is a $2500 in your purse for you. I want you to pay off those bad checks you wrote." My eyes grew big. No one had ever given me so much money in my life.

Tavares had hooked me up.

"Thank you for the money. I hope all goes well for you," I said as I gave Tavares a kiss on the cheek

The next day I woke up early in the morning to get ready for Tavares' graduation.

I was not a morning person, so it was not easy for me to be some place at 8:00 A.M. on a Saturday morning.

The graduation was being held in the arena. The arena was where most of the concerts and basketball games were held. I decided to walk because trying to find a parking space would have been a nightmare.

I day dreamed the entire graduation ceremony. I planned how I was going to spend the money that Tavares had given me. Of course he had told me to pay off the bad checks, but I wasn't thinking about those bad checks. That was going to be my summer time money.

After the ceremony was over I waited for Tavares. I waved my arms so he could find me. Tavares ran over to me and gave me a big hug. He was with a group of women.

"Hey this is my family. This is my mom, my girlfriend, and my Aunt Kee-Kee."

"Wait a minute, that is my Aunt Kee-Kee," I said as I ran over and gave Kee-Kee a hug. Aunt Kee-Kee was one of my favorite aunts. She lived in Atlanta and she was my cousin Ray-Ray's mother.

"Lori, I didn't know you went to school here."

"Wait a minute, Aunt Kee-Kee, Tavare's is your nephew?" I asked.

"Yes, he is my brother Oscar's son. You never met Oscar or his kids because Oscar has been in jail since you were a baby." Aunt Kee-Kee hugged Tavares.

"We are so proud of him." Tavares mother kissed him on the cheek.

Tavare's girlfriend was a short, skinny Asian girl. Her name was Sue. This was the girl that he was being so faithful to.

Tavares was my cousin. I couldn't believe it. I was so happy that we didn't sleep with him. I was extremely attracted to him, but I was so glad that I didn't cross that line.

Tavares moved away and we didn't keep in touch. I missed having him around. I couldn't believe that I had a cousin and I didn't even know it. I should have known if I did have a cousin he would have been a shady criminal. My whole family was crooked and I was to.

The warrant situation didn't come back to haunt me until 2 years later. I avoided the police those two years. I was so paranoid. I almost lived in fear. I didn't speed. I didn't get any parking tickets. I didn't give the police any reason to have to come in contact with me.

During the fall of 1996, I was walking down the street with my friends. As always, I was dressed in a very nice outfit. I was wearing a tight pair of jeans and a baby blue Guess sweater. I felt adventurous that day. I also was wearing a pair of blue contact lenses. The contact lenses matched my sweater and I thought that was cute.

Our destination was the video rental store on the strip. As we were walking in the store, a tall young man was walking out. The young man held the door for us. He was a tall, thin dusty looking man. He was ashy, as if he hadn't put lotion on his body for weeks. His clothes looked dirty, but he was wearing a gold chain. I could never understand why people would wear nice jewelry if their clothes weren't up to par.

The man smiled at me. I smiled for courtesies sake and entered the video store.

My friends and I spent about 30 minutes in the store. When we exited the store, the young man was still standing there. I pretended like I didn't see him and I walked past him.

"Hey, can I talk to you?" He grabbed my arm. I was startled.

"Please don't touch me," I said as I pulled my arm away.

"It's just you have such pretty eyes. I just want to talk to you. My name is Henry. What's your name?" He stuttered and he smelled bad.

"It doesn't matter. I have to go." I walked away. He started to follow us.

"Just tell me your name and I'll leave you alone." He was a pest.

"My name is Lori. Bye." I said my name with major attitude and started to walk faster.

When my friends and I were out of ear shot I commented on the situation.

"He was a dirty bum. He even smelled bad." I told my friend Sheree.

"You didn't have to be so mean," Sheree said with a smile.

"He was dirty and he grabbed me. He was all up in my personal space." My friends and I laughed about the incident.

Two days later as I was sitting in my dorm room my telephone rang.

"Hello." No one said anything. I hung up the phone. The phone rang again.

"Hello." I was getting scared.

"Hey Lori, its Henry." I didn't know any Henry.

"I don't know any Henry."

"How could you forget me. You met me outside of the video store the other day. I haven't forgotten you or those pretty eyes."

How did this freak get my phone number?

"How did you get my phone number?"

"I called the front desk of your building and I described you and told them your first name and the guy at the front desk gave me the number." Henry laughed on the other end.

"Please don't call again." I started to hang up the phone when Henry yelled out.

"Wait, I bought you a present. I bought you a necklace. Just let me see you and give you the necklace. I know where you live, let me bring it over." I was really scared. He hadn't threatened me but he was scaring me.

I hung up the telephone and called my resident assistant. The front desk worker who gave my phone number to Henry was reprimanded. My resident assistant suggested that I call the police.

I was scared. This Henry guy seemed crazy. I wanted to call the police, but in the back of my mind I remembered that I had the warrants. I couldn't call the police. The police would arrest me.

Henry left three messages on my voice mail that evening. He was begging me to let him come over. I didn't scare easily, but this guy was really scaring me. Why did he pick me out of all of my friends to harass? I should have never put on those blue contact lenses.

By my junior year of college, I had really cleaned up my act. I was getting good grades and I was working a legitimate job working in an office in the school library. The last thing I needed in my life was a whole lot of drama.

We didn't have Caller ID in the dorms. I couldn't just stop answering my phone.

The next evening Henry called again.

"Why don't you want to talk to me?" Henry said.

"I'm not interested. I have a boyfriend." I lied.

"I'll kill your boyfriend and then you won't have one anymore." This guy was nuts. I hung up the phone.

Over the next few days I did some investigating and discovered that Henry was not a SIU student. He lived in town and he had been in trouble with the law before. He had been arrested for sexual assault in the past. Why was he free and able to harass me?

My friends and co-worker begged me to call the police. I couldn't though. I could not go to jail. I had come too far to see myself go down over something stupid.

Saturday morning as I was sleeping I heard a knock on my door. None of my friends came over to my room without calling first. I walked over to the door and peeked out of the peep hole. I looked out the peep-hole and there was Henry.

I ran to my phone to dial 9-1-1. As I started to dial, I remembered the warrants. I hung up the phone. I stood very still. He continued to knock on the door. The knocking grew louder. I called my resident assistant.

"The guy is out there right now and he is knocking at my door." My resident assistant ran into the hall. The knocking ended and I heard Henry run away.

The resident assistant was still on the phone with me.

"Lori, he ran off. If you are this frightened you should call the police," she said. I listened to her advice. I couldn't tell her that I was scared to call the police because I had warrants for my arrest. I hung up the phone.

I spent the entire weekend holed up in my bedroom because I was scared of Henry. I had let one crazy guy disrupt my entire life.

Monday came and I had to face the world. I went to my classes and after my 10:00 A.M. class I went to work. I was sitting at my desk sorting a stack of paperwork when the telephone rang. My boss answered the phone.

My boss Debra was a thirtysomething single mother from Carbondale. She was a sweetheart. She had long flowing blonde hair and she looked like Farrah Faucett in her heyday.

"Lori, telephone." I couldn't imagine who would be calling me at work. I picked up my phone.

"Hello, Lori Baldwin."

"Why are you being so mean to me. I've only been nice to you and you are treating me real bad." It was Henry. He had found me at work. He was a stalker and he was good. How could this be happening to me? I hung up the phone. The phone rang again.

The library was a quiet, peaceful place. I couldn't have Henry bringing all of this drama to my job. The phone rang again. My boss answered the phone.

"Hello." She listened. I knew it was Henry.

"That's an awful thing to say!" Debra screamed into the phone.

"What did he say?" I asked.

"He said that he is on his way up here to kill you and all of us too! I don't want anything bad to happen to you Lori. I'm calling the police." Debra started to cry and she dialed 9-11.

"Debra don't cry, he's not going to kill me, he's not going to hurt anyone. He's just talking trash." I attempted to reassure Debra, but I couldn't even stand by my words. I didn't know what this guy was capable of.

Debra called the police. We sat there and waited for the police to arrive. In the back of my mind I hoped that the warrants would not catch up with me.

Five minutes later the Carbondale police arrived at the library. Debra explained to the officer what Henry had said during the phone conversation. I explained to the officer the events of the last few days. The officer filled out his police report very detailed.

"Anything else that you would like to add to the police report Ms. Baldwin?"

The officer asked.

"No, sir." The officer was a handsome young White man. He had dark brown hair and blue eyes. He reminded me of Mark Wahlberg.

"Ms. Baldwin, are you aware that you have two Jackson County warrants out for your arrest?" I didn't even see the point in lying.

"Yes, sir. That is why I didn't call the police sooner because I was afraid that I would be arrested for the warrants." Debra stared at me in shock.

"I'm going to have to arrest you I'm afraid." I took a deep breath. At least I would be safe in jail. The officer placed his handcuffs around my wrists and escorted me out of the library.

I was so embarrassed. I was being led away from my job in handcuffs and it seemed that everyone was staring at me. I wanted to scream from the top of my lungs. "It's not as bad as it looks."

I had my mug shot taken and I was fingerprinted at the police station. I felt like such a criminal. The police were nice to me. They didn't treat me like a criminal. I guess I wasn't the only young woman to ever be arrested for writing bad checks.

Debra bailed me out an hour after I was arrested. I was given a court date to return to plead my case. The police told me that they could not arrest Henry because they had no solid evidence. However, they did stop by his house and had a chat with him.

Debra was a very understanding boss and she did not hold the mistakes of my past against me.

Surprisingly, after that day, Henry never contacted me again. It still puzzles me to this day why Henry decided to stalk me. Sometimes I wonder if evil came to me because I had done so many bad things in the past.

The night before my court date I feared that I would be convicted. I faced up to a year in prison. Prior to my court date I retained a lawyer.

Court was not as dramatic as I envisioned it to be. The judge fined me $250 and ordered me to pay the stores the money I owed them. The judge also sentenced me to perform 250 hours of community service at a battered woman's shelter.

I had matured a lot since my bad check writing days. I realized that I had come to and had far too much to lose. I couldn't risk my future by playing games with the law.

When Your Enemy Bites The Dust

▼

Samantha Greer and I both attended the same high school. Samantha was probably the most popular girl at Morgan Park High School. Everyone liked her. She ran track, and she was a cheerleader. She was one of the few girls who had a car while in high school. She was one of those popular people who it was easy to hate. Her life was too perfect.

Her life seemed perfect, but she wasn't perfect. She had an evil side. I suppose to stay on the popular pedestal she had to bring down some little people. I was unfortunate enough to be one of the little people who she decided wasn't worthy enough to breathe her air.

My first run in with Samantha was during freshman biology class. I was sitting at my desk minding my own business taking notes. Samantha and the rest of the popular girls were all sitting next to each other chatting and gossiping while the teacher was writing on the board. Our teacher gave us a group assignment and he instructed us to get into pairs. Everyone paired up into groups.

I didn't have anyone to work with.

"Mr. Lee, I don't have anyone to work with," I said.

"Lori, get in the group with Samantha and Dee Dee," Mr. Lee instructed.

I did not want to work with these girls.

I moved my chair over to Samantha's desk and sat my notebook on the table. Samantha and Dee Dee gave me a dirty look. I guess they didn't want me in their group. I tried to break the ice.

"So, does anyone know what we are supposed to be doing?" I asked.

Samantha rolled her eyes and looked over at Dee Dee. Samantha stared at me straight in the face and said, "I don't like you. Nobody at this school likes you."

I didn't like her either. My feelings were a bit hurt because the whole class had heard what she said and they started to laugh.

I couldn't let her get the best of me like that. I tried to remain calm.

"What did I ever do to you?" I asked in an angry tone. "People do like me at this school."

Samantha pointed her finger at me.

"Well first of all," she said, "you dress like a ho. You always wear little short skirts and try to shake your butt when you walk. You always wear tight shirts trying to show off your little chest.

"Then on top of that," she continued, "you flirt with every guy at school."

The whole class laughed and cackled. A boy who we called "Yoda" tried to stir things up.

"Damn, Lori, are you going to take that?!" he asked.

The whole class was laughing. Mr. Lee didn't even care what was going on. Samantha thought she was so cool and so popular. I couldn't let her get the best of me.

I stood up and pushed her out of her seat real hard. She slammed to the ground, hitting her head hard on the hard school room floor. She grabbed her head in agony.

What happened next was like a chain reaction. All of her friends, male and female started to move toward me as if like they were going to beat me up. A tall boy named Sammy tried to swing on me. I ducked.

Samantha's friend Dee Dee screamed at me.

"You crazy loser," she shrieked. "I think she has a concussion!"

Samantha lay on the floor crying and holding her head. I didn't even feel bad. At the time I wished I could have hurt her more.

Then the security guard came and I was escorted out of class. I was promptly given a three-day suspension for fighting.

When I returned to school after my suspension, I was less popular than I was before I left. It seemed that someone was giving me a scornful look everywhere I turned.

But I did manage to make some new friends. Some of the self-proclaimed nerds took me in and worshipped me. The nerds couldn't stand the popular kids, and they admired me a lot for knocking Samantha Greer on her ass. They would ask me to tell the story over and over again.

Still most of the girls at school—especially the Black girls—avoided me like I was the plague. But I remained popular with about half of the boys.

I was approached by a handsome junior named Chauncey during my sophomore year. Chauncey was on the football team, and he was very popular with the ladies—especially the cheerleaders.

One day I was opening my locker when Chauncey came up to me.

"Hey, what are you doing this weekend?" he asked.

He was really handsome, with light brown eyes and a gorgeous smile. Good thing I was single at the time.

"I'm not doing anything," I replied. "Why do you ask?"

Chauncey smiled at me.

"My boy Eddie is having a party and I was wondering if you would like to go to it with me."

As if I would have said "no."

We exchanged phone numbers, and agreed that he could pick me up at my house Saturday night at around eight o'clock.

I was flattered that an attractive football player had asked me out on a date. Saturday evening I wore my favorite green skirt. I wore a nearly sheer white top and large hoop earrings.

Chauncey picked me up at 7:45 p.m. and we drove to Eddie's house. Chauncey drove a 1991 Nissan Maxima. It was his parents car, but they let him drive on the weekend. Chauncey and I laughed and talked about people at school.

"I heard that you beat Samantha up last year," Chauncey said, laughing.

"I did not beat her up," I protested as Chauncey pulled into Eddie's driveway.

"I only pushed her down on the floor. She was asking for it."

He agreed.

"Yeah, Samantha can be annoying at times," he said. "I used to go out with her." I nearly got whiplash as I swiveled my head around to stare at Chauncey. He used to go out with Samantha? I thought that I kept up with school gossip, but that was one bit of information that I didn't know.

I never would have agreed to go out with him if I had. Too late for that.

Eddie's party was packed with popular people. All of the football players were there, and so were most of the basketball players. The whole cheerleading squad was also in attendance, of course. A black light glowed, and the smell of beer and incense wafted through the single-family ranch style house. A DJ spun records in the corner.

It didn't dawn on me immediately that Chauncey might have been using me that night to make Samantha jealous. I had tried hard not to think of that possibility—although Samantha and her friends kept staring at just as hard.

But soon I didn't care. The music was good, Chauncey was great, and the night was young. We danced the night away.

The DJ finally played a slow song. Chauncey held me real tight as we slow danced to "I Wanna Sex You Up" by Color Me Bad.

But soon we were interrupted. I felt a tap on my shoulder.

I turned around then jumped in horror as Samantha threw a cup of red fruit punch all over my white top. She bolted toward her friends for protection before I could react.

My top was ruined and I was furious. But to my surprise, so was Chauncey.

"Now why did you do that?" he screamed at Samantha from across the room. "You are so ignorant! That's why I broke up with you!"

Samantha turned red with embarrassment. Tears began to stream down her face.

"Fuck you, Chauncey!" she screamed.

"How could you bring her to this party and flaunt her all in my face? How could you go from a classy girl like me to a trashy slut like her?"

She had looked so pitiful that at first I was going to let her slide for pouring the punch on my red shirt. I had pushed her down in biology class, so I was going to consider things as being even.

Now she had called me a "trashy slut." I just couldn't let that ride.

"Look here, bitch," I said as I began my tirade.

"I don't know why you think you are all that. I ought to kick your ass for messing up my shirt."

By now I was fully across the room and standing right in front of her. So Samantha took two steps and spit directly into my left eye.

She bolted again, but I jumped through the air and tackled her before she could get too far. I began smashing her head into the floor while her cowardly friends began to kick me in the back. The party had turned into an all-out brawl before Chauncey and his friends finally broke it up.

It was unfortunate that the evening had ended on such a sour note.

I later told Chauncey that it would be better if we didn't see each other again. If I had to fight Samantha Greer every time we went out, it wasn't really worth it.

It wasn't much of a surprise to me when Chauncey and Samantha started dating again one week after Eddie's party. I suppose Chauncey had only used me to make Samantha jealous. Anything otherwise was too much of a coincidence to ignore.

Samantha and I didn't have any more altercations in high school. She made my life a living hell, though. I hated her. I hated her more than anyone in the world. We regularly traded insults.

Sometimes I would be at my locker when she would walk past.

"Ooh—someone smells like fish," she'd shout so everyone could hear her. "It smells like tuna city! I guess Lori must be around."

Most of the time I just ignored her. I was a happy person and my life was going well. I wasn't going to let a shallow popular girl ruin my life.

One day during a sleepover bash at my house I took some old socks and made a voodoo doll. I taped the name "Samantha" on the doll and poked it with safety pins. My friends and I also recorded a song about how much we hated Samantha on my keyboard.

Samantha and Chauncey continued to see one another, although he would blow me a kiss sometimes when he would pass me in the hall. He was nothing but trouble, and I was glad that I had absolutely no interest in Chauncey.

Thankfully Samantha and I went our separate ways after graduation. I was on my way to Southern Illinois University at Carbondale. Samantha was headed to Purdue University.

Samantha's best friend Dee Dee was also planning to attend SIUC. But I could live with that. With no Samantha around, Dee Dee was completely powerless. When I saw Dee Dee around campus she was actually cordial to me.

But one day on campus during my sophomore year, I found myself walking straight toward Samantha Greer . She stared at me hard as she walked past. I stared back.

I soon found out that Samantha had transferred to SIUC to be with Dee Dee. I also found out that she was still dating Chauncey, who attended St. Louis University. He was less than two hours away.

Could Samantha and I coexist on the same campus? We did, although we rarely spoke to each other. We did a lot of staring, though.

It only took three weeks before conflict between the two of us began. There was a girl in my building name Kyiana that did hair. Every Saturday morning Kyiana's dorm room was jumping like a beauty shop as she handled client after client. One day as Kyiana was putting a pony tail in my hair she said,

"Hey Lori, I heard so many things about you. You are a little rough girl. You don't even seem like the type."

"What are you talking about?" I asked.

"This new girl, her name is Samantha, she was telling all the dirt about you today in the cafeteria. She was telling us how you used to fight all the time and how you used to dress like a hoochie," Kyiana said with a smile.

I didn't find things the least bit funny. Here I was minding my own business and Samantha was spreading rumors about me. I was not the same person that I used to be. College had made me stronger and I wasn't going to lie down and take a whole lot of shit from Samantha and Dee Dee.

I knew that Samantha and Dee Dee were roommates. They lived in the building next to mine on the 9th floor. That very same Saturday that Kyiana did my hair, I decided to pay Samantha and Dee Dee a little visit.

When I arrived outside of their dorm room I got the jitters. I was a little nervous. I didn't want us to end up having a physical confrontation. I swallowed a cup of courage and knocked on the door. I heard loud music and voices. I knew they were home.

"Who is it?" I heard Dee Dee ask from behind the door.

"It's Lori," I said as I leaned against the door. I heard the voices behind the door start to whisper. They turned the radio off. Dee Dee answered the door.

"Can I help you?" I peeked into the room and I saw Samantha sitting on the bed. "Samantha can I talk to you for a minute?" I asked. She was pretending to read a magazine.

"About what?" She said.

"Stop being so phony. You know about what. I heard that you have been talking shit about me." I did not have time to play games with this girl. I was rather loud with my comment and several other doors in the hallway opened up. A few girls that lived on the floor decided to peek out of their rooms to see what was going on. I didn't want to embarrass myself.

"Look Dee Dee, can I come in so Samantha and I can straighten this out?" I asked as Dee Dee stood guard at the doorway.

Samantha jumped up off the bed like she was all tough and everything.

"Look bitch, don't come to my room trying to start shit, anything I said about you was true!"

I pushed my way around Dee Dee and stood in the room face to face with Samantha.

"Samantha you are a petty little girl. High school was a whole lifetime ago. I have a life here. This time I'm one of the popular people. There is enough popularity on this campus for us both to shine. You don't have to try to bring me down to bring yourself up," I said.

Those words didn't seem profound to me when I said them, but the instigating girls in the hallway thought that I had told Samantha a piece of my mind. "You told her girl!" They chanted from the hallway. Samantha was thinking of a comeback, but I couldn't let her have the last word.

"Look, just pretend like you don't know me, and I will pretend that I don't know you."

I walked past Dee Dee and out of the room. I had made it through my entire freshman year with no problems from Dee Dee. Now Samantha was here, I was going through some of the same petty drama that I used to be a part of in high school.

The next few months were quiet. Dee Dee and Samantha went about their lives and I went about mine. I would see Samantha every Tuesday at 11:00 A.M. We both had a class in the same building. When the bell would ring we would walk past each other. She would stare at me, I would stare at her.

We both became well-rounded popular college students in our own rights. Samantha and Dee Dee joined a sorority. I just hung out with a bunch of cool people.

Occasionally, we would even speak to each other when our paths crossed around campus. Samantha was still dating Chauncey. Usually high school relationships didn't make it through college. I guess Chauncey and Samantha really cared for each other. They deserved each other. They both were nothing but trouble.

From word of mouth I knew that Chauncey and Samantha were still a couple. I didn't actually see them together until October of my junior year. Samantha's sorority was having a bowling and billiards social event. I didn't avoid the whole sorority, actually I had some friends that were in Samantha's sorority. My friends and I decided to attend. I wasn't very good at bowling or billiards. I was going to play things cool. I would just sit back and relax.

I was sitting on a bench next to a television monitor watching ESPN. Next thing I knew a guy came and sat down next to me. I didn't immediately turn around to see who he was. I noticed that he smelled very good.

"I know you missed me girl." I turned around. It was Chauncey. He had grown into a very attractive grown man.

"Hey what's up, you're down here visiting Samantha?" I asked. He shook his head.

"Yeah, her and her little sorority are having some events this weekend and she wanted me to attend. So I came down here to check her out."

I looked around the bowling alley for Samantha. I didn't want her to see me and her man sitting together. Samantha was at the other end of the bowling alley with her sorors posing for pictures. Samantha was wearing a pink shirt with her sorority letters on it. She looked really happy. Her and her sorors posed for several pictures and then Samantha grabbed her friend and soror Dee Dee to the side. They posed for a picture together and then gave each other a big hug.

"Well nice seeing you Chauncey," I said as I stood up to leave and he grabbed my hand, "Hey what building do you live in, I could stop by and see you before I leave."

I could have had sex with Samantha's man just to get back on her. He was sexy, but I wasn't even that type of person.

"Look Chauncey, I don't want any problems, I don't want to come between you and Samantha." I pulled my hand away. "I just was going to come by and check you out, you know talk about old times, you know you want me to come girl." "No, that's alright." I walked away.

As I was walking away from Chauncey, Samantha, Dee Dee and a couple of other girls in the sorority ran up to me.

"Were you trying to talk to my sorors man?" One of Samantha's sorority sisters asked me as Samantha stood there glaring at me.

"Uhmmm…can't she speak for herself?"

"Look, he was the one trying to talk to me, he asked me if he could come and visit me and I told him that I wasn't interested. Then I walked away," I said as I put my hand on my hip. Samantha chimed in.

"You are such a liar. Chauncey come here." She motioned for Chauncey to come over. Chauncey slowly got up from the bench and walked over to where we all were standng having a heated confrontation.

"Chauncey, did you ask her if you could come and visit her?" Samantha asked. Did she really think that Chauncey would tell the truth?

"No baby, she asked me if I would come and visit her and I told her no." He was such a liar.

"I have no reason to lie. And you know what? I don't want him. If you are that insecure about your man maybe you don't need to be with him," I said as I walked away.

"Stay away from Chauncey," Samantha shouted.

Whatever. I was sorry that I had even gone bowling. My friends and I left and went back to the dorms.

My life was good. I was getting good grades. I had good friends and I also was dating. By junior year, I was finally getting my act together. Every once in awhile I would see Samantha and Chauncey. For him to go to school in a whole different state, he sure was always at SIUC. That fall Samantha and Dee Dee's sorority performed in the step-show on campus and they won first place. Samantha was also featured in the school paper. They wrote a little article about what a well-rounded balanced student she was. She had a 4.0 G.P.A., she was the vice-president of the Black Student Union, she was the president of her sorority, she was a Resident Assistant, and she was on the track team.

They quoted Samantha saying,

*"I just stay focused. My education is very important to me.
I understand that I need to keep a good grade point average if
I want to get into a good medical school. My sorority is important because we do a lot of community service and help people. I love to help others. That is why I work so hard. I want
to see all of my dreams come true. I eventually would like to
become a pediatrician and help children in disadvantaged
countries. Or maybe I will discover a cure for AIDS."*

Well didn't she just sound like the most well-rounded student ever. She
wasn't nice. She was the super-bitch of the century to me. She was so
phony. I hated her. Maybe a part of me was jealous of Samantha. Perfect
grades, well-rounded lifestyle. Remember reading that article over and
over. It made me want to puke. No one was that perfect. I decided to save
the article. I cut it out and put it in my scrapbook.

It was a cold Tuesday evening in December. My last class of the day was
Film Analysis. The class let out at 5:30. It was a nice little walk from my class
back to the dorms and it was freezing cold outside. As I was walking my
neon green pager went off. It was my friend Sheree. I didn't have a cell
phone, so I would have to wait until I got back to the dorms to call her back.

When I made it back to the dorms I headed straight for the cafeteria.
Dinner ended at 6:00, so I didn't have much time to eat. As I was in the
food line waiting to be served a helping of fried chicken and mash pota-
toes, Sheree came running up to me.

"Hey Lori, you know that girl that you hated that went to the same
high school as you that goes to school here now, I forgot her name."

"Who Samantha Greer, what about her?" I said.

I just knew Samantha had started some more drama.

"She's dead." Sheree said. I dropped my tray of food on the floor. I was
in shock.

"What do you mean she's dead?"

"She had an asthma attack after a track team practice. She died on the scene," Sheree smiled as she shared the news of Samantha's demise with me. I was numb, I didn't know what to say or do.

"Lori, you didn't like that bitch anyway, now you don't have to worry about her anymore".

"Sheree that wasn't a nice thing to say. I mean we had our differences but I never wanted her dead."

"Hey you need to clean up that mess kid," the cafeteria worked yelled at me from behind the serving line. I picked up the tray and sat it on a counter. Food was spattered all over the floor. I didn't clean up the food. I just walked away as the cafeteria worker continued to yell at me.

I went back to my room and really tried to reflect on my life. Samantha was dead. I didn't answer my telephone the whole night. The phone rang constantly. I just let the answering machine pick up the calls. By the end of the evening I had 17 new messages. All of the calls were about Samantha. Some people called me to tell me that she had passed away. Some people called to claim victory, as if our clique had won something because one of my enemies was dead.

I wasn't happy that Samantha was dead. Actually, I was quite depressed. I had known other people my age to die. When I was in high school the boy that lived next door to me died of Leukemia. My cousin Tee Tee's boyfriend's brother was killed in a drive by shooting. I had never known another female my age to die.

The emotions that I was going through were hard for me to understand. Here was person that I didn't like, a person that definitely did not care for me, and here I was totally devastated that she was dead. I thought about Chauncey. I knew that he must have been devastated. I just imagined him sitting in a corner crying because his girlfriend was dead. Then I thought about Dee Dee. I knew that she must have been crushed. Samantha had been her best friend since the 2nd grade. Then I thought about Samantha. She was a beautiful girl. She had so many hopes and dreams that she would never get to accomplish. Here she was 20 years old, and dead. She would have no future. Her story was written and this was the final chapter. My enemy was dead, but I didn't feel victorious.

The next day the school newspaper read, "Junior, Sorority president and Black Student Union Vice-President Dies of Asthma Attack at Track Practice." Samantha's obituary read:

> *It seem's like just yesterday we were writing a featuring about how focused and well-rounded Samantha Greer was. Samantha Greer, a junior majoring in biology, died Tuesday after suffering a severe asthma attack after track practice at the East Campus Gymnasium. Paramedics arrived at the scene but they were unable to resuscitate the victim. Samantha had a history of asthma. The Campus Chronicle spoke with Samantha's best friend Dee Dee Jones. "I am completely devastated. I was the one that had to call her parents and her boyfriend and tell them the horrible news. Samantha always had her inhaler with her, but this time she didn't have it. Why would God take such a beautiful angel away from us". Samantha Greer is survived by her parents, two brothers, a fiance, and a host of friends. There will be a memorial service held at Carbondale Church of Christ at 7:30 P.M. on Thursday.*

I may have felt bad about Samantha dying but that didn't erase all of the horrible things that she had done to me while she was alive. I hardly saw her as a "beautiful angel". Why is it that when people die they only remember the good things about them? I'm sure that Samantha did have a good side, I just never saw it.

It was Wednesday, the day after Samantha passed away. I had to think of a game plan as to how I would approach this whole thing. My friends and Samantha's friend were waiting for some kind of reaction from me. That day as I walked through the Student Center I thought I should take the initiative to do something nice.

I knew that Dee Dee worked in the Computer Lab as a supervisor. I stopped in the bookstore and bought a sympathy card. I signed the card and went to the computer lab to deliver the card to Dee Dee. I walked to the back of the computer lab to the supervisor's station. Dee Dee was sitting at her desk crying. Her face was red and her eyes were puffy as if she had been crying for hours. I remember thinking to myself, "Why did she come to work?" I walked into the office.

"Dee Dee, I'm really sorry. I know Samantha was your best friend. I know that we all didn't really get along, but I just wanted to say sorry."

"Thank you," Dee Dee said tearfully. I handed Dee Dee the card.

I felt tears welling up in my eyes and I didn't want Dee Dee to see me cry. I quickly left the office. I exited the computer room and tears just starting flowing down my face.

I cried the whole walk back to the dorms. I thought about all of the fights Samantha and I had. I thought about the girl who was so happy posing for pictures with her sorority sisters. I thought about how devastated Samantha's parents probably were. The whole situation seemed unfair.

The next day I agonized over whether or not I should attend Samantha's memorial service. I called Sheree.

"Hey Sheree, will you go with me to Samantha's memorial service, I really feel like I should go."

"Lori, you are to nice. No, I'm not a phony person, I didn't like her, why would I go to her memorial service?" Sheree said in a sarcastic tone.

"Sheree, I just feel like I should go."

"Lori, you feel guilty. You and the girl argued all the time and treated each other shitty, now she's dead and you feel like you have to pay your respects".

Was Sheree right? I don't think I felt guilty. I truly felt bad about the fact that Samantha was dead. Samantha and I had been playing this "enemy" game so long, I didn't know how to act now that the game was over. I truly mourned the fact that she would never grow older. She would forever be 20 years old. She would never get married or have children. She would never become a doctor. She wouldn't discover a cure for AIDS.

I decided to attend the memorial service. I wore a pair of black pants and a black satin shirt. It was November and it was a cold evening. I wore a heavy coat. I was one of the first people to arrive. I sat in the very last row. I kept my coat on in case one of Samantha's friends told me that I was not welcome and requested me to leave. Church attendants carried in floral arrangement after floral arrangement. Samantha's friends and even a few family members soon filled the pews of the small church. Chauncey walked through the door. He was wearing dark glasses. He didn't notice me as he walked past me. I remember smelling his cologne. He always smelled so damn good.

The organist began to play a sad church song. Dee Dee and several of Samantha's other friends began to cry. The back door to the church opened up as the organist continued to play. Six pallbearers came into the church carrying a silver-pink colored casket. I thought memorial service meant no physical body? I wasn't good with being around dead people, it freaked me out very badly. I had never been to a young person's funeral.

The pallbearers placed the casket on the casket stand and opened the top portion of the casket. Inside of the casket laid Samantha. She truly looked like and angel. Her hair was curled tightly and her make-up was perfect. It almost looked like she had a smirk on her face. Dee Dee cried hysterically and Chauncey ran over and consoled her. A tall black man with a neatly trimmed goatee broke down and began to cry loudly. I later found out that he was Samantha's brother.

The whole memorial service was like a dream to me. I was physically there, but it was like I wasn't there. I could hear people talking but I couldn't make out the words. I was in a weird trance-like state. After the minister gave his sermon, they opened up the floor for family members and friends to pay their respects to Samantha. Samantha's brother spoke. Dee Dee and Chauncey were too devastated to speak. I felt like I should have said something, but I didn't know if it was appropriate.

I stood up and walked up towards the podium. As I made my way to the podium, Chauncey and Dee Dee glared at me and gave me a "you better not say the wrong thing" look. I looked into the sea of mourners.

"Samantha Greer and I were not the best of friends. We both attended the same high school and we ended up attending the same college. We had several run-in's with each other in life. Samantha was a good person to her family, her friends and her boyfriend. If she were here now, I would really try to make peace with her." I started to cry. I quickly regained my composure. "If she were here I would try to make peace with her. I can only hope that maybe one day we would have outgrown our petty little differences."

I stepped away from the podium. I didn't even sit back down. I walked straight out of the back door and left the church. I got in my car and cried for about two minutes. I started the car and drove back to the dorms.

Samantha was less than 30 semester hours away from completing her Bachelor's Degree. We would have graduated at the same time. During my graduation, they paid tribute to Samantha and gave her an honorary degree that her mother accepted on her behalf. I saw Chauncey at the graduation. He spoke to me, but we didn't hold a conversation.

Occasionally, I still think about Samantha. I'm not going to sit here and lie though. I still think about how she was a total bitch to me and made my life hell most of the time. However, I feel extremely sad that she is not here to live her life. She never got the chance to grow into and adult and to do adult things like have a family and career. And for that reason, I feel bad about Samantha dying.

LOSERS I HAVE DATED

▼

CHANCE

I met Chance the summer that I graduated from high school. I was driving down the street in my turquoise 1992 Toyota Paseo. I thought that I was unstoppable in that car. The car had tinted widows, hot rims, and a nice sound system.

My cousin Carrie and I would cruise around and listen to all of the cool music from 93' like, "Whoomp there it is", and SWV's "Right Here".

Carrie was my normal cousin. She didn't have a whole lot of drama going on in her life and she spent most of her time in the house watching television. We would always go cruising in the suburbs because we preferred the suburban boys to the city boys.

One day we were cruising around Country Club Hills, when we saw this tall, cute guy washing his car.

"He's mine, I saw him first," I said.

"No, I saw him first," Carrie said.

"Let's just let him decide," I was going to get this guy.

We were so young and crazy acting. We pulled the car over and started talking to the boy. When he saw us walking his way he smiled and stopped washing his car. I was wearing a tight black skirt and a black body suit. My hair was long, straight and black at the time.

"What's you name?" I asked him.

"That's not your real name," Carrie said.

"Why not? That is my name."

Chance was gorgeous. He had a smooth brown complexion and the most beautiful greenish gray eyes I had ever seen. I later found out that they were contact lenses, but at the time I thought they were real.

My cousin and I spent the afternoon watching Chance wash his car. When he decided to go and play basketball we went to the basketball court with him. We were totally sweating this guy to see which one of us he would finally give his phone number to.

We found out that Chance was 17 and that he was a senior at Homewood-Flossmore High School. The car that he was washing was his, a 1992 Nissan Maxima. He also had a motorcycle. We were so impressed that such a young guy had so many nice vehicles. Carrie and I were in an intense competition for Chance's attention.

Chance gave me his number and we set a date for the 4th of July of 1993. Chance planned all of the details. He only told me to "Be ready at 3:00"

On the day of our big date Chance drove to the city to pick me up. He was so gorgeous that I couldn't believe that I was sitting in the car with such an attractive guy. He drove real fast and played his music loud. He was so beautiful he could have been a model, but in reality he was a high school football and basketball player.

Chance had planned a beautiful day for us. We drove until we were at nice secluded area near the water. I soon found that the water was Lake Michigan and that we were in Wisconsin. There was a picnic going on.

"Is this your family?" I asked.

"Yes, this is my group"

I was not dressed to meet the family. Chance and I got out of the car. He held my hand and we walked towards the group of people.

"Mom, this is my date Lori."

"Hi Lori, nice to meet you," Chance's mother reached out to grab my hand.

"Hey mom is all of the stuff I asked for on the boat?" Chance asked his mother.

"Yes, Chance. I put the food in the kitchenette and I put the movies on top of the VCR."

Chance grabbed my hand and we walked toward the water.

"Are we getting on that boat?" I asked pointing to the luxury cruiser docked at the pier.

"You aren't scared of the water are you?" Chance asked as he grabbed my hand harder.

"Of course not."

We boarded the boat. The boat had a little downstairs area with a television and a kitchenette. I sat my purse in the downstairs area and Chance and I went up to the deck.

"Can you drive this boat?" I asked.

"Yeah, I can drive a boat."

Chance started the boat. We were speeding so fast and the air was whipping my beautiful hair out of place. We rode far out into the water until Chance's family having the picnic was only a spot in the distance. Chance stopped the boat and put the keys in his pocket.

We sat outside looking at the water. It was so beautiful. Chance and reclined in the chairs on the deck and stared at the sky.

"Chance why did you give me your phone number and not my cousin Carrie?" I asked. Chance looked over at me with his beautiful eyes and said,

"Do you want me to be honest?"

"Of course I do."

"Because you were the driver." I was so surprised that Chance said that.

"That's a terrible thing to say. I thought you were going to say because I was prettier or because you liked my personality."

"All of those things are true, I just wouldn't want to date a girl that didn't have a car of her own because I would have to drive her everywhere."

"I guess," I said.

Suddenly, Chance didn't seem as wonderful as I thought he was.

After about an hour of laying in the sun Chance and I went downstairs and warmed up the food that his mother had left on the boat.

"Did you all rent this boat for the holiday," I asked. Chance laughed.

"We don't rent anything. This is my parents boat," Chance said arrogantly.

I found myself very curious about Chance and his family. I didn't know very many black families who's teenage son owned a new car and a motorcycle.

"What do your parents do for a living?" I asked.

"Their doctors. My mom is a pediatrician and my dad is an obstetrician. That's why he is not here today. He is on-call at the hospital"

His parents were successful, he had manners, and he was gorgeous; what more could a girl ask for?

We put a movie into the VCR and turned off the lights. The boat rocked gently back and forth due to the motion of the waves. We were laying on the couch and Chance gently brushed against my face and kissed me.

We kissed for a long time and then Chance went for home base.

"Are you going to let me make love to you? I have a condom."

I thought about it. It had been a nice date. I was in the middle of lake Michigan on a boat. He was awfully cute. I was so easy.

Chance and I had sex in the boat, but something was really wrong with the whole experience. It didn't last long at all, and he was so anxious when he pushed up on me. He was grinding on me like a little frog. There was nothing gentle or romantic about it. I remember when it was over I thought to myself, "Did that just happen?" and "How could someone so gorgeous be so lousy in bed?"

After our brief sexual encounter Chance drove the boat back to shore. Night had fallen and the temperature was dropping. His mother had packed up the car and was waiting for Chance to return.

"Chance, you know I don't like you out in the boat when it gets dark. I'm glad that you brought yourself back to land. I was starting to get mad. Lori, did you and Chance have a nice time?"

I felt like such a dirty little whore.

"Yes, ma'am. We had a very nice time. Thank you for packing up such a nice lunch."

After our date Chance started to call me every day. He would make the drive from Country Club Hills to Chicago to see me whenever he had the opportunity.

We would have sex in my mothers bedroom while she was away at work. I taught Chance new things and eventually his sexual performance improved.

I knew our little fling would not last long because I was preparing to leave for college and Chance still had another year of high school ahead of him.

One afternoon I went to visit Chance. His parents were at work and Chance and I were holed up in his bedroom. His room was so nice. He had a 27 inch television and a VCR in his bedroom, and he had his own phone line. I wish that I would have had a set-up like that when I was in high school.

This particular afternoon we had sex in his room and fell asleep. All of our sex sessions were exhausting because I would try to teach Chance a new technique every time we had sex. It was only 1:30 in the afternoon and his mother wasn't due home from work until at least 4:00. We were sleeping in the bed when his mother burst through the door.

"Chance get up right now!" His mother screamed. I was frightened. Here I was a grown woman of 18 and I was terrified of someone else's mother.

"Lori, get dressed and get out of here. You are a little slut. I can't believe that you are in bed with my 15 year old son. Get out of here." His mother screamed at me.

Chance was15?

"What do you mean 15? Chance told me that he was 17 years old and that he was a senior," I said as I scrambled to put my clothes on.

"No. Chance just finished his sophomore year. He will be 16 on September 19th. You are an easy little girl. You are too pretty to be easy like that. You've only known Chance two weeks. Lori, I don't expect to ever see you over at my home again, and please don't call either."

By this time I had gotten dressed and was headed out the door. I had to ask. I was so stupid. I turned around and looked at Chance's mother.

"If Chance is only 15 how did he get a motorcycle and a nice new car? I assure you that Chance told me he was 17," I pleaded.

"Hey mom can I talk to Lori for a minute?" Chance asked.

"No, go back to your room. Lori, the Maxima is one of my cars that I let Chance drive. The motorcycle is his fathers. Please leave. Even if you thought Chance was 17 that still does not mean you should have sex with him after only knowing him 2 weeks. That is so slutty".

Chance's mother shut the door behind me. I wish I would have cursed her out. I couldn't believe Chance was so young. That does partially explain why he was so sexually inexperienced.

The day before I left for college I decided to call Chance to tell him goodbye.

"Hello, Chance"

"Hey, Lori, what's up, I miss you."

"Yeah, I just called to tell you goodbye," I said with a sigh.

I guess Chance's mom had been listening to our conversation because the next voice I heard was hers.

"Lori, didn't I tell you to never call my house again? Leave my son alone before I call the police on you." I hung up the phone.

A couple of years later I met a girl in my dorm named Felicia. One day she was telling me about her boyfriend from Country Club Hills named Chance. She showed me a picture and told me how he was "sweet" and "wonderful in bed" I didn't tell Felicia that I used to date Chance. I couldn't help but to think that my sex lessons with Chance helped him to be a better lover.

KYLE

I met Kyle the second semester of my sophomore year of college. Kyle was a campus security guard. There had been several sexual assaults on campus and he worked as an escort. I was leaving my Film History class when Kyle walked up to me. I kept walking and he walked along with me.

"Hey, I'm fine I don't need an escort. The walk to the dorms isn't too bad."

"You really should let me walk with you, it's not safe for a sexy young thing like you to walk alone in the dark. This is a dangerous campus."

I hadn't paid attention to the security guy until he called me sexy. He was tall, light-skinned and he wore glasses. I took another look at him as I walked. I tried to imagine what he would look like without the glasses and in regular clothes. I decided that he was cute, so I let him walk with me.

"So what is your name?" I asked the security guard as he walked me toward my building. I leaned over to look as him name tag but I couldn't read it.

"My name is Kyle, what's your name?" By sophomore year I had pretty much made a name for myself around campus. People either loved me or hated me.

I was a popular student, I wondered to myself if he was pretending not to know me, or if he really didn't know who I was.

"My name is Lori."

"Nice to meet you Lori. Do you have a boyfriend?" Kyle asked.

This guy didn't mess around. He went straight to the point.

"Why do you ask? Do you want to be my boyfriend?" I asked.

"Maybe. Just maybe we'll have to see."

We reached my dorm room. I prepared to enter the building.

"Lori, can I come back and visit you sometimes?" Said Kyle.

"I live in room 718," I said with a smile.

I didn't expect Kyle to come visit so soon. He came back that first day after his shift was over. I invited him in. Kyle was really cute without his glasses and without his uniform on.

"Where are your glasses?" I asked.

"I only wear them when I am working," He said.

We sat on my bed and watched the news on television. We had a long conversation and I learned a lot about Kyle. He was a junior and he was from Alabama. He lived off campus in a trailer and his major was English.

I was attracted to Kyle, but I didn't want to jump any to any thing with him. I decided to let him court me.

Over the next few weeks Kyle took me out to eat and we went to the movies. After three weeks Kyle and I had sex. It was the best. Kyle was very well endowed and he was very skillful with his tongue also if you know what I mean! If I knew that sex with Kyle would have been so good I would have gave him some on our first date.

I fell in love with Kyle. I was such a tough-skinned chick, or so I thought, I didn't fall in love easily. I fell hard for Kyle though. My friend Jeneva said that she "had a bad feeling about Kyle" and that she felt "he was hiding something."

I couldn't understand why Jeneva had her doubts about Kyle. She just thought it was odd that she was a junior and he was a junior and she had never heard of him, nor had any one she asked heard anything about him.

I didn't have the same concerns about Kyle. He was nice and he treated me good.

For Valentines Day, Kyle talked my resident assistant into letting him into my room so that he could decorate it. Kyle surprised me with huge bouquet of flowers and balloons on my dresser.

Two weeks after Valentines Day my aunt Opal died of breast cancer. She had been sick for several years. I wasn't that sad about my aunt dying because she had lived in South Carolina for my whole life and I had only met her about 5 or 6 times in my life.

Aunt Opal had a will and she left me $10,000 in her will. It didn't take long for me to get the money either. Her lawyer called my family and a few weeks later I received a cashiers check for $10,000 via certified mail.

I had never had that much money in my life. I quit the job that I had been working as an assistant manager at Taco Bell. I put most of the money in the bank. I kept $3,000 in cash on hand.

At the time I didn't even realize how much money $3,000 in cash was. I would walk around with the money in my shoes. Sometimes in class I would think to myself, "I have $3000 in my shoe. I'm a baller"

It didn't take me long to start flossin with my money. I took Kyle shopping and spent $500 on new clothes. Jeneva and I went on a shopping spree and spent $1500. We bought perfume, new leather jackets and got our hair and nails done.

I made the worst mistake in the world when I told Kyle about the money. Initially, I told him the money was left over from my student loan. I eventually told him the truth about my Aunt Opal and that I still had $7,000 in the bank.

Kyle became obsessed with my money. Sometimes at night when we would lay in the bed today he would plan my money.

"You know you could do a lot with that much money," He would say. I would not respond. You could just see the wheels turning in his head.

Kyle encouraged me to go to the bank and to put some of the money in a certificate of deposit. In retrospect I think he only went to the bank with me because he wanted to see how much money I had.

In the grand scheme of life, $7,000 is not that much money, but in a college town where you could rent an apartment for $200 a month and buy a nice meal for $4, that much money could go along way.

Soon the relationship that Kyle and I had started to sour over money. Whenever we would go out on a date he would expect me to pay. He would say,

"You're the one with all the money," Kyle would say.

Kyle became very bitter and jealous about my money. He would ask me to buy all kind of things about the money. I still owed $3,000 on my 1992 Toyota Paseo. I went to look at new cars. I was young, dumb and didn't look at the big picture. The Paseo was a nice car with low miles. It was only 3 years old and in excellent condition. It was customized and if I would have paid it off I would have owned it free and clear.

Being that I was young and dumb, I decided to go to a car dealership to look at new cards. I stopped at a Ford Dealership and fell in love with a 1995 Ford Mustang. The Mustang was cherry red. Fully loaded the car was $24,000. The car dealership talked me into some kind of deal. They would pay off the Paseo, give me $4,000 trade on it. I would put $5,000 cash down on the Mustang, which brought my balance down to $15,000; with a monthly car note of $320.

I didn't think about the future or the fact that between the $3,000 dollars cash that I had dwindled down to $1200 and the $2000 in the bank that my money was running thin. I didn't have a job and my expenses were mounting.

Kyle and I were doing good. He still asked me for money, $100 here, $200 dollars there, and I would always give it to him.

In May of 1995, I decided to move off campus into a house. The rent was $320 a month and Kyle was going to live with me. Kyle decided to go to Alabama to go and visit his family for two weeks. Summer school didn't start until June, so I decided to take a little trip to go visit a friend named Susie.

Susie lived two hours from Carbondale in a small town named Centralia. I didn't think it was possible for a town to be smaller than Carbondale, but Centralia was. Centralia reminded me of the small town in the movie "Footloose" I saw a couple of mixed people while I was there but I don't think I saw any other Black people during my visit.

Susie was a White girl that I met during my freshman year. She was short with blond hair and blue eyes. She looked very cherubic and had a chubby round face. She was doing well for herself in Centralia. She had her own apartment and she was expecting a baby.

We would drive around town (which was a very short trip) and look for fun (which we never found). The hang out spot in Centralia was the Mc Donalds parking lot.

We pulled into the parking lot and sit in the car with the music playing. This seemed very boring to me, but this was Susie's idea of fun.

"So this is what you all do for fun around here, huh?" I asked.

"Yeah. Now we sit here in the car, we look cute, we play cool music and some guys will pull up and start to talk to us," Susie explained.

We waited for about twenty minutes and no guys pulled up.

"I'm dating the really nice guy named Kyle Anthony." I said.

Susie turned around and glared at me.

"I know who Kyle Anthony is, he is such a loser!" Susie shouted.

"Gosh Lori, how did you get involved with someone like that!" Susie faked like she was going to bang her head on the steering wheel. I had never heard anyone say one bad thing about Kyle.

"This can't be the same Kyle, Susie. He's Black, you must be talking about a White Kyle." I said.

"No Lori, I only date Black men and so do my friends. The Kyle Anthony I know is a loser. LOSER!"

I was starting to get upset.

"Why is he a loser Susie?" I asked. Susie looked out the window and then she looked at me.

"If I told you, you wouldn't believe me," She said.

"Susie, I would believe you, you are my friend?" I said in frustration.

"The Kyle Anthony I know was married to this girl named Shanda. He and Shanda had 2 kids. He cheated on Shanda with a White girl named Natalie. Natalie is my friend. He had a baby girl with Natalie. Shanda and Natalie live in the projects on the East Side of Carbondale. They don't go to school and they are both on welfare. As far as I know he doesn't give either one of them money but I know he is still having sex with Natalie and Shanda. Because he goes and visits Natalie and then he goes right across the street to Shanda's. He says he is just going to "check on the kids", but I don't believe that and neither does Natalie,"

Susie explained as she slurped on her soda.

I couldn't believe what I had heard. Susie was right. I didn't believe her and I knew she was lying.

"I don't think it is the same Kyle," I said.

"See, this is exactly why I didn't want to tell you," Susie threw her hands up in the air.

We left the Mc Donald's parking lot and headed back to Susie's apartment.

That night we went to some whacked out club in the middle of nowhere named "City Nights". The club pumped old school dance tracks like they were new songs. The year was 1995 and they must have played "Pump Up The Jam" and "Push It" at least twice, and those songs were from the late eighties.

The next day I prepared to make the trip back to Carbondale. I washed my brand new Mustang and filled the car up with gas. In the back of my mind I thought to myself, "I don't care about Kyle, I have my car and I love the car more than Kyle."

Susie and I said our good-bye's.

"Now Lori, I will be in Carbondale in two weeks to visit my friend Natalie and I want to see you also. I hope that it is not the same Kyle, even though I am sure it is." Susie gave me a hug and I drove off.

When I got back to the house Kyle was home. I couldn't wait to see him and ask Him if Susie's allegations were true. I ran in the house and dropped my bags from the trip on the ground. Kyle was lying on the couch watching a basketball game. I turned off the TV.

"Kyle, is it true that you are married and have 2 kids by a girl named Shanda, and a baby by a White girl named Natalie too?" I asked.

Kyle started to look very serious.

"Who told you that?" He asked.

"It doesn't matter," I said. Kyle stood up off of the couch and grabbed me. He was scaring me.

"Who told you that?" Kyle asked as he shook me.

"You're hurting me," I screamed.

"It was that little White bitch Susie wasn't it?" Kyle said as he let me go.

"Well is it true?" I asked.

Kyle got very angry and slammed the remote control on the floor.

"I'm sorry I got upset. I didn't want you to go and visit Susie because I was afraid something like this might happen. Susie used to want to get with me but I wasn't interested so she went around telling lies on me," Kyle explained as he gave me a hug.

This was interesting information. Kyle had never mentioned that he knew Susie. I was starting to think that maybe Susie was telling the truth.

"So you are saying that nothing she said was true, it was all a lie?" Kyle sat on the couch and started to look very frustrated.

"Your friend is jealous of what we have. Are you going to let her ruin our relationship?" Kyle hugged me close. I wanted so much to believe that it was all a big lie, but deep down I knew that it was probably true. I loved Kyle and I didn't want to be alone again.

The next few weeks I kept my eyes and ears opened. I watched Kyle's every move for some kind of sign that he was being unfaithful or that he had a secret that he was keeping from me. Kyle treated me very different after I confronted him. He monitored my phone calls and wanted to know where I was at all times. He became very controlling and I feared he might turn violent towards me.

Two weeks later Susie came to town. Susie knew my address and she came over on a Thursday afternoon. Susie didn't come alone, she brought Natalie with her. Kyle was at work when the two women arrived.

"Come in" I welcomed them into my home.

"Lori, this is Natalie," Susie made the introductions.

Natalie was a shapely White female who wore a short African-American hair style. She was wearing a tank top and a pair of jogging pants. She had a gold tooth and was also wearing a big gold chain.

"So you are the girl that Kyle has been with. He told me he had a new girlfriend that was in school and that he was moving in with her," Natalie said as she looked at the pictures of Kyle and I on our coffee table.

"You and Kyle still see each other?" I asked Natalie.

"Yeah he comes over almost every day to see our daughter and half the time when he leaves my house he goes and sees that stank bitch Shanda. Now, I will tell you this much. Kyle and I still have sex sometimes, but it doesn't mean anything because I have a boyfriend who is locked down."

I was totally repulsed. Kyle was sleeping with the girl with the gold tooth that lived in the projects.

"Do you all use protection?" I naïvely asked. Natalie looked kind of dirty like she didn't care about protecting herself.

"Hell no, we gotta baby together. And I know he is still messing around with Shanda because this girl on the block that watches my daughter for me sometimes told me Shanda just had an abortion and that she was pregnant by Kyle for the third time."

This wasn't making sense to me. When did Kyle have time to do all of this? He was with me every evening and weekend. Then I thought about the fact that he wasn't even using protection with the other girls. I wasn't using protection with him because I was on the pill. I was so stupid.

"When does he come over to see you, I mean what time, because he spends a lot of time with me," I asked.

"Girl, I don't work. He comes over at like 9:00 in the morning and he plays with our little girl. I might cook something to eat. He'll leave my house at about 12:00. After he leaves my house he goes to Shanda's house. He leaves Shanda's house at about 1:45 and then he leaves for work. I think he works 2-8."

Natalie seemed genuine and I didn't feel like she was lying.

"How can that be when those are the hours that he is in school?"

Natalie burst into laughter and slapped herself on the knee.

"Kyle is not in school. He only works on campus. Gosh, he had really told you some stories. So he didn't tell you anything about me, Shanda or our daughter? What a bum".

The three of us sat there for hours talking. I knew that Kyle would be home soon and I wanted to see the expression on his face when he saw Natalie sitting on the couch.

I heard Kyle's car pull up. When I saw him turning the knob my heart froze. I was so scared. Kyle walked into the house and he saw the three of us sitting there.

"Natalie, what the fuck are you doing in my house?" Kyle shouted.

Natalie jumped up off the couch.

"Nigga you ain't gotta be fuckin' cussing at me. I came over here to tell Lori the truth about your dirty stankin hoe ass!" Natalie held her finger in Kyle's face.

"Natalie, don't start with me get out of my face," Kyle said pushing Natalie out of the way.

"Naww man because what you did wasn't even cool, denying your children?" Kyle got angry and pushed Natalie hard on the ground. Natalie hit her head on our end table and the lamp fell on to the floor. Susie ran up behind Kyle and kicked him in the knee. Keep in mind that Susie was 7 months pregnant. Kyle turned around and slapped Susie in the face and shoved her into the couch.

"Kyle what are you doing," I screamed.

"Lori, why did you do this? Why did you bring these bitches in our home? I would have told you the truth when I thought you were ready," Kyle pleaded. I started to cry.

"Kyle get out, I don't want you here, please leave," I screamed.

"This is my house to and I'm not going anywhere," Kyle yelled as he grabbed me and started to shake me.

"I hate you let me go, just leave, leave me alone," I screamed. I kneed Kyle in the nuts and he lunged toward my neck. Kyle held me in a corner and started to choke me. Natalie got up and picked up the half -broken lamp and hit Kyle in the back. Susie picked up the phone and started to dial 9-1-1.

"Hello, police. I am 7 months pregnant and this Black man just pushed me and slapped me. I am at 1423 East Oak. Please hurry. He is choking my friend," Susie yelled into the phone.

I was in pain from Kyle choking me, but I was conscious enough to remember that I didn't like the fact that Susie had described Kyle as a Black man. She made it seem like Kyle was a crazed Black man who had attacked a pregnant White woman when in fact he was just a pissed off Black man in a fit of rage.

Kyle heard Susie on the phone and stopped choking me. He grabbed his keys and left.

The police came over and we all made our statements and filed a police report. I called the landlord and he had a locksmith come over and change the locks.

I was so scared to be in that house alone. Summer school had not yet started and many of my friends were not in town. Susie was with Natalie. Although Natalie had came through for me when Kyle was choking me, I didn't feel like she was cool enough for me to go and hide out at her crib.

At 9:00 that night Kyle came home. He tried to open the door with his key. His key would not work. He went around to the back door. His key did not work. I was terrified. I thought he was going to come in the house and try to kill me. He banged on the window and banged on the door. I was terrified. I could have called the police because I knew the police were looking for him because he assaulted us, but I didn't want him to go to jail.

He left and went to a payphone and starting calling. Initially, I didn't answer the phone. Finally, I couldn't take it anymore.

"Hello," I whispered into the phone.

"Lori, why are you doing this?" Kyle asked.

"Kyle, you are married and have 3 kids. How could you just leave that out. I asked you when I came back from Centralia if any of this was true and you told me no. You are a liar and I don't want to be with you."

"Just let me come and get my things," Kyle pleaded.

"I'll pack your things up and take them to your friends house tomorrow."

I hung up the phone.

I was devastated that night. I curled up in my bed and listened to Mary. J. Blige's "My Life" CD until I fell asleep.

I knew that Kyle was pissed off at me but I never knew that he would do something so drastic.

The next morning I walked out of my front door. The first thing I noticed was my car. The front windshield was shattered. The word "BITCH" was spray painted on the hood. All four tired had been slashed.

I opened the car door. The leather interior seats were all slashed. The radio had been pulled out of the dashboard. The interior floor carpet looked as if it had been burned.

For some reason my first instinct was to start the car. I just remember thinking to myself, "All of this can be fixed, as long as the car starts."

I turned the ignition and smoke filled up inside of the car. I looked around to see where the smoke was coming from. It was rising from under the hood. The next thing I knew I saw flames. I jumped out of the car and the entire hood area of the car erupted in flames.

I sat on the steps and watched the car burn. My neighbor called the fire department. How did I sleep though Kyle destroying my car? The way that the house was arranged, the back bedrooms did not face the driveway. Kyle had a key to the car. I worried that he might try to steal the car before I was able to get the key back but I never thought he would have destroyed my brand new car that I had only made two car payments on.

Later that day, a tow company came and towed my car away. After examining the car they gave me an initial diagnosis. Kyle had not only put sugar in the gas tank, he also put sand in the oil fill tube. He also poured an unidentified flammable substance on the engine. When I started the engine, the sugar clogged the fuel injectors and killed the carburetor. The sand in the oil fill tube destroyed the piston and the chamber of the engine. The fire ruined everything else.

Basically what they told me is that the engine of my brand new car was destroyed. Between that and all of the interior damage, it would probably take close to $10,000 or more to fix the car.

That my friends is when I experienced my first nervous break down. I say I had the nervous breakdown because of the car. My mother says I had the nervous break down because of Kyle and our soured relationship. I loved that car. Losing that car destroyed me, especially since I owed so much money to the finance company. On top of that I only had liability insurance so I had no recourse.

I lost it. I went mental in the worst way. I'll have to save the details of my nervous breakdown for the sequel.

As for Kyle, the Carbondale police were looking for him for assaulting Susie, Natalie and I. The police told me that they couldn't touch him for destroying my car because they didn't have enough evidence. Kyle left town and moved back to Alabama.

NATE & REESE

I can honestly admit that I used to be a borderline basketball groupie. I was fascinated with basketball players. I would watch basketball games on television every chance that I would get. I had dated several basketball players in my life, but I never got serious with a basketball player until I met Nate.

The year was 1998. I was in Colorado visiting my father when I saw this tall gorgeous man in line at the same United Airlines gate as I was. I was preparing to take a flight to St. Louis so that I could drive back to school in Carbondale, Illinois. The guy kept looking back at me. When he would look my way I would smile. He was very handsome.

When I boarded the plane I don't know if it was a coincidence or a twist of fate, but we ended up sitting next to each other on the plane. We talked the entire plane ride. I discovered that his name was Nate. He was 22 years old and he was a senior studying psychology. Nate was very tall, he was six foot eight. He had thick curly black hair and light chestnut colored eyes.

Nate played basketball for the University of North Carolina and he had been in Colorado attending a basketball clinic. He lived in Raleigh, North Carolina, which was about 800 miles away from Carbondale. He desperately hoped to become a professional basketball player.

We talked the entire plane trip. When the plane landed in St. Louis we hugged and exchanged phone numbers. We would talk on the phone for hours. Nate was so sweet to me. He would always say,

"Lori, I hope you have sweet dreams all about me," Nate would say to me at the end of our phone conversations. Then we would get off of the telephone and I would play with my vibrator and think about Nate.

Nate was your classic bench warmer for the University of North Carolina. He had a nice body and the height to be a good power forward or college center, but he was always hurt. If it wasn't his ankle, he was having back spasms. All he did was complain about not being able to play or the coach working him to hard in practice.

Initially our relationship took place on the telephone for the most part. My first phone bill after we met was $400; Nate's was $350.

I was working as a web designer for a radio station in town and I took home just enough to pay my bills while I was finishing up school.

When Nate got his phone bill he asked me for money.

"If you don't send me the money my phone will get cut off," Nate pleaded.

I didn't have money to spare. However, at the same time I was young, dumb and I liked talking to Nate on my phone. He was my far-away boyfriend.

I sent Nate $200 towards his phone bill. He called me when he got the money.

"Lori, you didn't send the whole $350. My phone is going to get cut off. I can't have my phone get cut off. What if some team tries to call me and wants me to work out with them? Or what if my sick mother try's to call me. I just can't have my phone cut off." Nate tried to get me to see his point of view.

That was my first hint that Nate was straight out of "Loserville".

"If you can't come up with the other $150 then you have a problem, I was being nice sending your ungrateful ass what I did."

"Lori, I'm not like you, I don't have a job, or parents that can send me money, without that other $150 my phone will get cut-off."

I thought about what he said. He was such a bum. How did he pay his phone bill before he met me? If I weren't so stupid myself at that time I would have left him alone right then and there.

Nate and I continued to talk on the phone until the day came that his phone was disconnected. When his phone got disconnected he started to send me e-mail messages from the school computer lab.

Lori,

> *As you can see my phone is cut off. I only think that is right that since I was talking to you and ran up my bill that you are the one that should send me the rest of the money to get my phone cut back on. Well I hope that you are doing well.*

Nate.

He was such a loser with a capital "L". But at the same time I tried to look at the big picture. He was a basketball player, and he did have potential to eventually become a NBA player, which mean that he might be a millionaire some day so I continued to communicate with him. I didn't look at him as a serious boyfriend. Nate was in North Carolina and I was in Illinois. I was still doing my thing and I'm sure he was to.

He also irritated me because when we did talk on the phone he always had a pathetic story about his family, his friends, or himself. He thought he was unattractive, even though he was gorgeous. I felt like he was always trying to make me feel sorry for him.

With Nate's phone cut-off and me being where I was, I assumed that he and I were a thing of the past. Nate still needed my faraway companionship. He began to e-mail me everyday.

Lori,

    We lost today. I could have made a difference but coach didn't even put me in he game. I wish he just had the confidence in me to put me in the game. I know I am a good player, but if I don't get any minutes this season I know the scouts aren't going to look at me. I wish my phone wasn't cut off. I miss you. I hope you come to see me soon.

    Do you love me?

Nate

How could I love this dude? I didn't even know him, plus he was lame. On the one hand I liked him because he was tall, cute and he played basketball. But at the same time I was so irritated by him because he always was whining and complaining about something.

First, Nate asked me for money for his phone bill. Then he turned around and offered me money-to write a paper for him.

I thought that student athletes only asked people to do their homework for them in after school specials and TV series like "Beverly Hills 90210". Nate sent me an e-mail message about his term paper.

Lori,

    I have this paper that I need to do. If I get anything less than a "B" I will fail my class and I will get kicked off of the basketball team. I will send you $100 if you do the paper for me. If you agree I will send you the details and the money.

    P.S.

    I know we only met once, but I feel as if I've known you forever. I love you.

Nate

I thought about what Nate said. He touched a soft spot in my soul when he said he loved me. I agreed to do the paper. Here I was months away from completing my own college degree and I was writing a paper about "The Development of the Childhood Brain" for Nate. He sent the money priority mail. It's funny how Nate had money to send me to type a paper but he couldn't pay his phone bill.

I spent hours in the library doing research for Nate's assignment. When the paper was complete I sent it to him via e-mail.

I thought to myself, "I've done one paper for him, and that's the end of it." Nate was happy with the paper that I wrote for him. He got an "A". Soon Nate was asking me to write papers for him almost every week. On top of that he had me completing regular assignments, like answering review questions from the end of his textbook.

Nate would send me the questions. I would go to my school library, check out the textbook, complete the questions and send them back to Nate.

He sent me various amounts of money, $75 here, $150 there. I was starting to feel like Nate was using me to complete his homework.

I stopped replying to his e-mail messages. I didn't accept his collect calls. I was dating someone else and I had decided that I had enough of Nate.

A week before Thanksgiving break I opened the inbox to my e-mail and it was filled with messages from Nate with the subject heading of "URGENT". I opened the messages and they all said the same thing.

Lori,

I need you to write one more paper for me. I promise this will be the very last time. Basketball is taking up all of my time and if I don't turn in this paper I will get a "C" in the class and I will not graduate next spring. Instead of sending it through the e-mail maybe you can bring the paper. I would love to see you during my Thanksgiving break since I can't go home for the break because of basketball. If you want to bring a friend, my roommate Reese will be here too. If you drive, I will give you gas money.

Call me on my roommates phone at 555-9080

Nate

I thought about Nate's offer. Raleigh-Durham, North Carolina is a beautiful area. I had been there the year before with several of my friends when Jay-Z performed at North-Carolina Central's Homecoming.

It would be a nice road trip. Duke was close to the University of North Carolina. If I went with my friend Tammy (The only friend who I knew would be down for a basketball themed road trip), we would have a good time.

I wrote the paper and Tammy and I planned the road trip. My college experience included a lot of wild road trips. When you are young, and have no kids, it's easy to just pick up and hit the road.

We packed our cutest clothes and we listed to Ginuwine and 2Pac the entire 700 mile trip.

We arrived at Nate's apartment at 7:00 P.M. the Tuesday the week of Thanksgiving. Nate wasn't home but his roommate Reese was.

Reese was hot. Not only was Reese hot, he was exactly my type. He was about six feet tall and he was light-skinned with short curly hair. He was a pretty boy. He was in a fraternity, he was a Kappa. Reese also had striking green eyes, and they weren't contacts. Reese also was a bit thugged out. He wore a black doo-rag on his head and his pants sagged.

"So you are Nate's girlfriend?" Reese asked as Tammy and I sat on the couch chilling.

"Hell no, I'm not his girlfriend," I didn't want this cute ass guy to think I was taken.

"You mean to tell me you came all this way to see a cat that isn't you guy?" Reese said in a cute southern accent.

"We came to have fun," Tammy said as she puffed on a blunt Reese passed to her.

"Yeah, life is about fun. Having fun, that's what life is about," Reese said as he puffed on the blunt.

"When is Nate coming home?" I asked. Reese leaned back on the couch and propped his leg up on mine. I didn't tell him to move his leg. I wanted it there.

"Nate has a basketball game in Richmond. He'll be back in the morning or late tonight. I don't know. I don't keep tabs on Nate. He's a grown man. He comes and goes as he pleases," Reese leaned over and licked my bottom lip. It felt so erotic when he licked my lip that I felt my panties get wet.

I was really digging Reese, but I had come to see Nate. The phone rang and Reese got up to answer the phone in his bedroom. Tammy leaned over to whisper in my ear.

"You don't know what you are getting into," Tammy said in a soft voice.

"Tammy, the way I see things, yeah Nate is cute and all but I don't like him that much. We're only young one time. That's what being young is about having fun. We hang out, we shake our ass, and we mess around with men. When we get old, we are going to fondly look back on our wild memories from college"

Reese came back into the room.

"Hey, that was Nate on the phone," Reese said as he chewed on a tooth pick.

"When is he coming back?" I asked.

"Dude said they haven't even started the game yet. They have a hotel room so they will probably leave Richmond in the morning."

"Did you tell him we were here?" I asked.

"Yeah," Reese said with a devilish grin.

"What did he say?" I asked.

"He said "Don't fuck my girl before I get to," Reese started to laugh. Tammy laughed to. I smiled.

"Why did he say that?" Tammy asked.

"Because I always get his girls before he does. I don't know what it is, ladies just love me," Reese leaned over and laid his head on my chest.

"I know we aren't going to sit in the house all night, let's go out, I know there is something going on?" I asked.

"Yeah, no doubt. Do you all like Go-Go music? It's Go-Go night at this spot I hang out at do you want to ride out?"

"Yeah, for sure!" I said.

Reese changed clothes. He put on a white tee shirt and a pair of black Tommy Hilfiger jeans. His boots were Timberlands and he wore a red sweat-band around his head. I slipped into a simple black dress and Tammy wore a short Guess tennis dress.

"I'll drive," Reese said as he grabbed his keys and we followed him to his truck. Reese drove a red Ford Explorer. Tammy sat in the back seat and I sat in the front seat next to Reese. Reese popped in an Outkast CD and we sped down the high way.

As Reese was driving I thought about how attracted I was to him. He was definitely all player, but I was willing to play his game even if just for one night. I knew that I was in town to see Nate, but at this point I didn't even care if saw Nate or not.

We arrived at the spot and the club was jumping. The three of us lit the dance floor on fire and we drank all night. My girl was drinking Long Island Ice Tea and Reese was drinking Bacardi and Coke. As usual, I was knocking back straight Vodka shots.

I remember experiencing a euphoric feeling. My body was hot and I was grinding so close to Reese. I remember feeling his penis pressing against my behind as we were grinding on the dance floor and he felt rock hard.

On the dance floor I made up my mind that I wanted to sleep with Reese. What about Nate though? I didn't like him, but on the same hand I didn't want to seem like a total whore. Then I thought to myself, who cares? You only live once, and I wanted to have fun. Who cared? It's not like I had a real future with either one of them.

We partied the night away. When we left the club, Reese had his arm around both Tammy and I. One minute he would lean over and kiss me on the cheek, then he would lean over and kiss Tammy. He was such a player. The three of us had a blast that night.

When we got back to the apartment, we were exhausted. Reese held on to me and walked me straight to his bedroom. I will admit I was drunk, but I was still lucid enough to know what the hell was going on. I knew I was horny and that I wanted to be with Reese.

In the bedroom, I collapsed onto the bed. My head was spinning around and I felt like I was on cloud nine. Reese turned off the light and licked his lips. Reese climbed on to the bed and lifted my dress up. Reese held me tight and kissed me tightly. His body felt so good against mine. Gosh, I was feeling good at that moment. Reese gently kissed my thighs and started to lick my panties with his tongue. Reese pulled my panties off. He went down on me for what seemed like hours.

"Do you have a condom?" I remember asking Reese when I was ready for him. He pulled a condom out from under the pillow. I smiled. This guy was too much for me. I don't know if it was the alcohol or if Reese was just the bomb, because we had some of the best sex I had ever had in my life.

After we had sex I was exhausted and slightly hung over from drinking so much Vodka. I remember having this real deep conversation with myself in my head. I kept referring to myself as self in my conscious. It was a real whacked out mental conversation I had with myself.

"Self, am I a whore?"

"Self, I did just meet this guy and I screwed him"

"Self, who judges me besides God, it was good, I'd do it again."

"Self, What about Nate?"

"Self, what about Nate, he's probably fucking some chick himself."

"Self, maybe I am a whore, better yet a trip tramp slut"

"Self, who cares I am young and having fun, hey I used a condom, score 1 for Lori"

"Self, maybe, just maybe I should put on some clothes since I am laying in the bed butt naked."

Somewhere after the last "self", I fell asleep. I fell into a deep, drunken stupor of sleep.

I heard someone in the living room walking around. I thought maybe it was Tammy, but I heard keys and footsteps of a large person.

I heard a knock at Reese's bedroom door. I was conscious, but to drunk and tired to put on any clothes or to even get under the covers. I remember thinking to myself, "Fuck it, who cares, he's not my boyfriend. It doesn't matter."

There was another knock on the door. The knob turned. The door opened. The light came on. Reese woke up and turned over.

"Man, you can't just be coming up in my room like that, dog. That's some bullshit. I'm trying to get some sleep turn off the light," Reese mumbled. I heard a voice. I knew it was Nate. I pretended to be sleep.

"So you just couldn't keep your hands off of her. You can't leave anyone that is interested in me alone, can you Reese. Lori, you know Reese is a big player," Nate said. I pretended to be sleep.

"I saw your foot move Lori, I know you are awake. Did you bring my paper?"

Like I thought. He didn't give a fat babies ass about me, he was only interested in the paper in the first place. I pretended to just have woken up.

"I forgot the disk at home," I said. I had the disc in my purse, but I had changed my mind. I wasn't giving him anything.

"Oh, so you can come down here and fuck my roommate while I'm at the game, but you forgot my paper. I want you to get dressed and get out of my crib." That's when Reese jumped up. He was so thuggish at time I loved it.

"Look man, you may be my roommate and my boy and shit, but I am not going to let you disrespect this young lady. Player, don't hate the game. Your chick chose me. They all do. Maybe if you didn't act like such a little as punk they wouldn't get with me," Nate turned the light off.

"Reese, you are drunk and you know I can kick your ass but I won't."
Nate walked out of the room and shut the door.

The next morning I was so hung over. I didn't know if we should leave
and go back home or stay in Raleigh for the remainder of our vacation.
After talking to Reese we decided to stay as his guest. Nate didn't speak to
us the remainder of our time their. He spent most of his time at the library
writing his paper. Reese introduced Tammy to one of his frat brothers.
The four of us kicked it and had so much fun that week. On Thanksgiving
Day, Reese took us to Elizabeth City, North Carolina to his mothers house
and we had a wonderful Thanksgiving dinner.

Saturday after Thanksgiving, Tammy and I prepared to make the trip
back to Carbondale. We were sad to leave Reese and his friends that we had
met because we had so much fun. Reese and I knew that a relationship was
not in our future. However, Reese and I remained very good friends.

Oh yeah, Nate didn't give us the gas money to drive back to
Carbondale. I had to pay for the gas home with the $77 of credit I had left
on my Visa card.

It was a cold November and the ride home was a treacherous one. We
drove through the mountains of Tennessee in a snow storm. After 22
hours we safely made it back to Carbondale.

In a strange twist of fate, we didn't have an accident until we made it
back to Carbondale.

I was driving over a patch of snow towards the train tracks in the middle of town. The train signals were not working and we noticed a fast
Amtrak train approaching. I hit the brakes and the car would not stop
because we were on a patch of ice. Tammy and I jumped out of the car,
which was going about 45 miles per hour.

I landed in the street and suffered cuts and bruises. Tammy laid on the
ground clutching her arm. The car came to a stop on the train tracks. The
conductor feared there were people in the car. He attempted to stop the
train. The train almost came to a complete stop. The train gently bumped
my car and knocked it off of the tracks.

People came running out of a neighboring bar to see if we needed help.

It was sad that we ended our vacation on such a terrifying note. The whole scene seemed like something out of a movie. I saw the bright lights of the train, I attempted to stop the car and it wouldn't stop, I jumped out of the car at 45 miles per hour.

An hour later, I made it home. Blessfully, Tammy and I were safe. It remember walking into my apartment and thinking, "Why does crazy shit always happen to me?"

KEVIN

Fun boys are nice. A fun boy is a guy that is carefree about life. He has a car and a nice amount of money in his pocket. He doesn't stress out a lot and he loves to have fun. He is attractive and many times he may have more than one girlfriend. I wouldn't advise a woman to settle down with a fun boy. They are good for fun, but not too much else. When it comes to the real life stresses of bills and being responsible they fall apart and run the other way.

I made the mistake of falling in love with a fun boy. Kevin and I met in Atlanta during spring break. He was a sailor stationed on the U.S.S. Enterprise. Kevin was in Atlanta visiting his family. He was so attractive. He was about six foot four with a perfect complexion. He had not one zit or wrinkle. His face was perfect. He also had the most beautiful smile.

My friends and I were walking down the street and Kevin was on the corner sitting on his motorcycle. The bike was beautiful; it was a yellow Kawasaki Ninja. Kevin was by himself. He was just sitting on the bike watching the spring break crowd. He smiled at me and I melted. I'll never forget this. He got off of his bike and walked over to me and held my hand.

"What's up, I'm Kevin," he said as he grabbed my hand. His hand was so soft. He was gorgeous.

His eyes were deep medium brown and his hair was shiny and black. He was Black, but I later found that his father was Puerto Rican. That moment that he was holding my hand felt like and eternity and I never wanted him to let me go.

My friends walked across the street to look at some artwork that a street vendor was selling as Kevin and I stood on the corner talking. He explained to me that he was in the Navy. Kevin was stationed on a ship in the Pacific Ocean and he was only in the states for a few days. Kevin also told me that he had lived in Japan for three years. Kevin was 21 years old, 2 years younger than I was. I was attracted to him mentally and physically. He was worldly and intelligent. We exchanged e-mail addresses and promised to keep in touch. I took a picture of Kevin on his motorcycle. He was so cute. I couldn't wait to get the picture developed.

I thought about Kevin the whole ride back to Illinois after our spring break vacation. Although I had only spent a few minutes talking with him, I really liked him. I kept talking to my friends about him and they weren't very supportive.

"Lori, he was on a motorcycle, he is young and he is a sailor, do you know how many girls he probably met this weekend?" My friend Vicky was a hater. I daydreamed about Kevin as I looked out on the highway. I envisioned us living together one day and having kids, I hoped that he would be the one. I didn't even know him, but he met my preliminary qualifications. He was smart, he had a job, he was tall and he was attractive. At that time I wasn't looking for much more than that.

When I got back to my apartment the first thing I did was hop on my computer and send Kevin an e-mail message.

Hey Kevin,

> *It was nice meeting you. I hope you enjoyed your trip to Atlanta. I know that it may never happen, but I would really like to see you again one day.*
> *Keep in touch.*

Lori

Kevin had told me that he would be returning to his ship in a couple of days. His ship was stationed in the Japan. I sent my e-mail message on a Sunday night. About 6 days later I heard from Kevin.

Hey Ms Lady,

You don't know how good it feels to get e-mail messages. I am back in Japan. My ship is in port for the moment, but we will be heading to the Gulf in the next few weeks. I would like to see you again. It is not as impossible as you might think. The next time I get the opportunity to take leave I am coming to see you. I have never heard of Carbondale, but if you are there, I will find it. Please continue to write me, I get so lonely over here.

Your sailor boy,

Kevin

That simple e-mail message put me on cloud nine. Kevin and I continued to send each other e-mail messages. I didn't really look at him as a potential boyfriend. He was thousands of miles away on a ship in the middle of the ocean. I was in Carbondale, Illinois trying to finish graduate school. I felt like Kevin was one of my good friends. We had only met one time, but through our intense e-mail messages I felt like we knew everything about each other.

In April, exactly 12 months after we met in Atlanta, Kevin called me on the telephone. I was surprised to talk to him, considering that most of our communication took place via e-mail. He explained to me that he had a 14-day leave pass and that he wanted to come and see me in Carbondale. His ship was docked in Norfolk, Virginia and he was going to drive to Illinois. I was a bit hesitant. This was a man I had only met one time in my life. Sure we communicated via e-mail, but I didn't know him on a human interaction level. He was going to be in my little apartment for almost two weeks. He gave me a good vibe though. I gave him directions and 18 hours later he was at my doorstep.

Kevin was more handsome than ever. His car was hot to. He drove a shiny red 1996 Ford Probe with silver rims. I invited him in.

"Do you still like me after seeing me again?" Kevin asked.

"Oh course, I like you," I replied. The first night we played video games and I fried chicken.

"Man you cook, you are in college, you are the perfect girl for me," Kevin said with a smile. My heart melted. I couldn't believe this gorgeous guy was here with me, and on top of that he had drove 18 hours just to see me. Here he was in the Navy, stationed on a ship in the middle of the Persian Gulf and on his leave he decides to come and visit me. While we were eating dinner, Kevin stuck his tongue out at me. He had a shiny silver object in his mouth.

"Do you have your tongue pierced?" I asked. He stuck it out again. I had never known a Black guy who had their tongue pierced. Kevin was cool. I liked him.

I don't know how I managed to keep a job or make it through my junior. The entire two weeks that Kevin was in town I only went to work one day and I only went to one class. The rest of the time Kevin and I were together. We would play wrestle, go to the movies, drink and hang out with my friends. Oh yeah, I mustn't forget we had sex to. Kevin was probably one of the very best lovers I had ever had in my entire life. Even the sex was fun.

The world I lived in with Kevin those two weeks was a pretend world. In the real world, I had to work, go to school, and am responsible. When I was with Kevin, I didn't think about anything but our time together. Every day was like a party. He was child like almost. He just wanted to have fun all the time. Sometimes we would get in his car, turn up the music and just speed down the high way with no destination in mind.

Then sometimes we would pull over on the side of the road and have sex in the car. I never wanted out time together to end.

The day finally came that Kevin had to leave. I didn't want him to leave me.He didn't want to leave me. We hug and kissed for hours. I cried, he cried and we promised not to forget each other.

He gave me one last kiss and he said,

"Lori, I have to go, I'm sorry but I really have to leave," I let him go and I took one last picture of him before he left.

Remember I mentioned that fun boys were for fun and not for anything serious?

I learned that lesson the hard way. For some reason, when Kevin left I thought he was my boyfriend. We had grown so close; I couldn't see things any other way. We continued to e-mail each other. My messages grew more intense; his still were on a good friend level.

Dear Kevin,

   I miss you so much. I think about you all the time. I can't wait for you to come back to the states. My friends ask about you all the time. Do you miss me? We had so much fun together; I have never had that much fun with someone in my whole life. Write back soon.

Love,

Lori

Kevin didn't write me as much as he did before he came to Carbondale. Two days after I would send a message I would get a reply.

Hey Lori,

What's up? I like being on the ship. Sometimes I will go up
to the top deck and look out onto the ocean. It is so beautiful.
I wish you were here.

Kevin

Here I was pouring my heart and soul out to him and he replies telling me about the stupid view from the ship. Well, he did say that he wishes that I would have been there with him, so that's cool. I would write Kevin more than ever, and he replied less than ever. For every 3 messages that I would send, he would send back one. I even started to send him letters in the mail.

In September, six months after he had come to visit me in Carbondale, Kevin was preparing to come back to the states.

Lori,

Sorry I haven't written in awhile. My ship is preparing to
pull into Norfolk, VA and they had cut off our e-mail for a
couple of weeks. We pull in on the 23rd.
See you when I get back.

Kevin

See you when I get back. I came up with the wonderful idea that I would drive to Virginia and surprise Kevin. I was so excited about my plan. I glanced up at my calendar, it was September 20th. I didn't have much time to get ready. I had to get my hair done, get my nails done and get to Virginia. I didn't tell any of my friends about my plan because I knew they would call me stupid for making such a long drive unannounced. I packed plenty of CD's, a suitcase full of clothes and $400 in cash and hit the road.

The drive was nice. I had a lot of time to reflect and think about life. Over and over in my head I played the whole scenario in my head. The ship would pull into the pier, I would be there waving, Kevin would have on his white uniform. Just like in an *Officer and a Gentleman*, he would pick me up and hold me high in the air and give me a big hug and a kiss. I was so excited.

I arrived in Virginia and rented a hotel room. I was tired from the long drive. As I was unpacking I realized that I had left Kevin's cell phone and pager number back in Carbondale. Just in case I didn't see him getting off of the ship I had no way to get in touch with him. I couldn't take that chance.

It was September 22nd, the day before the ship was due to arrive. Kevin couldn't receive phone calls on the ship. I didn't have access to a computer to send him e-mail, and how could I endure he would get the message in time. What I did next was so stupid. I don't know what I was thinking. I called the Red Cross and told them that I was Kevin's fiancée and that I had an urgent message to relay to him. I left my name and the number at the hotel. I sat by the phone and waited.

Kevin called about 45 minutes later.

"Hello," he said in a panicky voice, "What's wrong?" He sounded really nervous. I was starting to think that my bright idea to call the Red Cross was not a good one.

"I'm here in Virginia and I had no way to get in touch with you so I called the Red Cross. I left your phone numbers back at my place," I said.

The phone was silent. I could feel the anger through the phone.

"You know I was working and the Captain came and told me that I had an urgent message. You know I thought my mom had been in an accident or something. That was real dumb Lori, real dumb, don't ever do that again," he was really mad at me.

"I'm sorry," I said.

"Why are you here?" Kevin asked in a serious voice. Wasn't this my fun boy? I had never heard him angry or talk in a serious tone.

"I wanted to surprise you when the ship pulls into the pier," I said.

"Don't come. It's going to be a mad house. 5,000 sailors are pulling in tomorrow. You won't be able to find me. Plus, my mom is supposed to meet me"

Kevin's mom was in town. This was not part of my plan.

"Well Kevin if your mom is in town maybe me and her can come up to the pier together?" I spoke in a quiet voice. I knew he wouldn't go for it.

"Look Lori, I don't know why you came down here. I didn't ask you to come," Kevin said in a pissed off voice.

"You did ask me to come indirectly, you said, "See you when I get back" in the e-mail message," I said tearfully. I had drove all this way for nothing. Kevin was acting like a jerk.

"Look Lori, I meant, see you at a planned time in the near future. Look I have the number to the hotel room. I'll call you when I get back. And please don't come up to the pier, you'll never find me, look I only was allowed 5 minutes for this call. I have to go." He hung up the phone.

I had made a mistake. I would have to live with it. I couldn't even sleep that night in the hotel room. I watched TV for most of the night. Why was Kevin so angry? I thought he would have been happy to see me. He had been out to sea for 6 months, I just knew that I would be the first person that he would want to see when he arrived on land. I guess I was wrong. My feelings were hurt.

The next morning I went to the pier to watch the ship come in. I knew Kevin had told me not to come, but I felt like I had to. I had come so far; I at least wanted to see him. If I saw him, I was going to try to apologize. I was wearing a shiny pink shirt and a tight black skirt. My hair was the bomb and my make-up was perfect.

The ship pulled in at exactly 9:30 A.M. The place was a mad house. Parents and children, pregnant wives, all of these people trying to spot their loved one in a sea of Navy personnel wearing white uniforms. I looked everywhere for Kevin.

Finally, I spotted him, and I guess someone else spotted him at the same time. This Hispanic girl with long flowing black hair ran up to

Kevin and gave him a big hug. He leaned over and kissed the girl. They looked so in love. She was too young to be his mother; she was probably a girlfriend. I could have walked away and never looked back, but that just wasn't in my personality.

I walked up to Kevin and the girl who were now talking. The girl lifted up her shirt and showed Kevin her stomach. The girl's stomach poked out a little. She looked pregnant, not real big and pregnant, but big enough to tell that she was pregnant.

I stood there watching for a minute. The girl noticed I was staring and looked over at me. Then Kevin noticed me.

"Hey Lori, what are you doing here?" he asked.

"Who is this?" I pointed at the girl.

"This is Amber, my girlfriend from Atlanta," Kevin said.

Amber his girlfriend from Atlanta. His pregnant girlfriend from Atlanta.

"And who are you?" Amber asked.

"I'm Lori", I started to say more, but Kevin interrupted me.

"This is Lori. Remember I told you that I had a good friend that sent me e-mail all the time? This is her."

So that's all I was. A good friend that sent him e-mail.

Amber seemed nice. It wasn't her fault that her man messed around with me. Amber extended her arm to me and shook my hand.

"It's very nice to meet you. Kevin relies on e-mail to keep his spirits up when he is out to sea. I don't have a computer so I am unable to write him. But I send him long letters everyday. This is my baby, I love Kevin," she held Kevin.

I was devastated. Seeing Amber look so happy with Kevin, whom I didn't really love, but only wanted to be with because I had so much fun when I was with him.

"Hey Amber, will you wait right here? I'm going to go walk Lori to her car," Kevin said.

"That's fine. It was nice meeting you," Amber said as she waved at me. Amber seemed so sweet. I couldn't even be mad at her. I was a bit jealous that she had Kevin.

Once we were out of Amber's earshot I really dug into Kevin,

"I can't believe you had a girlfriend all along. You lied to me, you misled me, I can't believe I came all this way," I breathed hard as the tears ran down my face.

"Lori, I never lied to you. I never asked you to be my girlfriend. The only time you asked me if I had a girlfriend was when we first met, and at that time I didn't have a girlfriend. Amber and I hooked up after I met you. I got her pregnant the last time I was at home. When I left Carbondale, I stopped in Atlanta and spent a week there." Kevin explained.

He was such a liar. He did tell the truth about some things. He never did ask me to be his girlfriend.

I reached my car and got in and slammed the door. The window was down and Kevin leaned over.

"You look real nice today. Look, I'm sorry. I'll come by and visit you. You are at the Comfort Inn, right?," he asked.

"Yeah," I said as I wiped away tears.

I drove away. I was crying so hard I could barely see the road. I went back to the hotel, packed my belongings and hit the road.

I was so hurt. Kevin was fun, but I didn't see any real future in our relationship. I just enjoyed his company so much. I don't blame Kevin for the way that things unfolded as much as I blamed myself. He was right. He didn't ask me to drive to Virginia. He never asked me to be his girlfriend. Kevin was a fun boy. He was someone to hang out with, someone that was just for fun. I guess I never wanted the fun to end.

I made the mistake of trying to cling on to someone who wasn't trying to cling on to me. I was trying to put Kevin under my spell but it didn't work. I wanted more from him that he was willing to give. In life, we have to understand that people are only ready to extend themselves to someone else if they are ready.

Kevin and I e-mailed each other from time to time over the next few years. Him and Amber did not settle down. It turned out that he wasn't even the father of Amber's baby. Sometimes when I get bored I still think about all of the good times that Kevin and I had those two weeks in Carbondale. When I really think about it, life is about the good times that you have with people. Although, Kevin and I didn't have happily ever after, we did have our two weeks together in Carbondale.

IMANI

---▼---

Imani was the best friend that I have ever had my entire life. Imani and I met during my junior year of college. Imani was a native of Boston, Massachusetts. When I met Imani, she was 23 years old, a year older than I was. Imani was a very pretty girl. She had a dark complexion and thick hair that she always wore in braids.

Imani transferred to SIUC during her junior year. Prior to attending SIUC she was a studying Education at the University of Jamaica. Imani wanted to complete her Bachelor's degree in Black American Studies. There are not to man schools that offer that degree. Imani decided on SIUC because it offered that program and because it was inexpensive.

My major was film production. During my junior year SIU brought in a guest lecturer to teach an African American Film course. The course was limited to 15 students due to the limited classroom space the Cinema & Photography Department had. I was one of the first students to sign up for the class, which quickly filled up and closed.

On the first day of class our teacher, Xavier Rawls, an African American independent film maker introduced us to the history of the Black film. Mr. Rawls provided the class with some background knowledge of the 1920 Oscar Micheuax film "Within Our Gates". As he prepared to show the film, a young woman opened the door.

"May I help you?" Mr. Rawls asked the young woman.

"I'm sorry that I am late but I couldn't find the building," the young woman sat down in the first empty seat that she found.

"Are you on the roster? What is your name?"

"Imani Phillips, no I'm not on the roster, but I would really love to take this course."

"I've already talked to the department about this class. The roster is locked in at 15, and there is a waiting list," Mr. Rawls explained.

Imani counted the chairs in the room.

"There are 18 chairs in the room, why is the roster locked in at 15 students? I just want to learn," she explained. She had a good point. The class laughed. Mr. Rawls smiled.

"You have a good point Ms. Phillips. I'll see what I can do about getting you enrolled in the class." Mr. Phillips turned off the lights and started the film.

After the class let out I exited the building and prepared to walk back to the dorms. Imani walked fast to catch up with me.

"Hey are you walking back towards the dorms?"

"Yes," I said. I wasn't sure why she had chose to walk with me.

"You see it's dark, and I don't remember the way back to the dorms," she explained. I hadn't seen the girl around campus before.

"Are you new here?" I asked.

"Yeah, my name is Imani. I just transferred here from the University of Jamaica."

"What brought you to SIU of all places?" I asked.

"Well SIU has a good Black American Studies program," Imani said.

As we walked back to the dorms we chatted. We decided to go to the cafeteria and eat dinner together. I discovered that Imani was pretty cool. We had a lot in common. We both had one brother and we both came from divorced families. We also both had an appreciation for hip-hop music.

We sat in the cafeteria talking until we saw the football team came in. We both pointed out which players we thought were attractive. I also saw my friend Jeneva walk in. Jeneva was a senior. She was very intelligent. She was in a sorority and she stayed out of trouble. She spent most of her time in her books or with her boyfriend Kurt who was a football player.

I motioned to Jeneva to come over.

Jeneva came and ate dinner with Imani and I. I introduced the two women and they seemed to hit it off. I met Jeneva during my freshman year, but we didn't start hanging out a lot until the summer before my junior year. I used to be pretty wild and out there. Jeneva couldn't be associated with someone like me at that time. It wasn't good for her reputation. I couldn't blame her for keeping her distance.

Turns out that Imani lived in my building on the same floor as I did. It didn't take long for Imani and I to become the best of friends. We would talk on the phone for hours. Imani had a very outgoing personality. She spoke to everyone she saw.

Imani had lived a very sheltered life with her parents. In college, she found the opportunity to be free and to express herself. She was 1000 miles from Boston and she was young woman in full blossom. Imani also had a very unique style of dress. She wore a lot of African clothes. Even if she were wearing a regular pair of Levi's she would spice them up with a bright colorful top.

I think one of the reasons Imani and I bonded so well is because we had both been loners so long in our lives. I spent most of my free time in my room writing or watching movies. Imani wrote in a journal in her free time. At the time we were both single. Imani had broken up with her long time boyfriend before she came to SIU. My relationships never lasted beyond 90 days, so I was single at the time.

On the weekends, Imani, Jeneva and I would hang out in my room and watch movies or just have "girl talk". Jeneva was the only one of us that had a boyfriend. Imani and I were "single and ready to mingle"

Friday and Saturday night was our time to party. We would usually go to the clubs on the strip or to the football teams keg parties. Imani was a nice looking girl, so of course she was popular with the boys. I was pretty popular with the opposite sex myself. When the two of us go together there was never a dull moment.

On Saturday, September 7, 1996, Imani and I went to a bar in town to watch the Mike Tyson fight. The fight was on pay-per-view and we couldn't order the fight in the dorms. Neither one of us were interested in Mike Tyson or the fight. We didn't even know how they took score in boxing. We knew that their would be a lot of guys at the bar watching the fight, and for that reason we made sure that we would be there.

We met these two cool guys at the bar. I can't remember their names because I was drunk, but they were cool. We rode around in their car and we went to Denny's and got something to eat after the fight.

Imani was a free spirit like that. Sometimes we would do things that for all intense purposes were not safe, but if we had a "good vibe" we would do it. Sure those guys could have killed us or raped us, but we didn't even think about that.

Later that night when we returned to the dorms we found out that Tupac Shakur, my favorite rapper had been shot. I was so sad and depressed. Imani spend the night in my room keeping me company because I was so upset. Seven days later Tupac succumbed to his wounds. Jeneva thought I was stupid for mourning someone that I had never met, but Imani understood my pain.

It didn't take long for me to consider Imani my best friend. She was the only person I had in my life that was always there for me. When I was upset about a boy or a film project I was working on she was always there for me. We planned our futures together. After graduation, we planned to move to California together. I was going to pursue my film career and Imani was going to attend graduate school at USC.

We both really enjoyed our African-American film class. We aced the course and both got A's. Surprisingly, this was the first class I had ever taken that had an African-American theme. Imani, being a Black American Studies major, taught me a lot of things about my culture that I should have known.

Imani previously attended the University of Jamaica, so it was no surprise to me that she smoked weed. I didn't care that she smoked, I just knew that smoking weed wasn't for me. Before we would go out to a club, Imani would smoke a blunt, and I might drink a half of a bottle of Vodka straight. We were young, we didn't have any kids, and we were just having fun.

The spring semester of 1997 was supposed to be the semester that I was to graduate from college. Being that I was a film student, I had to complete my final thesis, a film, in order to graduate. I didn't have the money to produce a spectacular film. On top of that I had a total mental block, I had no idea what I was going to make my film about.

Spring semester Imani and I decided to move off-campus. We moved into an apartment building in the middle of town and rented one-bedroom apartments right next to each other. Jeneva also moved off-campus and she moved into an apartment across the street from ours with her boyfriend Kurt.

I was happy. I had friends. I still had no boyfriend, only occasional sex partners now and then. But with my good friends nearby, I didn't even long for male companionship like I normally did.

One of my "only one time" sex partners was a guy named Gavin. Gavin was cool. He was a fraternity boy and he was really popular around campus, especially wit the ladies.

I knew Gavin because I had seen him around campus from time to time. One day he came up to my job at Pizza Hut and starting flirting with me. He was sitting at table 1A with a group of his friends.

"Hey girl, can I get a free pizza?" He asked.

"No, you have to pay like everyone else," I said.

"Well can I get your phone number then?" He asked. I gave him the number but I never expected him to call.

Gavin called and we would talk on the phone for hours. He was cool. He was more of a friend that a boyfriend. One day he invited me over to his house. We were drinking and just hanging out.

Gavin lived in a junky frat house. He invited me to his bedroom and we played video games and listened to music. Then Gavin did the sweetest thing. He took out a pen and a pad and started writing.

"What are you writing?"

"A song," he said as he scribbled in his notebook.

"A song about what?"

"Shh…I need to concentrate, it's a song about you," Gavin said as he wrote faster.

I went through some of Gavin's belongings on his dresser, he didn't mind, and he continued to write.

"Okay, I'm finished. I wrote this little rap about you, now don't laugh."

"Well let's hear it," I said with a smile. Gavin held the paper up in order to read it and started to recite the little rap he wrote for me.

"Lori, oooh Lori, you remind me of a story,

With your ghetto booty and your pretty eyes,

Like all women I know you probably lie,

That doesn't matter though, because tonight it's you I'm havin

Because you have to give up the draws to Gavin," Gavin burst into laughter.

I fell out on the floor laughing. Gavin fell on the floor laughing with me.

"Gavin, that rap didn't even rhyme that good and it was so silly," I said laughing.

"That doesn't matter. It was from the heart, that's what counts."

We had both been drinking so maybe that is why we were so free with ourselves. That night Gavin and I had sex in his bedroom. I was kind of out of it but from what I remember it was good.

When we woke up the next morning, we both had a feeling that we had done something that we weren't supposed to have done. Gavin and I had so much fun together and we clicked so well, I thought that it would be best if we just stayed good friends. Plus, I knew that Gavin was a big player around campus. I didn't regret having sex with him, it was just one of those things that I did that I didn't think much about after it happened.

Imani was my best friend. We shared everything, but we had never shared men-until Gavin. After Gavin and I had sex, he and I became closer friends. We never had sex again or even came close to being intimate. We just became very close friends. To this day, I can honestly say Gavin is the closest male friend I have ever had.

Gavin often stopped by my apartment to hang out. Imani was my girl, so she was there most of the time. I had seen Gavin flirt with many women during the course of our friendship, but it stung a little bit when he started to flirt with my best friend.

One day I was frying chicken and invited Gavin and Imani over for dinner. Gavin spent the whole evening trying to put the moves on Imani. She knew that I had been intimate with him and she knew that he was a player, but she went along with the game.

"Imani, why don't you have a boyfriend?" Gavin asked while he was chewing on a chicken wing.

"I don't know," Imani said as she took a sip of her soda.

"Are you going to let me come and visit you tonight?"

"Why should I let you come and visit me?" Imani smiled at Gavin.

"Because girl, you know you want some company"

I couldn't stand to hear anymore. Why did I care if Gavin was flirting with Imani? I had told myself a million times that I didn't like Gavin, that he was just my good friend, but I would get so jealous when he would flirt with Imani.

Not to my surprise Gavin and Imani "hooked up" She even had the nerve to call me and tell me the details.

"Lori, guess what?"

"I did it with Gavin, it was so good. I mean it was great," She giggled into the phone.

"That's nice," I said in a flat tone of voice.

"What's wrong with you?" Imani asked.

"Its just you know Gavin is my friend, you know he is no good and you know I had sex with him, so why did you have sex with him," I said in flat tone of voice.

"Lori, he's not your boyfriend. Are you jealous? If you like him you can have him back, it isn't worth messing up our friendship," Imani said.

Imani was right. Gavin was not worth messing up our friendship. I just didn't understand why she would follow up behind me like that.

In April of 1998 I turned 22 years old. I planned a party and invited all of my friends. I invited Jeneva and Gavin, and even my old pals Sheree and April. Imani and I cooked chicken, we made macaroni and cheese and we bought a huge cake. We decorated my apartment and we had plenty of liquor.

I was so excited about my birthday party. I put my hair up in a great big ponytail. I put on my favorite hoop earrings and I painted my body with body glitter. I wore my favorite pink dress and a pair of high heel white gym shoes. When I came out of the bedroom after getting dressed Imani stared at me in awe.

"Ohmigosh, Lori look at you. You look so cute!" Imani walked over to me and pinched me on the cheek.

"Lori, your hair is so cute and you are sparkling all over. You look like a doll. Like a little Sparkledoll!"

"Thanks," I blushed.

"That's your new nick-name Lori, Sparkledoll," Imani said with a smile. I did look like a little glittery doll.

We told people that the party would start at 6:00. 6:00 came and no one knocked on the door. 7:00 came and 8:00 came and no one arrived. Imani and I sat there watching the food get cold. By 9:00 we resolved that no one was coming. We decided to eat the cake. Imani sang happy birthday to me. She was my friend. She was the only person with me at my party. It may have just been the two of us but we danced, ate and drank and had a good time.

The next day I all of my so-called friends were telling me why they messed my party. Gavin said that he was "pledging some new potential frat brothers," Jeneva said, "she forgot", and everyone else had one excuse or another.

Imani and Gavin's fling was starting to die down. He wasn't really Imani's type; he was just someone that she was messing around with.

May came and I didn't graduate. I wasn't any closer to graduating than I had been when the semester started. I just was stuck when it came to an idea for a film. My department had placed two requirements on film students wishing to graduate. Prior to graduation the senior student must complete a feature film and a term paper that would accompany the film.

I promised myself that I would spend my summer working on my film. I decided that the only type of film I could afford to produce would be a documentary.

I needed a subject or a story to follow for my documentary film. I came up with several ideas. My first idea was a documentary film about the life of an SIU janitor. After filming for three days I decided that made for a very boring film.

June rolled around and I still had not shot one reel of any substantial footage. One Saturday Imani and I were swimming at the Campus Lake. It was a beautiful sunny afternoon. The temperature was 90 degrees and we were having a good summer. We would go swimming any opportunity that we could.

The lake was about 30 feet deep in the middle. Imani and I would swim to the middle of the lake and just float there and look at the sky and the beautiful surroundings.

"Imani, I'm never going to graduate. I need to start on my film," I said.

"Sparkledoll what kind of film are you going to make, a documentary right?" Imani loved to call me by the nickname that she had given me. I gently kicked my feet in the water as we floated in the water.

"I want to make a documentary film. A real cutting edge documentary, not some boring old PBS documentary," I felt so at peace in the lake.

"Why don't you make a film about yourself?" Imani said. I thought about what she said.

"I got it. I can make a film about the life of a female Black college student. I can follow her to class and interview her and just film everything about her life."

"Yeah, that is a good idea, Lori. I'll help you if you need any help," Imani said.

"I need more than help. I want you to be the star," Imani would be perfect.

"Me, if you want me to be in your film I will," I was glad that Imani agreed because if she hadn't I would have hounded her about until she gave in. I was relentless like that sometimes.

We laid in the middle of the lake floating for about 30 minutes. We could feel the sun turning our dark skin even darker. Our eyes were closed and we were just chilling in the middle of the lake. We felt some ripples in the water. I thought it was Imani kicking the water.

"Imani was that you?" I asked.

"No, girl I thought it was you," Imani said as she looked around.

We opened our eyes and there were two great big black ass water moccasins circling us in the water.

"Oh shit!" I screamed. Imani started to scream. I think we may have scared the snakes to. If we could have run we would have, but we were in 30 feet deep water. We started to swim as fast as we could. I got a cramp in my side, I just knew I was going to drown. Imani almost had an asthma attack. The people who were sitting on the beach of Campus Lake didn't why we were in the middle of the lake freaking out.

When we reached the shore we were so happy we started to hug each other. We had been so scared.

The next day I started filming Imani. I would film her getting ready for her summer school class. I would film her walking to class. She would always talked directly into the camera.

"This is me walking to class. My first class of the day is African-Literature."

"Act natural," I would say off camera.

I decided to name my documentary "90 Days". I would film Imani everyday for 90 days. I would catch the ups and the downs and edit the film into a 90-minute feature. Imani liked being filmed. After the first couple of days she started to act completely natural in front of the camera.

The weekend of the 4ᵗʰ of July there was a big reggae concert in Carbondale. Imani and I went to the concert together. When we got there I met up with a guy that I had been dating named Dante. The concert was free (our favorite price) and it was in the park on campus. Dante was 24 (2 years older than I was), and he was out of college. He lived in Carbondale with his cousin. I had known Dante for years, but this was the first time that we had dated. Honestly, the best thing about our relationship was the sex. Outside of sex, he got on my nerves. He was always complaining about the state of the world or some other bullshit I wasn't trying to hear.

The reggae band performing had arrived earlier in the day on a tour bus. Imani and I saw the group unpacking their equipment.

"Lori, look at that guy he is so cute, look at his dreads," Imani pointed to a short brown-skinned man with long shoulder-length dreadlocks. The man was wearing a tank top and a pair of blue denim shorts.

"I bet he is in the band. I want to meet him after the concert," Imani said.

The reggae concert was on point. It lasted late into the night. Dante and I danced together and Lori puffed on a blunt as she danced. She flirted with the guy she had seen earlier. Turns out he was a drum player for the reggae band.

After the performance the band started to load up their equipment and the crowd started to dissipate. I had taken most of the evening off from film-ing, but I just had to film Imani trying to pick up the reggae drummer boy.

"Lori, are you going to come with me to meet him, I'm scared to go over there by myself?" I looked around for Dante. He was talking to some of his friends.

"Sure, I want to film this," I said as we walked toward the stage.

We walked up onto the stage and basically cornered the drummer.

"Pretty lady, I saw you in the audience," the guy leaned over his drum kit and gave Imani a hug.

"You have an American accent. I just knew a dreadlocked brother like you was from Jamaica or the Bahama's, especially since you play the reggae music so good," Imani said in her best Jamaican accent.

"No Miss lady, I am from Cincinnati, Ohio. What is the pretty ladies name?"

He grabbed Imani's hand.

I should have known if we would have a reggae band in Carbondale, they would be from somewhere like Ohio. I didn't even know they listed to reggae music in Ohio.

"My name is Imani, and this is my friend Sparkledoll. Don't mind her filming, she is working on a school project," Imani patted me on the head.

"Sparkledoll?" the guy said.

"My name is Lori, don't listen to her, what's your name?"

"My name is Greg."

After we all had made our introductions, I saw that Imani was comfortable so I left her and Greg alone and I went to find my booty call buddy Dante to make sure that he was coming over to my apartment that evening.

"Dante, are you ready to go?" I asked as I found Dante sitting on the curb like a little nerd. Dante was a nerd at times, but he was very well endowed, and for that fact, I kept him around.

"Yes, sweetie, I'm ready. I saw you and your girl up their talking to that dread-locked cat."

"Imani likes him," I said.

Dante and I prepared to walk to the car. I called for Imani.

"Imani are you ready?"

"Greg is going to take me back to the crib."

"Are you sure?" I asked.

"Yeah, I'm straight," Imani said as she waved to us.

It was one thing letting other college students that were strangers take you home, but this guy was from Ohio and played in a band that was just passing through town. I didn't want to seem like I was hating so I didn't say anything. I left with Dante.

Dante and I went back to my apartment and had sex, and as usual he left afterwards. I usually wanted him to leave. Sometimes I would wake up and look at him and think, "Why am I in bed with him? He doesn't stimulate my mind, he isn't that attractive," and then I would look down at his penis and it would all become clear why I was with him.

It was about 2:30 A.M. went Dante left and went home. I decided to go across the hall and check on Imani. I knocked on the door. She was holed up in the room with the dread-locked boy. She opened the door just a crack and said,

"I'm busy," Imani said with a giggle through the half-opened door.

"I can see" I peeked in and saw Greg sprawled naked across the bed.

The next day at about 1:00 in the afternoon I decided to go visit Imani and get some footage about the night before. Much to my surprise when I went to her apartment Greg was still there. Didn't he have to go back to Ohio?

Imani invited me in. Greg was laying on the bed in a tank top and a pair of boxer shorts. Imani was wearing at tee shirt and a pair of underwear. I filmed them together.

"Imani, Greg, so you all are digging each other?" I asked. Imani smiled.

"Greg, don't you have to get back to Ohio, when does your bus leave?" I asked.

Greg puffed on a Black & Mild cigar.

"They left. I'll take the Greyhound bus back to get some clothes and then I am coming back here to stay with Imani," Greg said as he puffed on the Black & Mild.

How could she just invite this complete stranger to move in with her?

"What about your job with the band?" I asked.

"Oh, I only got paid $35 a gig. I can find a better job here. Maybe I can even start my own band," Greg reached for Imani's hand.

This guy was a hobo looking for a home. What kind of person can just through away their whole life in one night? Didn't he have a job, bills, and responsibilities? Obviously, not. He moved in with Imani, and that is when everything started to change.

It didn't take long for Greg to become a major influence on Imani. Imani, who used to smoke weed occasionally, now became a heavy weed smoker. Then she cut off all of her hair because Greg said he wanted is women "To be natural". It was so fast that things changed. Imani was with Greg all of the time. She never had time for me. Whenever I tried to film her, he was there. He was ruining my documentary film.

Imani thought that I was jealous of her and Greg's relationship. That was not the case. He just seemed like such a bum to me. He didn't work. He lived off of her and her student loan check.

Imani and I still had time to talk. Sometimes Greg would go play basketball or he would go out looking for a new band. It's like I was losing my best friend. Everything in her life had to do with Greg. Every time that we would meet I would film our time together. Everything she said always started with Greg said.

"Greg says I should get a tattoo of Bob Marley on my back, he says that would look nice."

"Greg says I should get my clit pierced. He says I should get my tongue pierced to."

"Greg says I should stop wearing deodorant because the man puts chemicals in the deodorant that gives us breast cancer."

By the time October came around I was still shooting my film. I already had over 300 hours worth of footage, but I didn't feel like I had the right scenes to tie my movie to an end. By now I saw Imani less and less. The only time that she had time for me is when Greg would make his weekly trip to Ohio on the bus.

Greg would go home every week. He said that he would go home to "earn money". I once questioned Imani about Greg's trips.

"Did you ever stop to think that maybe he has a girlfriend in Ohio?"

"Lori, stop hating. How could he have a girlfriend and be here with me all the time?"

"Anything is possible," I said.

Imani was nothing like the person she used to be. She was dirty and smelled bad due to the fact that she didn't wear deodorant. Her hair was short and nappy. Not that anything is wrong with a short Afro, but she didn't keep her fro up. She had gotten the Bob Marley tattoo on her arm instead of her back. She also had gotten her lip pierced. Imani had completely changed her life because of this man.

The landlord would complain about the smoke coming from Imani's apartment. He also took notice that Greg was living with Imani and his name wasn't on the lease. Imani was tired of the landlord's complaints, so she made plans to move into a cheaper apartment on the East Side of Carbondale.

Dante and I didn't spend as much time together as we used to because he had taken a job in Atlanta. He would still come and visit me twice a month. One day the visits just stopped. I was busy trying to edit the footage that I had together to complete my film in time for a December graduation. In early November, I got a letter from Dante. I was surprised to get the letter. It had been almost 6 weeks since I had heard from Dante. I was anxious to open the letter.

> *Dear Lori,*
>
> *Hey what's up? I hope you are fine. It is very important to me that I write you this letter. I just wanted to tell you that I never liked you. I was not attracted to you and I was only with you because the sex was so good. One day I just decided that good sex was not worth me wasting my gas to go all the way to Illinois to see you. I hope you aren't made and I hope I didn't hurt you. Are we still friends?*
>
> *Dante*

I couldn't believe the letter that I was holding in my hand. It was a tremendous blow to my ego. No one had ever said something so mean to me in my life. I read the letter over and over again in disbelief. Then I thought about things. Dante felt exactly the same way about me that I felt about him. My feelings were really hurt by that letter.

I was in a hurry to make the December graduation deadline so on November 15th I turned in the edited footage that I had of Imani. My teacher, Mrs. Burrows, a very harsh film critic, told me that my film was "too raw" and that it needed to be "edited tighter". I couldn't apply for December graduation. I would have to wait until May.

The fact that I wasn't going to graduate threw me into a deep depression. Imani and Greg had moved away and I never felt more alone in my life. I still had Gavin, but he didn't have much time for me. He settled down with a sophomore girl named Charmaigne and settled down. Charmaigne didn't like me because she didn't understand the friendship Gavin and I shared. I still had Jeneva, but she was in graduate school and she didn't have much time for a social life.

Imani and I were still friends but we conducted most of our friendship via the telephone. One evening I got a late night call from Imani.

"Hello" I mumbled into the phone.

"Sparkledoll"

"Imani, what's going on?"

"I'm pregnant," Imani mumbled.

"Is this a good thing or a bad thing?" I asked.

"It's a good thing," Imani said.

"What did Greg say?"

"I didn't tell him yet."

"When are you going to tell him?"

"Tomorrow."

"Good luck. Hey, can I film it? Would you mind?"

"Well, I was thinking it was a private moment, but if you want, you can come over and film it."

The next day at 4:30 I went over to Imani's new apartment to film Imani telling Greg her big news. Imani's new apartment was on the East Side of Carbondale. The apartment was cheap and shabby, definitely a step down from her previous apartment. The place was so run-down there was a whole in the kitchen floor.

I sat down at the kitchen table and filmed Imani and Greg on the couch. I noticed a crack pipe and a needle in the ashtray on the table. I didn't say anything about it to Imani at that time, but I did film it.

"Greg, guess what?" Imani playfully pounced on Greg.

"I'm pregnant," Imani said as she held the positive pregnancy test in her hand. Greg gently pushed Imani off of him.

"Are you sure?" He said in a pissed off tone of voice.

"Yeah, I'm sure," Imani's tone of voice dropped.

"Are you sure it's mine?" He asked. Imani looked over at me.

"Lori, turn the camera off because I think it's about to get ugly up in here."

I turned off the light to the camera, giving the appearance that I had turned the camera off, but I continued to film.

"I can't believe you would ask me something like that," Imani cried.

"Well I don't know who you have been with I had to ask"

"Lori, can you come over another time?" Imani asked.

"Sure" I knew that my presence was no longer wanted. As I exited the apartment I heard Imani and Greg arguing.

When I got home I called Jeneva right away. She was surprised.

"Now why did that girl go and get pregnant by a bum like that. He doesn't have a job; he can't even take care of himself. How is he going to take care of her and a baby?"

"I don't know Jeneva, the whole thing is crazy. She hadn't been the same since she met him. She dresses all weird now and she doesn't take care of herself anymore. Today when I was over their I saw a crack pipe and a needle on the table."

"What! Do you think Imani is doing more than just smoking weed?" Jeneva uttered in disbelief.

"Jeneva, all I know is that Imani hasn't been the same since she met Greg."

The next day I called Imani to see how things were going with her.

"Hey girl, what's up?"

"Lori, he's gone," Imani cried into the phone.

"What do you mean he's gone?"

"He left. He went back to Ohio and I don't think he's coming back," Imani cried.

The phone went silent and I could hear Imani crying hard on the other end.

"I'm on my way over," I said as I hung up the phone and left my apartment. I jumped in my car and drove to Imani's house.

I didn't knock, I walked in. Sitting on the floor was Imani. She looked a mess. Her face was puffy and swollen from crying. She was looking at pictures that she and Greg had taken together. She was listening to Erica Badu and burning incense.

"Lori, he's gone, and he's not coming back," Imani started to cry and I got down on the floor next to her to comfort her. I held her close and let her cry on my shoulder.

"Imani, maybe he's just in shock. Did he say he wasn't coming back?"

"He said he had to go home to sort things out," Imani started bawling.

"Well maybe it's better that he is gone. Look at you. Look at where you are living. Do you really need him? I know he is the father of your baby, but you don't even have to have this baby if you don't want to. Maybe it's better that he is gone, now you can get your life back together," I said as I gave Imani a hug. Imani clearly didn't like what I said.

She pushed me off of her. Imani walked over to the couch and buried her face in her arms.

"You don't understand. He means everything to me!" She yelled.

"He is my whole world. I'm his queen, he is my king, I can't live without Greg," Imani said as she squeezed her wrist.

Imani had been drinking. The empty Tequila bottles were on the floor. She was flipping out.

"Imani, you lived before him. You can live without him. What did he ever give you besides sex? He had nothing to offer you but some bullshit ass conversation and some sex. When you tell him that you are pregnant he runs off. You don't need a man like that. In a few months you will be graduating from college. Don't throw your life away because of this man," I begged.

"Sparkledoll. I will die without him," Imani said staring at me with a blank stare.

"He is not worth killing yourself," I tried to reason with Imani.

"I won't have to kill myself, my heart will be broken and I will just die."

Two weeks past and Imani hadn't heard from Greg. I was preparing to go home for Christmas break. I will still a bit bummed that I wouldn't be graduating that December, but I was worried about Imani. She was so depressed about Greg that she skipped most of her final exams.

A week before Christmas, Jeneva and I were eating a pizza when Imani knocked on the door. When I opened the door I barely recognized her. She was so skinny and her eyes were sunken in. Her clothes reeked of marijuana and alcohol. She walked into my apartment and sat on the couch.

I stood looking at her in amazement. She was a shell of her former self.

"Imani, why are you drinking and doing drugs and you are pregnant?" Jeneva asked.

"It's not going to hurt the baby. I don't even care."

"When you have a retarded baby you'll care. That's terrible. You should really be ashamed of yourself. You are a pretty girl and you have really let yourself go." Jeneva didn't hold back." one bit.

"Thanks for the lecture Jeneva, but I came to see Lori."

"I'm about to go anyway, I'll see you later Lori. Call me.

Jeneva grabbed a slice of pizza and exited the apartment.

"What's going on Imani?"

"Lori, I told you he wasn't coming back."

"Imani, I know it's hard, but just let it go."

"Lori, I need your help," Imani said as she pulled a couple of wrinkled pieces of paper out of her pocket.

"I need you to take me to Ohio. I have to see Greg. I don't know exactly where he lives but I found these numbers on my phone bill and I have this bill with an Ohio address that his mother sent here to him."

I looked at the documents.

"Imani, Ohio is like 9 hours from here. Why don't you just call him?"

"Just help me this one time Lori, and I will ever ask you to help me again. If I had a car I would make the trip myself."

Despite everything that happened Imani was still my friend. She had always been there for me; I couldn't let her down.

The next morning at 6:00 A.M. Imani and I packed up my car and hit the highway. Driving to Ohio, we had a lot of fun. I even had the opportunity to do some filming when we stopped along the way. We laughed and joked and it was almost like old times. She wasn't high. The things we joked about weren't even that funny when you think about it.

"Girl, what if I get there and he is like, "Bitch get off my doorstep," Imani said with a laugh.

"Or what is he is like married and plays the stupid role. Do I know you from somewhere, I don't think I know this woman baby, she's lying," I laughed.

After two or three of our "too close to reality" jokes Imani would hold her head down and cry silently. I didn't know why it was so important for her to make this trip to Ohio. I understood that she was pregnant with Greg's child, but he couldn't provide for her and when she needed him the most he ran off. At first I thought she was seeking closure. However, I soon realized that what Imani wanted was Greg.

We arrived in Ohio at 1:30 in the afternoon. It was a very cold, snowy and icy December day.

"Okay, we're here. Now what?" I said as I looked at Imani holding the crumpled up pieces of paper in her hand.

"Well I have this phone number and I have an address. I got the phone number off of my phone bill, I don't even know whose phone number it is."

"Imani, we didn't come all of this way to make a phone call, we could have called from Carbondale. Let's try to find this address," I was getting more pissed off by

the minute. How did I let myself get into this wild adventure? It was freezing cold and I was tired because I drove the entire trip because Imani was tired and was experiencing motion sickness.

We went into a gas station and bought a map. We drove around for about an hour looking for the address on the piece of paper and we still couldn't find it. We eventually ended up asking a truck driver to give us directions.

1933 Hill Circle Drive was the address on the crumpled bill addressed to Greg.

The house was a shabby looking ranch style house. We pulled up in the driveway. I looked over at Imani.

"Are you getting out of the car?"

"Lori, I'm scared. Will you come with me?"

It was freezing outside. I really didn't want to get out of the car, but I went along for moral support. Imani and I walked up the steps and rang the doorbell. A fat older black woman with a Jheri curl opened the door.

"Who are you looking for?" The woman asked.

"Hi, we are here looking for Greg," Imani said.

"Greg ain't lived here in 8 years," the woman said.

"Are you his mother?" Imani asked.

"Yes, and who are you?" The woman looked Imani up and down.

"I'm his girlfriend from Illinois. Do you know where I can find him at?"

The woman looked at me, and then she looked at Imani.

"I'm sorry" The woman slammed the door and you could hear her turn the lock.

We stood there in disbelief.

"Lori, please tell me this woman didn't just slam the door in our face," Imani said.

I patted Imani on the back.

"Yes, my friend, I think she did."

I walked down the stairs and got in the car. Imani followed my lead. We sat in the woman's driveway for a minute plotting our next move.

"Well we still have the phone number." Imani whispered. She could tell I was getting pissed. I was cold, tired, and the only thing I wanted to see was my warm bed.

"Imani, just give it up. We're going home."

"Lori, we came this far. Maybe he and his mother don't get along," Imani kept the faith.

"Maybe he has a life here that you are not a part of," I said.

Imani started to cry.

"Look, I'm sorry Imani, I didn't mean to hurt your feelings. We'll go find a payphone," I said as I started the ignition.

Imani and I drove to the gas station that we bought the map from so that she could use the pay phone. Inside of the gas station it was so warm and toasty. Imani put .35 cents in the pay phone and started to dial. I stood next to her as she placed the call.

A woman answered the phone. Imani assumed that the woman was a sister or a friend.

"Hello, may I speak to Greg."

"Who is this?" The woman asked.

"This is Imani," Imani said with confidence.

"Imani, Greg who the fuck is Imani and why the hell is she calling my house," the woman yelled in the background.

"Babe that's just some girl playing on the phone hang-up," Greg said in the background.

"I'm not hanging up shit Greg, Imani where do you know lying as Greg from," the woman asked.

"I'm his girlfriend from Carbondale," Imani said in a soft voice.

"Carbondale. Girlfriend. This is Linda, Greg's wife and the mother of his two children. We have been separated because he is a bum and can't keep a fucking job. If you want his Black ass you can have him." Linda said with an attitude.

"Don't talk like that baby, you know you love me," Greg shouted in the background. Imani hung up the phone.

We silently walked back to the car. Imani didn't say anything the first 4 hours of the ride home. She just cried. Then she broke her silence.

"Lori, I can't believe he is married with two kids," Imani stared out of the window.

"I can, I just knew something wasn't right about him. Why was he always making those trips to Ohio?" I don't know if that was exactly the right thing to say at the moment, but I didn't want to hold back anything.

"Lori, why do you think he just left like that, just because I got pregnant?"

"Well Imani, maybe he left because you were his young college girl-friend. You didn't pressure him and you all didn't have any real responsi-bilities. When you got pregnant everything changed. I mean, that's just my guess. I don't even have a boyfriend, so I'm not expert on the opposite sex," I offered the best advice I could.

When we got back to Carbondale, Imani and I went our separate ways. I prepared for my final exams and Imani slumped into a deep depression. She ended up failing most of her classes because she skipped her final exam. She would just spend the day in bed. I knew she was pregnant and pregnancy does weird things to your hormones, but I couldn't understand why she just couldn't pull things together.

I could understand her fears about being single and pregnant and dis-appointing her parents. Imani was 23 years old, she had to accept the fact that she was an adult and she had to face the consequences of her actions. If she didn't want to have the baby she could have had a legal abortion ver-sus killing the hurting the baby by drinking and smoking weed.

Christmas break came and I went to Chicago to visit my mother. Honestly, I didn't even think about Imani too much. I was tired of seeing her depressed. I just wanted her to be my old friend again. The happy Imani. The girl I could talk to on the phone for hours with.

January rolled around and I was looking forward to a May graduation. I only had one class and my film to worry about. I would call Imani from time to time, but I got tired of hearing her talk about he same things.

"Lori, I'm never going to see him again am I?"

"Sure Imani, you'll see him again. Why do you want to see someone who doesn't want to see you?"

"Lori, you've never been in love like this. I feel like I can't breathe without him.

Every night I dream that he is just going to walk through that door."

Imani would always start to cry at this point. Then I would say.

"Well I was just calling to check in on you." Then I would hang up the phone.

Imani slipped deeper and deeper in depression. She resumed going to classes, but would often where the same outfit day after day. Her pregnancy was starting to show a little bit. Gavin would call me and ask me if, "I had seen how bad Imani looked." Jeneva was also concerned. One day the three of us decided to pay her a visit.

It was February 8, and we had been in school about three weeks. Gavin and Jeneva couldn't stand each but they came together so that we could try to help Imani.

We didn't call first; we just arrived at her doorstep. It took Imani about 3 minutes to answer the door.

The apartment was a mess. Dirty clothes were everywhere. Pictures of Greg covered the floor. Incense was burning and there was a strong scent of marijuana and alcohol in the air. Tequila and vodka bottles were lined up along the counter. Always a filmmaker, I had my camera rolling.

Imani was surprised that Gavin was with us. She tried to put on some make-up.

"Imani, girl what's going on?" Gavin walked up to Imani and gave her a hug as she was standing in front of the mirror putting on make-up.

Imani hugged Gavin tight as though she was love-starved for male attention. Jeneva and I looked at each as if we were thinking the same thought.

"I thought you had forgotten all about me Gavin. You never call,"
Imani said.

"You were living with the dreadlocked guy. How would I look calling
over here?"

"I guess you're right." Imani started to look sad again. Now it was
Jeneva's turn to ask Imani about her life.

"Imani, look at this place. I am scared to sit down a roach my jump up
and try to crawl on me. Girl, I ought to call your mother right now,"
Jeneva said in disgust.

"Jeneva, leave me alone I have enough problems," Imani shouted.

"Look, Imani. You have got to get some help for your depression. You
can't just let yourself go like this. You're 4 months pregnant. If you are going
to have this baby, you can't bring a child into the world like this" I said.

"True dat," Gavin agreed.

The three of us sat there for hours trying to make some kind of break
through with Imani. Imani gave too much energy to males. Jeneva and I
would make good points about things and she would ignore our com-
ments. But if Gavin made the same comment she would agree with him.
10:00 P.M. rolled around and we left. I don't think we made any progress,
but Imani promised to try to get better.

I thought that Imani was depressed, but I never quite knew just how
depressed that she was, or just how far that she would take things.

The next two months Imani stomach grew bigger and bigger and she
sank deeper and deeper into a depression. Imani never did tell her parents
that she was pregnant. They were worried about her because she had
stopped calling home, but she begged them not to come and visit. I was so
immersed in editing my film that I didn't have adequate time to help
Imani through her depression. I was lost. I didn't know what to do. I
begged her to get help. I offered my advice. I didn't know what else I could
possibly do. I had reached a final cut of my film on April 2, 1998, almost

a full two weeks before the deadline for me to make the May graduation deadline. I ended the film with a montage of footage I shot at the beginning of the filming process and a combination of some of the later footage I shot when Imani was going through her depression.

April 9, 1998 was the most surreal day of my life. It was a beautiful spring day in Carbondale. The weather was nice and the sun was shining. I was so happy. My film was done and I was looking forward to my future. I was walking through the Student Center when one of Imani's classmates walked up to me.

"You're Lori right?" The girl asked.

"Yeah," I said curiously.

"You know Imani is in the hospital," the girl said.

I felt my heart start to race.

"What happened?" I asked in a panic.

"Nobody knows. Some people said she tried to kill herself, then some people said she had a heart attack, but I know the baby died. They say that she was dead when the paramedics arrive, but they brought her back to life," the girl said nonchalantly as if she was relaying gossip.

I felt so bad. I was crushed and I was a panicked mess. I left the Student Center and ran to my car. There was only one hospital in Carbondale and I knew that is where Imani was.

It still seems like yesterday. I remember all of the events that took place in my head so vividly. I walked into the hospital. I walked up to the information desk and asked what room Imani was. The woman pointed to the Intensive Care Unit.

I walked into the unit and I passed all of the rooms. The rooms were all filled with older people and then I came across room 13B. Inside of the room was Imani lying in a hospital bed with tubes and machines hooked up to her. Inside of the room sitting in a chair crying was Gavin.

I had never seen Gavin look so distraught in his life. He held his head down low and stared at the ground. He looked up when I came into the room. There was only one chair in the room, so he stood up to give me the seat.

I looked at Imani. Her skin was a dark color and she looked like she already was dead. It seemed like the machines were moving her chest, but her life was gone.

"Gavin, what happened?" I was literally in shock.

Gavin walked over to the window and looked out of the hospital window. It's almost as if he couldn't look at me because he didn't want me to see him cry.

"Imani called me and said that she didn't feel good. She wanted to know if I could take her to the clinic on campus. I told her that I had to take Charmaigne to the grocery store, and that after that I would come by and pick her up.

I waited too long. I came like 2 hours later and no one answered the door. I had a bad feeling so I went around the back and peeked in the window. That's when I saw her lying on the floor. I went to my car and called 9-11. The paramedics arrived and broke the door down."

"Gavin, what had happened?"

"Lori, I'm trying to tell you. They couldn't find a pulse. Her eyes were rolled back in her head and she was foaming at the mouth. I thought she was dead. That was yesterday. I've been here every since," Gavin held his head in sorrow.

This was probably the worst thing that had happened to me in my life. I was so upset. I was so upset and distraught I couldn't cry. I was in complete shock.

"Gavin, did she try to kill herself, what happened?"

"The doctors said she was in complete cardiac arrest when she arrived. They worked on her for 17 minutes before they got her pulse started. They are still running tests. They haven't told me anything.

I relieved Gavin and told him to go home and that I would call him if I heard anything. I called Imani's parents and they prepared to make the drive from Boston to Illinois.

Later that evening Imani's doctor came in to see me.

"Your friend is very, very sick."

"What happened?" I asked.

"We are still running tests, but this is our initial diagnosis. Your friend has suffered a severe stroke. We checked her medical records and she had not received any prenatal care. She had developed high blood pressure. She was drinking and doing drugs, we even found a very, very small, small amount of crack cocaine in her system. All of these factors, combined with being 6 months pregnant, led to her having the stoke," the doctor paused and read Imani's chart.

"Now we ran some tests to monitor her brain activity, and we have detected very minimal brain activity," the doctor hung the chart next to Imani's bed.

"Is she brain dead?" I asked.

"Well, technically, yes. Your friend could not function without the machines she is hooked up to. Her kidneys have failed and she is not breathing on her own. It is too early to make any decisions. We need to see if she will progress. Are the parents on their way?"

"Where is the baby?"

"We removed the baby and disposed of it," the doctor said coldly.

"Oh yes, the parents are coming. They are driving."

The next few days were extremely hard on me. It seemed as if it took Imani's parents forever to make it to Illinois. I stayed in her room 24 hours a day. I just knew that she would wake up.

The doctors came and brought only bad news. They had determined that Imani was "brain dead" and that is she lived she would be a "vegetable" due to the extensive brain damage.

After conferring with the doctors Imani's parents decided to remove the life support. Her parents decided to remove the machines on a Wednesday. A minister stood by to read Imani her last rites.

The life support machine was removed and Imani continued to breathe. The doctors who had little faith in her recovery.

"Most patients breathe out of habit from the machine for a few minutes and then they stop."

I waited for three hours. Imani continued to breathe. Her parents were extremely overjoyed, but I remember not being happy at all. A part of me wanted Imani to die. What kind of life would she lead as a vegetable? I remember her parents saying, "A piece of life is better than no life at all"

Several days after the breathing machine was removed Imani started to open her yes and move around. It was very weird though. Her eyes seemed blank, as if there was no soul in her body. Her body movements were jerky and unnatural. She still seemed unconscious.

Three days before my graduation Imani's parents moved her to a rehabilitation center in Boston. Imani could breathe on her own and her eyes were open, but she couldn't talk or walk. At the rehab facility they taught her a few small words and over the course of the year she learned to walk again. But her mind was gone. She didn't remember anything about college or her life. Jeneva, who was a grad student in psychology, said that she thought Imani was blocking out her painful past.

Imani improved but she never returned to her normal life. She lived in the rehabilitation facility for a year and now she lives at home with her mother. She cannot work and she speaks very child-like. She answers questions with one-word answers and she still had not learned to read again. Doctors felt that between the stroke and the loss of oxygen to her brain when she was in cardiac arrest left her severely brain damaged.

Jeneva and Imani's parents were very happy that she was alive. I wasn't. Maybe I was selfish. I just didn't want my friend alive if she wasn't going to be the way she used to be. To me, Imani is dead. I can't call her up on the phone to gossip. She didn't move away with me after graduation.

I try to look for a life lesson in every experience that I have. I think I learned that you should never become so involved in another person, male or female that you will completely lose yourself and your will to live in the process.

Oh yeah, my film. I got an "A" on my film. I sent a copy of my finished film to Imani's parents. I thought it would bring them some joy to see their daughter happy. The film also would help them understand how Imani became such a different person because the film chronicled how she changed after she met Greg. I still have a copy of the film. I don't watch it. It's too painful.

It hurt me very badly to go on with my life and to become and adult without Imani by my side.

A Very Long Ride

On May 14, 1998 I graduated from college. I completed my Bachelors of Arts degree in Film Production. My college graduation was very bittersweet. It was a special day because my parents, who had been divorced for ten years attended my graduation together. Graduation was a very emotional day for me. As I sat in the stands in my black cap & gown tears streamed down my face. I couldn't believe that I had actually survived all of the crazy things that I had been through in my life. It was bittersweet because my best friend Imani was not by my side with me. When they called her name her brother accepted her degree in her honor.

As I sat in the stands I thought about all of the boys I had dated. I thought about all of the counselors in high school that used to tell me that I was a loser and that I would never amount to anything. I had graduated from college. This was huge for me. It was a milestone, and I had done it all by myself.

After graduation I went out to dinner with my parents and my brother. Dinner was nice.

"Lori, you still haven't told us about your plans for the future," my father asked during dinner. I chewed my steak and thought of a good answer.

"Well. I have an internship. I'm going to move to California and work for Paramount in Studio City, California," good answer.

"How much does this internship pay?" My mother asked.

"It doesn't pay anything," I said as I looked into my plate.

"How will you survive who are you going to live with?" My father asked. I was suddenly inundated with questions.

"Trust me. Everything will work out fine," I said.

I didn't have an internship. What I did have was a promise from an intern at Paramount. The intern, a SIUC alumni, told me that if I came to California, "She would see what she could do" about getting me an internship. The truth was that I was leaving the safety net of Carbondale and heading into the wild unknown.

The day after graduation my family left. I stayed behind to pack up my apartment and to plan my move to California.

The Paseo was six years old and I knew that it would never make the drive to California. I decided to pack all of my belongings into the car and ship the car as freight. I didn't have any furniture. Most of my belongings consisted of my clothes and my computer.

Shipping the car was going to run me $750 dollars. I only had $1300 saved up. Financially, I was not prepared to make a major move. I felt like I had to go to California. I couldn't see myself staying in Carbondale. At the same time, I couldn't imagine moving back to Chicago. Chicago is a wonderful city. But I just didn't feel like it was the place for me. I had always wanted to move back to California. I was determined. I had to make this move. I had faced uncertain situations before in my life and they always turned out okay in the end. Making this move was a risk I would have to take.

Two weeks after graduation, I shipped the Paseo to California. I purchased a one-way bus ticket to California. The bus trip from Carbondale to California was going to take 4 days. I couldn't imagine taking such a long bus trip. I took solace in the fact that I had a notepad and 30 of my favorite CD's.

The bus departed from Carbondale at 1:30 in the afternoon. I remember looking out the window as the bus drove past my old dormitory. I had changed so much since I had first arrived in Carbondale. I had really become a woman during those five years.

As the bus left Carbondale, I had a strong feeling that I would never see Carbondale again.

I sat on the bus and listened to my CD's and looked out of the window as the bus rode down the highway. One thing I always hated about riding the bus is that the person that sits next to you always feel like you are obligated to hold a conversation with them.

Our first layover was in St. Louis. The bus arrived at the St. Louis bus terminal at 4:00 P.M. and was not scheduled to depart until 6:00P.M. The bus station in St. Louis is next to a KFC. I walked across the street and bought a chicken dinner.

After I finished eating I walked back across the street to the bus terminal. I saw a cute guy talking on a cell phone. The guy was about 5 foot 11 and he was wearing a yellow jogging suit. He smiled at me when he saw me. I prepared to board the bus and I thought to myself, "I hope he sits next to me."

I was one of the first people to board the bus and I found a seat towards the back of the bus. My mother made me promise to sit behind the driver, but I preferred to sit toward the back.

The cute guy made my dreams come true when he walked up to me and said,

"Can I sit here?"

"Of course." I said with a smile.

I played It cool at first. I didn't want to flirt too much. I just wanted a cute guy to hang out with on the bus. I was headed to California and chances are I would never see this person again once I got off the bus.

I later found out that his name was Elgin. He was 23 years old, and he claimed that he was on the 1996 U.S. Olympic Track Team. I don't know if he was lying or not, but even if he was lying, that was a pretty original lie. He as headed to Colorado.

We talked for awhile and then I fell asleep. He let me lay my head on his shoulder. He was so sweet and smelled so good. I was such a loose girl. Here I was laying my head on the shoulder of a man I met on a bus a few hours prior. He could have been a murderer, but he was cute, so I pushed those thoughts to the back of my mind.

When the bus arrived in Kansas City, Missouri, Elgin and I got off of the bus to stretch out feet. It was a beautiful night and we stood outside of the bus holding hands.

"You have the most beautiful lips," Elgin said as he caressed my face. He was really handsome.

"Thank you," I said.

"Can I kiss you?" Elgin asked. I smiled. Elgin leaned over and kissed me. I remember thinking to myself, "I hope that all of these people on the bus think that I know him from somewhere and that I am not just kissing a complete stranger." I was kissing a stranger. It felt good.

Despite graduating from college, I still had that urge to walk on the wildside. I liked to play with fire. Maybe I hadn't been burned bad enough in the past, but I loved to take risks.

Back on the bus, night had fallen and I was tired. I fell asleep on Elgin's shoulder. As I slept on the bus, I dreamed. I dreamed about the life Ii was leaving behind and the life I was about to enter. I was so frightened. I was headed straight for the unknown. Who would I stay with in California? How far would the less than $500 I had in my pocket get me?

Elgin departed the bus the next day in Colorado. He gave me his phone number and asked me to "Keep in touch." I wrote his phone number down on the first page of my notebook just to make sure that I wouldn't lose it.

The next day on the bus was so boring. I decided to start writing my memoirs. I wasn't famous and chances were that no one would ever see what I was busy writing. As I wrote, I felt the most tremendous weight being lifted off of me. I couldn't believe the spiritual release that I was feeling.

America is such a beautiful country. Until I took that long bus ride, I never realized how beautiful the land that we live in is. For example, Utah is one of the most beautiful states that I have ever seen. Prior to my trip, the only thing I knew about Utah was that Mormons lived there.

The bus stopped in Salt Lake City for 3 hours. My body was so tired of the constant motion and cramped quarters of the bus. I decided to call

Elgin while I was in the bus station in Salt Lake City. I was just curious. I had a strong feeling that he had given me the wrong phone number.

I dialed the number. A woman answered.

"Hello, may I please speak with Elgin?" I asked.

"I'm sorry, this is the YMCA and no Elgin is here," a man said on the other end. I hung up the phone. What a bum. He probably just wanted some girl to kiss on the bus.

I still had no idea what I was going to do once I got to California. I had a friend named Shelby who told me that I could stay with her for a few months until I found a steady job. I was rather apprehensive about taking Shelby up on her offer because I hadn't seen her in years.

The bus left Salt Lake City. The bus was super-crowded and it smelled really awful. A tall woman with flame red hair had boarded the bus in Salt Lake. The woman's make-up was very exaggerated and she must have been wearing the biggest hoop earrings that I had seen in my entire life.

I was exhausted and I could not sleep on the bus. I had felt safe enough to sleep the day before on the bus with Elgin. I turned on the little light on the bus and continued to write my memoirs.

The woman with the red hair was moving from seat to seat. I didn't know what she was doing. The bus was dark. The third time that she moved seats, I really took notice. What was she doing? I suppose the woman sitting next to me noticed my curiosity with the woman.

"She's going from seat to seat performing sexual favors for men," the lady pointed at the woman.

"Get out of here!" I said.

I watched the woman closely. She would sit next to a man. The man would hand her money and she would lean down as if she were laying on his lap. This was wild, I didn't know that things like this happened on the bus.

I couldn't fight the sleep anymore. I said a quick prayer and fell asleep. I was awaked by the scream of a redneck man.

"Hot damn, that's no female, that's a man!" The man screamed. I sat up straight and looked around. The man was standing in front of the bathroom and he was holding the red head woman by her throat.

"Let me go!" The red head woman screamed.

"How do you know that there is a man?" A Mexican man asked.

"I was in the bathroom with her and I felt between her legs. That is no female," the man said with a scowl.

This could get ugly I thought to myself. Several of the men started to yell at the red head woman.

"Are you a queer?" They chanted.

I sank down in my seat. Could my life get any stranger. I was on a Greyhound bus, in the middle of the night, with a bunch of weird people arguing with a woman that was possibly a man.

I feared for this woman or man, because the men on the bus were ready to pulverize her. The bus driver pulled the bus over to the side of the road. I stared out of the window into the black night.

The bus driver walked to the back of the bus. The bus driver was a big burly Black man.

"I don't know what all of this commotion is about, but I am not having it. I want it to stop now, or I am putting all of you off right here."

Everyone went back to their seats and the bus was quiet for the rest of the night.

Our next big lay over was sin city, Las Vegas. I had never been to Las Vegas before. We arrived in Las Vegas at 5:00 AM. And the city was alive and full of life. I got off of the bus in Las Vegas and was amazed at the hustle and bustle of the city.

I was due to change busses in Las Vegas. My bus wasn't scheduled to depart until 11:00 A.M. I put my small suitcase in a fifty cents locker and hit the streets.

Something about walking around the streets of Las Vegas at 5:30 in the morning made me feel extremely sexy. I felt like the character Sera in

Leaving Las Vegas. I felt powerful. I felt like I owned the streets. I wasn't scared. I was so impressed by the lights and the fact the city truly never slept.

My first order of business was to get something to eat. I went to the first casino I found and ordered s steak and shrimp dinner. The steak and shrimp dinner only cost me $3.99.

After I finished my meal, I went straight for the casino. All of the machines were ringing and making noises. Almost every slot machine was taken. I had about $500 in my pocket. This was all of my money in the world until I found a job and received my first paycheck. Gambling should have been the furthest thing from my mind.

I promised myself that I would only gamble with $40. That was it. If I lose the $40, I lose it. If I win, I walk away with a few extra dollars. I sat down at a twenty-five cent slot machine and inserted two twenty-dollar bills. It didn't take long for me to get hooked. I was winning like crazy. Before I knew it I had an $80 credit. I had doubled my money.

My dad always told me that the real money in Las Vegas was at the tables. I didn't know anything about Blackjack, but Roulette didn't look to hard. I collected my $80 credit from the slot machine and moseyed on over to the Roulette table.

I lost the entire $80 in two spins of the Roulette Wheel. I should have walked out of the casino and went back to the Greyhound Station. At this point, technically I was only out of the $40 I had initially invested into my gambling.

I was hooked. I went back to the slot machine. I inserted more money. I would always win. Since I was winning at the slot machine you would think I would just stay there? I would collect the money I won at the slot machine and take it to the Roulette table where I would lose it all.

By 8:30 A.M, I had gambled away all but $40 of my savings. I sat on a bench in the Greyhound Station completely depressed. Why was I so stupid?

What was I going to do? How could I be so irresponsible? I may have been older and wiser but I still did dumb shit from time to time.

I boarded the bus headed toward sunny California. I was rather relaxed the remainder of my bus ride. Sure, I had blown my money, but if things got to bad I would have to ask my parents for some money. I'm sure they wouldn't mind helping me considering the fact that I was a new college graduate.

The bus crossed the California border.

"Welcome to California," The bus driver spoke into the loudspeaker. I smiled and looked out of the window. I had made it. I thought about my dreams as a young girl. I had always wanted to move back to California and here I was. I was back in California. I was alive. I was going to make it.

The Los Angeles Greyhound terminal was a dirty, grimy place. I reached in my pocket and pulled out the business card for the freight company that had shipped my car. I hoped that I would have enough money to take cab to pick up my car. I thought to myself, "If all else fails I can always sleep in my car."

The freight company was in Sherman Oaks, California. The cab to Sherman Oaks coasts me $27. Joe's Freight was a nationally recognized freight company. I paid the cab driver and walked out of the cab.

The freight company was on a huge lot. Cars and trucks were everywhere. I walked into the air conditioned office. A woman was sitting next to a water cooler with her young son. A twentysomething man was behind the counter staring at a computer screen.

I smiled and walked up to the counter. I was feeling real good. I don't know why I felt so good, considering I was down to my last $10.

"Hi, My name is Lori Baldwin. I'm here to pick up my car. It's a turquoise 1992 Toyota Paseo. I shipped it from Carbondale, Illinois," I handed the attendant my wrinkled receipt.

"Ms. Baldwin. We were expecting you."

The attendant typed into his computer. He stared intensely at his computer.

"Jeff, can you come and look at this," he called a man who was sitting in a back office.

"What's wrong?" I said.

"I need to talk to my manger, that's all." The man motioned for his manager. I had paid the bill in full. I prayed that I didn't owe them money because I didn't have any money to give them.

The manager and the attendant stared at the screen. They then went in the back office and made a few phone calls.

"We'll be right out Ms. Baldwin." They yelled from the back office. I sat in the office reading a People magazine. I didn't know what was going on, but I didn't have a good feeling about what was going on.

The attendant and the manager walked up to the counter.

"Ms. Baldwin can we speak with you for a minute?" The manager asked.

My stomach dropped as I walked up to the counter.

"Ms. Baldwin. There was an accident in Kansas. The truck that was hauling your automobile caught on fire. It seems your car and the belongings inside of your car that you had insured were destroyed." This couldn't be happening.

"You've got to be kidding me. All of my clothes were in there and I loved that car," I cried.

"Ms. Baldwin, we are extremely sorry. Things like this rarely happen. We see that you purchased $30,000 worth of insurance on your car and the belongings. We process all insurance checks out of our national office. Your check will be here in approximately 10 days. I spoke with our district manager and he told me to put you up in the Holiday Inn across town. We will foot the bill. We will notify you as soon as your check is available for you to pick up," the manger explained.

My tears turned to a smile. $30,000! Sure, I had lost my car and all of my belongings in the process, but I was going to have money to buy new things.

I checked into the Holiday Inn and took a nice, long bath. My body felt so dirty after that long bus ride.

I climbed out of the tub and laid on the bathroom floor and let the heat lamp dry my nude body. I sat up and painted my toes. Music was playing and I had a renewed feeling about life. For the first time in a long time, I really felt like I was going to make it afterall.

That night I purchased a newspaper and started pricing apartments and used cars. I ordered a pizza from room service and watched a repeat of "Sex & The City" on HBO.

As I fell asleep I started to cry. It was so hard for me to accept that I had survived all of the madness that I had experienced in my life. Life is so precious and I had been so reckless with mine in the past. At that moment, I determined that I would learn from my past and make the most of my future. I couldn't even sleep. I thought about Imani. I thought about Cherry. I even thought about Samantha. So many people I knew were not having the opportunity that I was. I was a college graduate and I was about to start my career. For the first time since I was 7 years old I said my prayers. I was blessed to have survived my long journey to adulthood.

ABOUT THE AUTHOR

---▼---

Sparkledoll-Always Into Something is the first novel by an exciting young writer. Dorrie Williams-Wheeler is a multi-talented genius. She wears many hats. She spent three years as a film major and completed her bachelors degree in Liberal Arts in 1997. Dorrie penned the scripts *Keeping It Real-A Hip Hop Love Story* (1996) and *Friendship Beyond Color Lines* (1998), both scripts were considered for production by major studios.

Aside from writing, Dorrie next greatest passion is design. Dorrie is an accomplished web and graphic designer. She has designed web sites for entertainers, athletes, and for small businesses. She has her own web design business, which can be found on-line at www.sparkledoll.com.

Dorrie completed her Masters of Science of Education Degree from Southern Illinois University at Carbondale in 1999. She also develops interactive learning tools. She has taught at several higher learning institutions on the East Coast.

Dorrie Williams-Wheeler lives in Virginia Beach with her husband Craig and their son. They are expecting their second child in the spring of 2001.

Dorrie enjoys the pop music of the 80s. She developed the popular web site www.imissthe80s.com. A child of the 80's, she list her favorite music group as Duran Duran and her all-time favorite television show as Jem & The Holograms.

Sparkledoll-Always Into Something, is a personal book for Dorrie. Many will draw comparisons between Lori and Dorrie, but they are two very different people.

Ask Dorrie why she named the book Sparkledoll, and her business is named Sparkledoll Productions, and she will say, "I wanted a word that was unique attached to my book."

Her future goals include becoming a member of Mensa and seeing one of her scripts made into a movie.

Sparkledoll is unique and this is not the last that the world has heard from Dorrie Williams-Wheeler.